The Darkest Part of the Night

David Spell

Volume Two of the Zombie Terror War Series

This is a work of fiction. Any similarities to events or persons, living, dead, or fictitious are purely coincidental. No part of this publication can be reproduced or transmitted in any form or by any means, electronic or mechanical, without permission in writing from the author.

Published in the United States by DavidSpell.com.

ISBN: 9781549852985

To the brave men and women in blue who work everyday to protect our society from the predators.

They are the Thin Blue Line.

"Despite what your momma told you, violence does solve problems." Chris Kyle

Kris 'Tanto' Paronto: "I never really get scared. Is that weird? Whenever bullets start to fly, I always feel protected. You know, like it's...As long as I'm doing the right thing, God'll take care of me. But that's crazy, right?"
Dave 'Boon' Benton: "Not any more than everything else you say." From the film *13 Hours*

"I looked up and saw a horse whose color was pale green. Its rider was named Death, and his companion was the Grave. These two were given authority over one-fourth of the earth, to kill with the sword and famine and disease and wild animals." (Revelation 6:8)

"Praise the LORD, who is my rock. He trains my hands for war and gives my fingers skill for battle." (Psalm 144:1)

Chapter One

East of Atlanta, Monday, Three days after initial attacks

Amir al-Razi checked into a nondescript hotel just off of the interstate. He paid with cash for two nights and kept the baseball cap that he was wearing pulled down low on his head. He kept his sunglasses on as well. The Indian clerk asked for his ID but Amir said that his wallet had been stolen. She handed him the key without any more questions.

Amir backed his rental car into a parking space and walked up the stairs to his room. He carried a plastic bag of food and water that he had bought at a twenty-four hour convenience store and he had a black duffel bag slung over his shoulder. A skinny drug dealer wearing a Bob Marley tank top stepped in front of him on the stairwell and asked him what he needed. Al-Razi pulled up his shirt and let him see his pistol.

"I need you to get out of my way," he said, quietly. The drug dealer scurried off.

As he was unlocking his door, a rough looking prostitute stuck her head out of the room next to Amir's.

"If you need anything, handsome, you just come knock

on my door," she said with a forced smile.

He didn't even acknowledge her as he stepped inside his room.

He flipped on the television to continue watching the coverage of his team's attacks and the others that had been launched throughout the country. The jihad had begun. As he watched the news, however, he began to understand that the attacks that he had orchestrated in the Atlanta area had only been partial successes.

The previous Friday night he had launched four teams of jihadi soldiers. Twenty-four warriors of Allah had been unleashed on Atlanta. One group, led by his lieutenant, Farouq Farhat, had attacked the Arbor Place Mall, just west of Atlanta. He witnessed part of that attack from his car in the parking lot. Amir had seen Farhat gunned down by Centers for Disease Control Enforcement Agents. They had also shot and killed the rest of his soldiers, but only after the martyrs had shot and infected many people inside the mall.

A second team was stopped on the interstate before reaching their target in downtown Atlanta. They were going to attack an outdoor hip-hop concert in the heart of the city. Two of the CDC police officers managed to stop their van and kill all six of them before they could execute their attack.

Al-Razi had watched the videos on the news. Just two of these federal police officers were able to stop his entire team of trained warriors. It was some consolation to hear that the officers had been wounded, but the reports on the

—

news indicated that their injuries were not severe.

His third team made it to their target at the Six Flags Over Georgia amusement park. Another CDC officer engaged the van containing six more of his soldiers, killing two of them before they could get inside. The other four were able to get into the park to kill and inflict the bio-terror virus on many. The police managed to eliminate his people quickly but, by then, they had already done much damage.

Amir's fourth squad had the most successful attack. They targeted the Atlanta Braves Stadium as the crowd was heading in for a 7:00pm baseball game. They were virtually unopposed and were able to kill many with their AK-47s before the virus took effect in the terrorists. Their rifles were no match for the police working security at the stadium. Four officers were killed and three others were wounded.

All of his men had been given a syringe loaded with the latest version of the zombie virus. Their instructions were to inject themselves five minutes before their attacks commenced. They did not know it was the zombie virus, but had been told that the injection would deaden them to pain and allow them to keep fighting, even after the police shot them. After the chemical took effect in them, they continued their assaults by biting and chewing on their victims, infecting them also. The police eventually killed all six of his soldiers, but by then they had infected many of the American infidels.

The initial death count in the Atlanta attacks was over

five hundred. Of course, new reports were coming in all the time of people who had gotten infected and then gone home to die or to turn into zombies later. These in turn, attacked their family and friends, continuing the spread of the virus. Now, three days later, the number of deaths was pushing towards a thousand in and around Atlanta.

In some cities, such as Los Angeles and New York, though, the numbers of dead were much higher. They were reporting that entire neighborhoods had been infected. Suicide bombers had blown themselves up in crowded areas. The bomb materials had the virus mixed in with the shrapnel. Not only were many people killed by the explosions, many of them were also infected and quickly turned into monsters. National Guard units had been activated in several locations to help law enforcement contain and control the crisis.

Amir had chosen not to use suicide bombers in these initial attacks. Americans were terrified of mass shootings so he chose to unleash his soldiers, armed with AKs and plenty of ammo. When the drugs in the syringe took affect, his men had died and reanimated as instruments of Allah's wrath. While not complete failures, al-Razi knew that the death toll in his attacks had been kept lower because of the quick response of the CDC Response Teams, as well as the local police.

Al-Razi wondered what his handler was thinking. Imam Ruhollah Ali Bukhari had suggested that Amir use suicide bombers but he had chosen to go in another direction. Many infidels had died in Atlanta so Amir hoped Bukhari would not be angry.

The terrorist was happy with the results but would have been happier with more dead Americans. His hatred for the United States ran deep. He hated their arrogance and their affluence. He hated that they put pressure on the United Nations and the international community to prevent Iran from having a nuclear program. And he especially hated their friendship with Israel. Maybe one day, Amir could spread the zombie virus among the Zionists, as well.

He had always had a plan for a follow-up attack but had hoped that the first teams that he had launched would be sufficient. Since they were not, he would begin working immediately on implementing Jihad Atlanta, Phase Two. It would take him a couple of weeks to get his people and plans in place. That could actually work to his advantage. The Americans would be so focused on combating the infected that were already among them, he should be able to launch the second phase without any interference.

This next wave of terror would involve targeting schools. He would begin working this week on a major attack at a large high school outside of the city. He also had plans to strike two of the large universities near Atlanta. These soft university students would experience a taste of holy war that would turn their campuses into graveyards of the walking dead. He still had a sufficient quantity of the virus to bring devastation to the enemies of Islam. Al-Razi knew that Bukhari would be pleased with Phase Two. The next few days should be very interesting, he thought.

John F. Kennedy International Airport, New York,
Wednesday, 1100 hours

Alejandro "Hollywood" Estrada shook NYPD
Detective Frank Walsh's hand, got out of the unmarked
detective car, grabbed his suitcase, and walked into the
airport terminal. The limp was almost gone, his right leg
almost healed.

His time in New York had been short but he was glad
he had come. His friend and co-worker, Marco Connolly,
had been the first CDC officer to be killed in the line of
duty. He had been attacked by three zombies the week
before and overpowered. Marco had managed to shoot one
of them before succumbing to his wounds. Alejandro had
killed another one of the infected before they had turned
and attacked him, as well. His kevlar pants had kept the
creature's teeth from penetrating his skin, but the bite left
him with a deep bruise just above his knee. Assistant team
leader, Jimmy Jones, had killed the third zombie but there
was nothing they could do for Marco.

Estrada was thankful to have spent some time with
Connolly's family in New York. He had attended the
wake, as well as the funeral. His boss, Rebecca Johnson,
and his team leader, Eddie Marshall, would have liked to

have been there but they were in the middle of dealing with the zombie virus and the aftermath of the terror attacks in Atlanta.

Hollywood had flown to New York on one of the Department of Homeland Security's small corporate jets. All commercial flights had been shut down for several days throughout the country after the bio-terror attacks in several major American cities. Now, he was flying back to Atlanta on a commercial flight. The terminal was packed with people trying to get on a plane but his federal police status had gotten him a flight without any problems.

His first stop inside the airport was the TSA office. He had the letter that Rebecca had emailed him from one of the assistant directors of the DHS authorizing him to carry his weapon on the flight. Estrada's 9mm Glock 17 was in a hip holster concealed by his navy blue blazer. He had two extra magazines for the pistol, a set of handcuffs, and his folding tactical knife. Of course, dealing with the Transportation Security Administration was on the same level as getting a root canal, even with an official letter and his own federal law enforcement credentials.

George Carter was ready to get home. He had come to New York as he had been doing regularly for the last several years. He was an IT Specialist who came to the Big Apple once a month to visit his biggest client. George could and did solve most of their problems remotely from his office in Atlanta. This particular client, though, liked having George visit them to give their IT issues his personal touch. And, they were willing to pay the extra costs to have him visit.

He had flown up the previous Thursday morning and should have flown home on Friday afternoon. With the nationwide terror attacks on Friday afternoon, however, his flight had been cancelled. Today was the first open flight that he had been able to secure.

George had served in the Army for five years as an Information Technology Specialist. After taking an honorable discharge, he had used the GI Bill to go back to school and get a Computer Science degree. Even at fifty-nine years of age, Carter had managed to stay relevant in the ever changing IT field. And his customers loved him.

He had spoken to his wife several times over the weekend. She assured him that they were fine. The attacks had not affected them. They lived in an affluent neighborhood north of Atlanta. His wife told him that their two sons and their families were fine, as well. George hadn't seen any of the "zombies" that they were talking about on the news but he had heard the police sirens almost non-stop around Manhattan. He had also learned from the news that a suicide bomber had blown himself up in a crowded subway station fifteen blocks from his hotel.

George was relieved that his family was OK, but he was still stressed at being stuck in New York. He had never liked the city and hated being there any longer than he had to be. He felt his blood pressure rising. Or at least he felt the symptoms the doctor had shared with him that indicated his blood pressure was too high. His head had been hurting for the last couple of days and he had started feeling dizzy that morning.

He was on medication to keep his blood pressure under control. He had ordered a new supply the previous week, before coming to New York, throwing it into his suitcase to have if he needed it. Now he needed it. On top of the stress of being away from his family, he hated flying. It was part of the job but he still didn't enjoy it. He was a big man and he was never able to get comfortable in those airline seats.

After getting through the security line and getting to his gate, George opened his carry-on bag and removed the medicine bottle. He was only supposed to take one pill but he took two instead. He felt terrible. He must have slept wrong the night before, he thought. His left shoulder and arm were both feeling a little numb.

He began to feel better almost immediately as the medicine started to take effect. The pressure in his head began to ease and the pain in his shoulder started to subside. Just a few more hours, he thought, and I'll be home.

The TSA Supervisor let Alejandro know that there was no Federal Air Marshal on his flight. He would be seated towards the rear of the plane so that he would have a clear view of the cabin. A New York Transit Police Officer walked Estrada around the security line and pointed him towards his gate.

He decided to board with the last group. If he was the

de-facto air marshal, by getting on last he could scan the flyer's faces for signs of trouble as he walked to his seat. He didn't see anything or anyone out of the ordinary. There was a big black man, seated ten rows up from him on the aisle, who looked like he was having some problems. He had glanced up at Estrada and nodded at him. Hollywood had noted the perspiration on the large passenger's forehead.

Military and law enforcement guys always seemed to recognize each other. He had an obvious military bearing, but didn't look like he was feeling well. That was one of the problems with flying, Alejandro thought. If there was someone with the flu on the plane, they could also inflict it on the rest of the passengers.

The reprieve that George experienced after taking his medicine was short-lived. By the time he got on the plane, he was feeling much worse. He was hot, he was sweating, his head was hurting, his left shoulder was throbbing, and he was having trouble catching his breath. He reached up and turned the small fan on all the way. I'll just close my eyes and take a nap, he thought. When I wake up, I'll be home with my wife.

He noticed the young Hispanic looking man walking down the aisle towards the rear of the plane. That must be the air marshal for the flight, Carter thought. He has that, 'I'm a cop or soldier,' look to him. As the plane started moving, George closed his eyes to rest.

What Carter had no way of knowing was that the

medicine he had consumed had been tainted with the zombie virus. Part of the initial attack was that several Iranian operatives, with a background in science and medicine, had been able to add the bio-terror chemical to hundreds of medical packages which were then sent out to unsuspecting people all over the country.

In George's case, the medicine intensified the symptoms that he was already having, causing him to have a heart attack. The virus was in his blood stream. As the airliner nosed into the air, George Carter gasped and then died.

Chapter Two

35,000 feet, Wednesday, 1215 hours

Before takeoff, Alejandro was in his seat at the rear of the plane checking emails on his smartphone. A young, pretty flight attendant stopped in the aisle next to him. "Can I get you anything?" she asked, her hand resting on the back of Hollywood's seat.

He looked up and saw her smiling at him. A nametag identified her as Isabella Rodriguez. Estrada had always gotten tongue-tied around girls and as he looked at Isabella, he couldn't think of anything to say. He tried to formulate an intelligible response.

"Sorry, I was just checking my email," he finally managed to stammer. "I don't think I need anything right now. So, are you working on this flight?"

She laughed. "Yes, this my route. New York to Atlanta and back. What about you?"

"No, I don't work on this flight. I work at our office in Atlanta." He felt hot. I'm making a complete idiot of myself, Estrada thought.

Isabella laughed again. She didn't see a wedding ring on his hand. The flight crew had been told that a federal law enforcement officer would be on their flight and that he would be armed.

The flight attendant had seen him get on and thought that he was really nice looking. He carried himself with such confidence as he walked through the airplane. Now, he was having trouble putting his sentences together.

"Okay, well, I need to get back to work, but I'm here if you need something," she said, her eyes sparkling.

"Thanks for checking on me. Maybe I'll need something later."

As Isabella walked away, Alejandro put his head back on the seat and closed his eyes. That's probably one of the prettiest girls I've ever seen, he thought. She wanted to talk to me and I couldn't think of anything interesting or funny to say. She probably thinks I have mental issues or that I didn't want to talk to her.

After the flight got airborne and leveled off at the cruising altitude, one of the other flight crew came down the aisle. She wasn't as pretty as Isabella but was smiling in Estrada's direction. She stopped suddenly about ten seats up.

"Sir, are you OK?"

The young woman had seen George Carter slumped over in his seat. There was no one seated next to him. He was seat belted in but the angle that he was slouched over at just didn't look right. The attendant put her hand on his shoulder and shook him. Nothing.

She reached over to check the pulse on his neck. There wasn't one. His body was still warm, actually, he felt hot to the touch, but there was no heartbeat. The attendant rushed towards the front of the cabin to get some help and to grab the portable defibrillator. A call came over the PA asking if there was a doctor or nurse on the flight. No one moved.

Alejandro didn't know what he was supposed to do. If he was the fill-in air marshal, he was supposed to stay incognito. He remained in his seat and watched Isabella, the other female flight attendant, and a male flight crew member rush back to work on the unconscious or dead man.

They undid his seat belt and pulled him onto the floor in the aisle. The problem was, Carter was a really big man and the aisles were very narrow. They were having trouble working on him as the male attendant was prepping the defibrillator. Isabella looked back at Estrada. It was obvious that she needed something. He got out of his seat and walked over to them.

"Sir, would you please go to the back of the cabin and get that backboard? It's laying against the rear bulkhead. We're going to need to move him to the rear of the plane where we'll have more room to work."

Alejandro rushed to the back to get what they needed. He found it on the other side of the cabin, at the end of the other aisle. As he was picking it up, he heard a scream. He dropped the board and hurried back to the other side of the plane.

All four members of the cabin crew were in the aisle trying to help the unconscious man. An older woman, who appeared to be the crew supervisor, had joined the other three attendants who were crouched over their patient. The male attendant was holding the defibrillator. Several passengers were out of their seats, crowding around, trying to see what was going on. The older woman was trying, to no avail, to get them to sit back down.

Before they could shock him with the defibrillator, though, the bio-terror chemical that had been added to George's medicine reached his brain. Isabella heard a growl coming from the man's throat.

"I think he made a noise," she said.

The other female attendant leaned over George's face with her ear to see if should could hear anything. George's eyes popped opened and he lunged upward, trying to bite the girl's throat. Startled by the sudden movement, she screamed, falling backwards against a seat.

George turned towards her and bit down on her right forearm. She screamed again but was able to rip her arm out of his mouth. Thankfully for her, she was cold natured, wearing a long sleeve blouse, a sweater, and her navy blazer.

Isabella saw the attack on her colleague and instinctively pushed herself backwards into an occupied seat. A businessman grabbed her and pulled her into his lap, away from the crazy-acting man on the floor.

Carl, the male flight attendant, put his hand on Carter's chest and said, "Sir, calm down. You're going to be OK now."

George was trying to get into a position where he could get up. He was wedged pretty tightly on the floor of the aisle. When the attendant put his hand on his chest, Carter thrust his head forward and caught the young man's hand in his mouth.

Carl gasped in pain as George's teeth clamped down on his right hand. He tried to pull free and could feel the teeth ripping into his flesh and bones. Blood began pouring out of his torn hand.

"Let go of me!" Carl yelled.

The big man seemed to bite down even harder. George reached out and grabbed Carl behind the neck and started pulling him down towards his mouth. Carl was still holding the portable defibrillator in his left hand. He raised it high and slammed it down onto George's head. The plastic shattered and opened several cuts on the big man's face. The force of the blow loosened Carter's grip and Carl was able to pull his hand free and scramble backwards.

The Flight Crew Supervisor, Janette, saw the blood and the damage to Carl's hand and ordered, "Go to the front of the plane and grab the first-aid kit and work on that."

She looked at George, still struggling to get up, and told him, "Sir, you need to stay down there. You've assaulted two members of this aircrew and you'll be arrested when we land."

Carter continued to growl. His mouth was opening and snapping closed. He managed to wiggle around enough to where he had some room to get to his feet. The passengers seated nearby pressed inward, towards the window seats.

Alejandro ran up to where George was trying to stand. "Federal Police Officer, everybody needs to stay back," he said, holding up his ID. "This man appears to have been infected with the zombie virus. I need everybody to stay in their seats. If you get bitten, you'll get infected to."

He drew his Glock but kept it pointed at the floor. What happens if I shoot him in a plane at thirty-five thousand feet? he thought. I know I can make the shot but what if I happen to miss or the bullet goes through him and hits the wall or ceiling?

Estrada issued a verbal challenge to the man large man in front of him. "Sir, you're under arrest. Stop and get down on the floor, now!"

George turned at started for Estrada. Alejandro could see that his eyes were glazed over. He raised the pistol and was about to take the head shot but he saw several people crowding into the aisle directly behind the infected man. The shot would be too dangerous.

Alejandro backed up and yelled, "Everybody get out of the aisle!"

No one moved except the infected man pursuing the police officer in front of him. Several people had their smart phones out and were recording the incident. Thankfully, the zombie was focused on Estrada.

There were plenty of innocent people that he could have easily grabbed. Estrada continued to back towards the rear of the plane. He bumped into someone. Now, people were standing in the aisle behind him, as well.

He couldn't shoot but he had to do something quickly. The big, growling man was shuffling slowly forward but he would be on top of Estrada in a matter of seconds. The officer quickly holstered his pistol and pulled his Benchmade folding knife out of his pocket. He flicked the knife open and took a step towards the zombie.

Carter reached out with his right hand to grab the officer. Estrada caught his reaching arm with his left hand and pulled the infected man towards him. He had the knife an icepick grip and fired a backhanded strike with the blade towards the zombie's face, aiming for his right eye. Because he was so much bigger than Estrada, though, the strike was a little off and caught him below the eye. For a human, the strike would have ended the fight and possibly even have been fatal.

For a zombie, though, the knife strike only slowed him down momentarily. The blade had not managed to penetrate into the brain. George reached across with his left hand to grab the officer again.

Alejandro stepped backwards, pulling his knife free. The people who had been in the aisle behind him had scattered. The zombie continued forward towards his prey, dark blood dripping from the hole in his face.

Estrada fired a powerful front kick into his knee. There was the sound of cracking as the bones fractured and

George stumbled, falling forward into the aisle. Alejandro backed up again so the man wouldn't fall on top of him.

He was even with the rear restrooms now, almost to the bulkhead. Time to end this, he thought. As the zombie struggled to get back to his feet, Estrada stepped in and brought the knife down onto the top of his head. The tanto blade pierced his skull and entered his brain. Carter collapsed facedown on the floor. This time, there was no more movement.

After cleaning his knife with alcohol provided by the crew, Estrada took off his blazer and scrubbed the blood splatter off his hands and face. Isabella draped a blanket over the dead man until they could put him in a body bag. She came to the back of the plane as Alejandro was drying his face and hands. She walked over and stood next to him.

"Are you OK?" she asked, a tremble in her voice.

"I'm good," he said. "What about you? That's not something you see everyday, huh?"

She shook her head and leaned against the bulkhead, closing her eyes and wrapping her arms around herself.

"I've seen the news reports but I thought those were isolated incidents. He tried to kill us and you. I thought he was going to get you."

Hollywood flashed a smile. "Not me. I'm a zombie killer."

Estrada wasn't sure what to say next so he decided to be honest.

"Hey, I'm sorry about earlier. When you came by my

seat, I, well, I've always been pretty shy around girls. I freeze up and don't know what to say. But, I thought maybe, sometime, you might have dinner with me?"

Did he really just ask her out? He felt hot again.

"That would be nice," she smiled. "I'd like that. I'll give you my number before we leave. Now, let me get back to work."

Alejandro went to check on the rest of the crew. The girl who had gotten bit, Lisa, was holding her arm. She was sitting in one of the front jump seats and appeared to be in shock. He had her take off her jacket and sweater and roll up her sleeve.

The infected man's teeth had not pierced her flesh. It was red and turning purple but she would be OK. She would have a nasty bruise and a sore arm for a few days. He had the same thing on his leg the previous week.

Carl, however, was another story. His hand had been mangled. Janette, the supervisor, was working on the wound. Alejandro noticed approvingly that she had put rubber gloves on. Carl looked up at Estrada with fear in his eyes.

"Am I going to die?"

"Nobody else is dying," Estrada said. At least not yet, he thought.

He spoke to Janette. "What's the pilot going to do? Are we going to continue to Atlanta?"

"I'm not sure. He was talking about diverting to Charlotte."

"Can you ask him if he can continue to Atlanta? The

CDC has been working non-stop on creating a treatment for this. I can get them to send the latest formula to the airport to treat him," he said, motioning at Carl.

Janette nodded and got up and walked over to the phone that would allow her to call the pilot.

"How you feeling?" he asked Carl.

"It hurts bad. He really messed my hand up. If I live, I'll probably need surgery. Man, I'm hot. I think I have a fever. Do you think I'll turn into one of those things?"

That was a distinct possibility, Alejandro knew.

"The CDC scientists told us that a person's immune system has a lot to do with what happens after they've been exposed to this. It affects different people in different ways. There's no way to tell what's going to happen with you. Could we buckle you into your seat, just to be safe?"

Carl nodded and sat back in his jump seat and allowed Hollywood to strap him in. He looked pale and sweat was pouring off of him. Janette had cleaned the wound, put an antibiotic ointment on it, and bandaged it tightly in gauze.

"I'm going to have some medicine waiting for you at the airport," said Estrada. "The anti-virus vaccine is experimental. I can't make you any promises if it will help or not. At this point, though, you probably don't have anything to lose by taking it."

Alejandro pulled out his smart phone and called his team leader, Eddie Marshall. One of the benefits of having a specially modified, government issued phone was that it would work almost anywhere. He gave him a quick rundown of the incident and asked him to have a dose of the vaccine delivered to the airport. Eddie told him he would contact the FBI and have them respond to handle the investigation.

Janette looked at Estrada. "The pilot said he'll continue to Atlanta. Can you help us bag that man in the aisle?"

"We need to leave him like he is until we land. He's part of the crime scene and they'll want to take pictures of him where he's lying. Sorry."

She nodded and walked towards the other end of the plane. Alejandro started to follow her but Carl put his good hand on Estrada and said, "Hang on. You might want to hear this."

He turned and knelt in front of the injured man. Carl lowered his voice and said, "Isabella, that cute flight attendant? She told us that she thought you were really good looking and was hoping to get to know you, if you know what I mean."

Alejandro smiled. "Cool, thanks, man. I've already asked her out."

"Smooth," said Carl, "Very smooth."

CDC Headquarters, Atlanta, Wednesday, 1245 hours

Team Leaders Chuck McCain and Eddie Marshall unpacked the boxes that their new equipment had come in. The long table in their briefing room was covered with new uniform polo shirts, kevlar pants, and jackets to replace those that had been damaged the week before.

There were also heavy tactical body armor and chest rigs that they could carry their extra rifle magazines in.

The terrorist attacks from the previous week had shown the teams that they needed to invest in some new gear. Their soft body armor was only designed to stop pistol rounds. Andy Fleming had gotten hit by a fragmented AK-47 round that punched a hole through his body armor and then punched a hole in him. He was very fortunate that it was only a bullet fragment.

Each officer now had a heavy tactical vest that would be able to stop rifle rounds. These vests would also add another layer of protection against zombie bites. The chest rigs would allow each officer to carry their rifle magazines and other equipment in a much more accessible position. A black kevlar helmet would protect their heads.

They were also being issued a small trauma kit. Andy wasn't the only officer to have been wounded. Scotty Smith had gotten shot in the shoulder and had received several cuts on his face from flying glass when their windshield had gotten shot out. The wound to the shoulder left a deep gouge where the bullet had grazed him. The trauma kit contained a tourniquet, a trauma bandage, a packet of blood clotting solution, and other first-aid items.

The teams had been working, using only their specially modified cell phones for communication. They were encrypted and secure but communication had not been as easy as they had hoped it would be. Now, they were being issued individual radios that would allow them to talk to each other and their base more quickly.

McCain had received a call the day before from Gunny Powell letting him know that he could come pick up the threaded barrels and the suppressors for the teams' Glock pistols. Powell was a Marine armorer turned Class 3 firearms dealer who had added suppressors to their Colt M4 rifles. Now, the officers would have suppressed capability for their pistols as well.

Chuck had been a police officer outside of Atlanta for twenty years. A large part of his career had been as a SWAT officer. After taking an early retirement package, he had signed up for two one-year contracts as a law enforcement advisor to the United States Army.

Because of his SWAT background, he was assigned to a Special Forces A team. He worked with the same team for both of his contracts. In Afghanistan, he saw first-hand the benefits of having suppressed weapons. Many of the soldiers he worked with had suppressors on their rifles to reduce the noise and the muzzle flash of their shots.

As a Team Leader for the CDC Enforcement Unit, McCain had noticed that the zombies were drawn to noise. They had gotten all of their rifles fitted with suppressors. Now, they would have them for their pistols, as well. These would be carried on their duty belts and screwed onto their 9mm Glocks when needed.

The teams were also in need of some new vehicles. Out of their four Chevrolet Suburbans, three of them sustained damage in the terrorist attacks the previous week. One of Team One's SUVs had been declared totaled. It had been shot up by AK-47 fire and then wrecked on the interstate when Scotty Smith rammed a vanload of terrorists to keep them from reaching their destination.

A second Suburban had also been shot up in the terrorist attack at the Arbor Place Mall in Douglasville. Team Two members Eddie and Jimmy hadn't been hit, but their vehicle took almost thirty rounds of 7.62x39 bullets in the engine and passenger compartment. That vehicle would also be replaced.

Luis García had pursued a van load of Islamic terrorists into the Six Flags Over Georgia amusement park. Two of the six terrorists opened up on Luis and a Cobb County police officer with their AKs. García killed both of the terrorists but his vehicle took several non-critical hits on the passenger side. That Suburban was being repaired.

Rebecca had ordered two new vehicles to be delivered today. She had found black Ford Police Interceptors at a local car dealership that catered to police departments. These were also equipped with blue lights in the grill and windshield and sirens.

Chuck and Eddie had just gotten back from lunch when Rebecca found them. "How's the new equipment? Does the order look right?"

"It sure does," answered McCain. "Now, we're just waiting on them to deliver the two new vehicles."

"I'm really glad we got this heavy body armor and the helmets," added Marshall. "Fleming and Smith were very lucky last week."

Johnson nodded. "Yes, they were," she said.

"Considering what we had to deal with, we were all very lucky."

Eddie felt his phone vibrate. "Alejandro's calling. I'll be right back." He stepped over to his office.

Chuck watched Rebecca. Her blonde hair was pulled back in a ponytail. She was close to five ten and worked out regularly. Even in her black CDC Enforcement polo shirt and gray cargo pants, she looked great.

"What's the latest from the rest of the country? Any more zombie outbreaks?" he asked her.

"Local police are trying to control the outbreaks in their areas. Our CDC officers in other cities are also doing a good job of containing it and killing the zombies. It just seems to be spreading so fast."

"Any intelligence on where al-Razi might be? With him still out there operating, it's just a matter of time until we get hit again."

"I know," said Rebecca with a sigh. "For the moment, anyway, he seems to have disappeared. He just made Number One on the FBI's Most Wanted list. His picture is all over the news. Maybe we'll get lucky and someone will see him and call it in. Remember, he's a trained intelligence agent from Iran. He knows how keep a low profile."

Marshall hurried back into the room and looked at Rebecca. "Boss, we need to go to the airport. Alejandro had to kill a zombie on his flight from New York."

"Is he alright?"

"Yeah, he sounded OK. He said that one of the flight

crew got bit but hasn't turned yet. They have him strapped into his seat. He's asking if we can bring some of the latest experimental anti-virus with us. The kid that got bit doesn't have anything to lose. I figured you'd want to bring in the FBI to help with this one. There are a lot of people that are going to need to be interviewed."

She nodded. "Definitely. Let me go talk with one of the people upstairs about that anti-virus and then we can go. I'll call the FBI on the way."

"I guess TSA doesn't screen for zombies yet, huh?" said Chuck. "That must've been something, shooting one six or seven miles up. And imagine how loud that had to have been in that enclosed space."

"That's what makes this one kind of unique," smiled Eddie. "He didn't shoot it. He killed it with his knife."

"With a knife?" exclaimed McCain. "That's pretty impressive!"

"He told me he wanted to shoot it but the passengers were crowding into the aisle taking video. He had to stab it in the top of the skull instead."

"Let's not tell Scotty," said Chuck. "He'll take it as a challenge and try and outdo him the next time we run into some of those things."

Atlanta Hartsfield-Jackson International Airport, Wednesday, 1400 hours

Before landing, Alejandro asked Janette if he could address the passengers. They needed to know what to expect when they landed in Atlanta. Whatever they were hoping to do that afternoon was probably going to get put on hold.

"Ladies and gentleman, my name's Alejandro and, like I said before, I'm a federal police officer. My agency has been in the middle of these terror attacks that have used this terrible virus as a weapon. I'm sorry that you had to witness this today but I'm very glad that no one else got hurt.

"I wanted to let you know what to expect in Atlanta. The FBI will be investigating this incident to make sure that I acted appropriately and to make sure everything is handled in the right way. Of course, they'll want to interview you and view any videos or photos you have of the incident. Please tell them what you heard and saw and cooperate fully. At this point, we don't know how this man got infected but I'm sure that the autopsy and toxicology reports will give us more information.

"I'd also like to thank the flight crew," he continued, making eye contact with Isabella. "Two of them were injured, one of them seriously. They did a great job trying to render aid to this man who turned out to be infected. We are fortunate to have such professionals taking care of us. Thank you."

At this, the passengers erupted in applause. As the adrenaline wore off, everyone realized how much worse this incident could have been. Most of the people on the flight seemed to appreciate what Alejandro had done. Several of the men shook his hand and thanked him for stopping the threat. A few of the women thanked him, also. And, of course, he overheard a few people loudly saying that he had overreacted and had killed a sick man. They were going to tell the FBI that this was a clear case of police brutality and that the officer should be arrested.

True to her word, Isabella gave him her phone number. She told him that she was a New Yorker but was in Atlanta several times a week. He was looking forward to getting to know her.

Several FBI agents boarded the plane at the gate in Atlanta. Rebecca and Eddie were with them. Eddie was Alejandro's direct supervisor. Rebecca oversaw the Atlanta office for the CDC Enforcement Unit. The FBI agent in charge of the investigation gave instructions to the passengers. They had had the airport clear out one gate area in the terminal to use to conduct their interviews.

Paramedics also boarded the plane and loaded up Carl for transport. He was in and out of consciousness and gave no response as the medicine was administered to him. They quickly secured him to the stretcher with restraints and got him out of there.

Rebecca and Eddie came over to Estrada and the three of them stepped to the rear of the airplane. Johnson put her hand on his shoulder and said, "How are you doing, Alejandro?"

He hung his head and appeared to be getting emotional. "That blazer cost me a hundred and fifty dollars and now it has infected blood on it. I think I'm going to need therapy,

Boss."

Rebecca and Eddie both laughed. "Did you really kill a zombie with your knife?" Marshall asked.

"I didn't want to, but I couldn't get a shot at him. The aisles were full of idiots taking video. I didn't want to shoot one of them so I got to use my East LA knife skills. I think I'm going to be the latest YouTube sensation."

Four hours later, the interviews were concluded. Alejandro had done a walkthrough of the incident with an FBI agent and had given a statement. Rebecca had one of the CDC Clean Up Teams respond to the scene.

The Clean Up Teams were four person teams trained in forensics, evidence collection, and crime scene processing. They all had both local and federal law enforcement experience and had received supplemental training from the FBI. They would take pictures and process the scene. They would also remove George's body for an autopsy.

Alejandro saw Isabella glance over at him from time-to-time as he talked to Rebecca. Isabella was still working and serving her customers. The airline had provided drinks and snacks for the passengers to have while they waited to talk to the FBI.

After the interviews were concluded, Estrada saw Isabella gather her things and start to leave. He walked over to her before she could get away.

"So, are you going to work tomorrow?" he asked.

"No, the airline is giving us a free day here in Atlanta. After that flight, though, I'm not sure that one day off is enough."

"Well, maybe, if you don't have anything else, maybe you would do something with me? We could see some of the city and have dinner?"

She looked down and seemed to be thinking about it. "That sounds like a nice day. But, you have to tell me, who's that blonde lady?"

"That's Rebecca. She's my boss's boss. Why?"

"Because she's so beautiful. I didn't know if you guys were, you know…"

Alejandro laughed. "No, she's just my boss. She's a great person, but I think she and another one of the guys in our office may be dating. They keep it pretty quiet. But for me, I'm not seeing anybody. Like I told you, I'm pretty shy. What about you? I bet you have a guy in every city."

Isabella laughed and punched him lightly on the arm. "No, I don't. I'm not like that. I haven't met the right guy. And, I work a lot."

"Carl told me that you thought you might've met the right guy."

Her face flushed. "Oh, yeah? What did he say?"

"Maybe I'll tell you tomorrow."

CDC HQ, Thursday, 1400 hours

One of the reasons that the CDC's response teams had been so effective was their high level of training. If they weren't following up on leads of their own or assisting local or other federal law enforcement agencies, they were usually training. Today, the officers were working with their new equipment at a local police department's shoot house. Alejandro had a date with Isabella a little later, but he had been out of action for a while and was glad to be back with his teammates.

Rebecca was missing this training to catch up on some of her administrative responsibilities. The phone on her desk rang. When she answered, Dr. Nicole Edwards asked her if she could come upstairs. Dr. Edwards was one of the leading epidemiologists at the CDC and headed up the team that was trying to create a vaccine for the zombie virus.

Hope surged in Rebecca's heart as she exited the elevator and walked down the hallway to the laboratory. Maybe they have made some progress on a vaccine, she thought. Up to this point, their best efforts had produced a few experimental versions that had not worked. The experimental vaccine that had been given to flight attendant Carl, for example, the previous day had not cured him. He had hung on to life for around eighteen hours before passing away in the hospital. He had not reanimated as a zombie, but he had still died.

One of the epidemiologists who had been assigned to the vaccine team, Azar Kasra, had turned out to be an Iranian agent providing intelligence to Amir al-Razi. They had also discovered that she had sabotaged the vaccine research and set it back several weeks. Kasra had been captured and arrested when she tried to infect Chuck

McCain. Her plan had been to infect him by sticking him with a syringe of the zombie virus and then to infect as many of the CDC executives and scientists as she could before being killed or arrested. At the moment, she was being interrogated by a CIA team in a remote location.

Johnson stepped into the lab and saw Edwards talking with a group of white-coated scientists. When she saw Rebecca, she smiled and walked over. Nicole's wavy brown hair hung around her shoulders.

"I have some good news," the scientist said. "Not great news, but definitely good news. We've found a chemical solution that will kill the virus on contact. With you guys being up close and personal with so many infected, I've been concerned that one of you might get infected through blood splatter."

"That's great," Rebecca said with a smile.

Inside, though, she was disappointed. She was hoping to hear that they had had a breakthrough in their vaccine research but this was better than nothing.

"I know it's not as good as finding a cure or creating a vaccine," said Dr. Edwards, "but it'll offer a little more protection to you and your people and it's something that we can pass on to local police, paramedics, and medical personnel who come in contact with infected people."

"So, how did you find something that would kill this thing on contact?" Johnson asked.

"Well, we've been using a chlorine solution to kill Ebola for years. We tried that and had some success with the zombie virus. It kills it but not right away. We experimented a bit and were able to increase the potency.

"I have some for you to take with you. Use it full strength on any blood splatter or saliva and let it stay for a minute or two. Then, just wash the affected area with soap and water."

Edwards picked up a cardboard box off of a table and handed it to Johnson. It contained twelve plastic bottles of the liquid.

"This solution will kill the virus on any surface. From your skin to your clothes, even your shoes, it'll do the trick. Hopefully, this will help protect you and your guys."

As she took the box, Rebecca smiled at Nicole. "Thanks for looking out for us. I really do appreciate this and the officers will, as well."

"Just doing our part. You and your guys are out there on the front line and don't think we don't appreciate it." Dr. Edwards lowered her voice. "And, I think all of us up here feel guilty about Azar. We should have caught on to what she was doing. She almost killed Officer McCain. I'm in charge and am responsible. I just feel terrible about the whole situation."

Johnson looked into the scientist's eyes. "Nicole, she was a professional intelligence agent. Don't feel bad. She had all of us fooled. She was good. And, for what it's worth, Chuck ended up getting the better of that exchange."

When Kasra had tried to infect McCain with the zombie virus, his kevlar lined pants had prevented the needle of the syringe from penetrating into his leg. When he felt the poke and saw what she was doing, he had punched her and knocked her across the hallway. When Azar had attempted to pull a revolver on him, he had dropped his knees into her back and twisted the gun out of her hand, breaking one of her fingers.

"Where is she now? Is she in jail here in Atlanta? Is there going to be a big trial?" Edwards asked.

"All I can say," Johnson deflected, "is that she's in custody and is being subjected to a very thorough interrogation."

Nicole nodded and gave a shy smile. "Well, Officer McCain is one good looking man and I know none of us wants to see that body wasted as a zombie."

Rebecca laughed and caught herself blushing. "Thanks for this, Nicole," holding up the box, and turning for the door.

Chapter Three

"I think that's enough," Amir said, looking up at Mohamud Ahmed.

Mohamud picked up the box of soft drinks and slid it into the open back doors of the red and white Coca Cola van. Twenty-five bottles of each type of soft drink, twenty-five bottles of water, and twenty bottles of a sports recovery drink had been treated with the zombie virus.

It was a time consuming process. Amir, working with heavy rubber gloves, would open the drink, breaking the plastic seal. He used a dropper to add several drops of the bio-terror formula to each bottle. Ahmed, also wearing gloves, then applied a few drops of glue to the plastic seal and screwed the top back on.

This was not a perfect process but they felt that it would work. Most of the American high school students that

Amir had met were clueless and he didn't think that they would pay much attention to the seal as they unscrewed the top from their drinks.

Now, it was up to Mohamud to make his normal delivery to the school in the morning. Al-Razi had been given Ahmed's name and information from one of the local mosque leaders. The imam had assured him that Mohamud was trustworthy and wanted to strike a blow for Allah.

The imam told him that Ahmed was a Somalian refugee who had managed to get a job as a route driver for Coca Cola. He appeared to be living the American Dream. In reality, he was waiting for the right opportunity to fight back against the United States and to gain some vengeance.

His father, brother, and an uncle had all been killed by American Special Forces. His father and uncle had died in the Battle of Mogadishu at the hands of American Rangers and Delta Force. Mohamud was only seven years old at the time. His brother had died just a few years earlier. He'd led a group of pirates that preyed on ships that strayed too close to the Somali shore. Two boatloads of pirates had attempted to board a ship that looked like an easy target.

It was their bad luck that this boat was a bait ship with an American SEAL team on board, just waiting for someone to attack them. Mohamud's brother and all the men with him were killed. The second boat managed to flee. Several of those pirates were killed or wounded as well, but a few of them managed to get home to tell the story.

Helping Amir was a great opportunity to gain the vengeance that Mohamud sought. He knew that he would have to flee after this. It would only be a matter of time before his face and name were plastered on every television in America.

The van was loaded. Ahmed would be at Peachtree Meadow High School before the students arrived. He would replenish the drink machines, making sure the bottles that had been tampered with were positioned so that they would be purchased first. They had picked this particular school for three reasons. First of all, it was one of the biggest high schools in the state with almost four thousand students. Secondly, it was in a very affluent part of the suburbs. This would be a blow to the very heart of the decadent Americans. And thirdly, because the school was forty-five minutes from the heart of the city, the response time for the CDC response teams, the local police and other responders should be significantly slower.

Amir had Mohamud's cell number and had given him the number for one of his prepaid phones. If everything went according to plan, al-Razi would contact Ahmed for a meeting. If Mohamud pulled this off, Amir would allow him to participate in the next attacks as well. Now, it was time to check into another cheap hotel and wait for tomorrow.

Peachtree Meadow High School, Northeast of Atlanta, Friday, 0900 hours

The police responded quickly to a report of a fight between students inside the school at 0815 hours. The School Resource Officer had been the first one on the scene and had immediately requested backup and an ambulance. He radioed in that he had a male on top of another male who was biting and ripping his neck with his teeth.

When the attacker did not respond to verbal commands, the SRO drew his taser and fired it into him. The two prongs struck the student in the back and the electrical charged surged through him, having no effect. Instead, he pushed himself off of his victim and attacked the officer.

Students crowded around the hallway to watch the fight. A few of them tried to help the boy who had been attacked as the blood gushed out of his ripped neck onto the floor. A teacher pushed his way through the crowd and began applying pressure to the large wound on the boy's throat.

The SRO was much bigger than the attacking student and easily threw him to the ground and tried to handcuff him. He managed to get his left hand cuffed but then the crazed boy sunk his teeth into the officer's right wrist. The resource officer couldn't pry the young man's teeth off of his arm so he started punching him in the head with his left hand.

The officer's weight kept the student pinned to the floor but he couldn't break the grip of his bite. The pain was excruciating as the boy chewed on his wrist. Punch after punch landed on the student's head but they didn't seem to faze him. One of the punches to the boy's skull broke bones in the officer's hand.

The resource officer reached and managed to get his collapsible baton off his belt. With his broken hand, he couldn't flick the baton to get it open. He could barely even grip it, but he was able to drive the tip of the metal baton into his attacker's mouth and pry his teeth loose, breaking several of them in the process. When his arm was free, hands grabbed at the officer and pulled him back to safety.

The attacking student, growling loudly, lunged at the next closest victim, a young girl with red hair, a freshman, wearing a skirt. He managed to sink his teeth into her calf. She screamed but could not get her leg free. She slapped ineffectively at her assailant as his teeth dug into her flesh.

Jeffrey Bell, a massive offensive lineman for the football team, had gotten to school late. The high school junior was rushing to get to class. He knew that if he got suspended again, he would get kicked off the team. If he got kicked off of the football team, he would have to face his father and he didn't want to even think about that.

He heard yelling in the hallway ahead. When he turned

the corner, he saw the crowd. The injured police officer was being helped to his feet. Jeffrey noticed that one of the officer's hands was dripping blood. The floor of the hallway was coated in the red liquid.

Directly in front of him on the floor, a student appeared to be dead. His throat was ripped open and he was lying in a growing pool of blood. A teacher continued to press on the jagged wound on the boy's neck.

A girl was screaming and other students were trying to pull a male student off of her. He was biting her leg and Jeffrey could see the blood seeping out of the wound. He quickly accessed the situation, dropped his book bag and stepped up to the girl.

"Get off of her!" he yelled at the attacker.

Jeffrey hated bullies. He had been bullied when he was younger and much smaller than he was now. He didn't really understand what was going on, but he could see that this guy had hurt several people.

"Hold onto her," he said to those around the girl. "I'm going to try and kick him off."

He aimed a kick at the attacker's ribs. The force of the blow to the body broke two of the zombie's ribs and got its attention. He released his grip on the girl's leg and started to stand up. Bell grabbed the crazed student by the collar and the back of his belt, easily lifting him off the ground.

The infected boy tried to bite Jeffrey on the arm but his teeth only connected with the material of Jeffrey's football letter jacket. Bell saw the guy trying to bite him and he threw the growling attacker face first into the concrete wall. The sound of the impact of his head on the wall sounded like a melon being smashed.

The blow fractured his skull, sending several pieces of bone into his brain. The infected body slid down the wall onto the bloody floor. With its brain damaged, the zombie was now really dead.

Jeffrey suddenly felt the weight of what he had just done. A ball of fear landed in the pit of his stomach. Sometimes he didn't realize how strong he was.

"Is he OK? Somebody see if he's OK," he said, motioning to the kid he had just thrown into the wall.

Another student spoke up, "No, everybody stay away from him. I think this is the zombie virus that we've been hearing about."

The student with his throat ripped open began to move. His eyes opened and he grabbed at the teacher who had been trying help him. His mouth was moving but with his voice box damaged, no sound came out.

The teacher wasn't sure what was happening. Should he try and help the boy to the clinic? The now infected student got a hand on the man's tie and pulled him down to his mouth. He missed the throat but sunk his teeth into the teacher's cheek.

The students in the hallway backed even further away. They had all just watched this young man murdered in front of their eyes and now he was alive and attacking a teacher. The students began to flee in different directions. Jeffrey watched as the teacher tried to free himself but felt paralyzed by fear. Then, he started running, too.

The SRO and the girl who had gotten bit had been helped to the clinic near the front of the school. The officer managed to give the police dispatcher an update and tell her that instead of just being a fight between two students, they had a homicide. He had not seen the murdered student reanimate as a zombie, so responding officers had not been alerted to this new threat.

By now, multiple calls were pouring into the police 911 center. One call came in of a teacher attacking a student. Another caller said a male student had attacked a female teacher and was killing her in the classroom. Still another said that two teachers were attacking a third one near the teacher's lounge. It looked like they were chewing on her throat. These calls were all coming in from different parts of the school.

The next two police cars were on the scene within five minutes. The two young officers rushed into the school to assist the resource officer. But, when they got inside, the principal met them and said he needed them in the library. A student was assaulting the librarian.

When they reached the library, the principal opened the door and pointed inside. The officers could hear growling and chewing sounds from behind a wooden counter in the middle of the room. They moved cautiously, one with his taser and the other with his pistol in hand.

As they rounded the corner, a male student with shoulder-length hair, wearing a long black coat, was on top of an elderly black woman. She was obviously dead and he was chewing on her throat. Blood covered the young man, the victim, and the floor.

"Police! Don't move!" one of the officers challenged.

The boy turned, gore dripping out of his mouth, and threw himself at the two officers. The one with the taser fired. The two prongs struck him in the chest but didn't slow him down.

Both police officers started backing up, trying to create some distance. They could see the blood on the boy's face, clothes, and hands. He was just about to grab the officer with the taser when his partner fired his pistol.

It's a misconception that police are trained to shoot to kill. In reality, they are trained to shoot to stop the threat. Police and military are trained to shoot at the center mass of their targets, the chest area. It is the largest area, it contains the most vital organs, and shots to that region usually stop the person. Unless that person has been infected by the zombie virus.

The officer fired two, three, four times into the young man's chest. The shots slowed him down but did not stop him. Instead, he changed directions and launched himself at the officer who was shooting at him. He managed to get off one more shot to his chest before the boy was on top of him, clawing at his face. He managed to sink his teeth into the side of the officer's face.

The second officer reached for the attacker before he could bite his partner's throat. He grabbed the back of his long black coat and spun, throwing the boy across a table. As the zombie student got to his feet, the officer quickly holstered his taser and drew his pistol. He put the front site on the young man's face and fired one time as he lunged forward again. This time he fell to the floor with a bullet hole in his forehead and did not move.

Additional police officers responded to the high school, including the shift sergeant. He quickly grasped that this was becoming a major incident. There were reports from inside the school of at least six dead and multiple injured. He asked that the SWAT team be mobilized.

Students continued to flee the school with horror stories of what was going on inside. Some of the students who began to fill the parking lot had bite wounds to a hand, an arm, or a leg. Some of these stayed for treatment, while many other injured teens simply got into their cars and drove home.

Even though there were no reports of armed attackers, the police treated this like an active shooter situation. Teams of four officers were sent in to try and locate and neutralize attackers and rescue the wounded. Paramedics were escorted in as the ambulances began to arrive. The biggest challenge that the police faced was that they were dealing with multiple attackers so they weren't sure where to start in neutralizing the threats inside the school.

Local police departments were slowly starting to wake up to the serious threat the zombie virus posed, but it is tough to go against one's training. The idea of shooting unarmed people contradicts everything that these officers had been taught. This was intensified even more because they were confronting teenagers. These were someone's children.

The first team of four officers who entered the school were told that several students were attacking others near the cafeteria. The officers made their way cautiously down the hall. The noises of a struggle and growling sounds were coming from around the next corner. The police approached cautiously and peeked into the hallway.

Six teenagers turned zombies had five victim's bodies pinned to the floor. Blood covered the bodies, the zombies, the walls, and the floor. Two of the creatures were ripping apart a woman, probably a teacher. The other four each had a student that they were working on. All of the victims were obviously dead.

The first officer gasped. "Oh, my God!" he exclaimed. "Everybody, down on the ground," he ordered the assailants. "Now!"

As one, the six zombies got to their feet and charged the officers. Their hesitancy to shoot unarmed people cost all four of them their lives. Only one officer managed to get off a shot, catching one of the zombies high in the leg. The shot broke his femur and dropped him to the floor. The zombie behind him, though, managed to get his hands on the officer's head and his teeth on the officer's neck. The one with the broken leg crawled forward so that he could feed as well.

A police radio broke squelch asking if the officers were OK. There would be no answer.

CDC HQ, Friday, 1030 hours

The two Atlanta CDC enforcement teams sat in the briefing room watching the drama unfold at Peachtree Meadow High School. The large television monitor on the wall showed scenes of unprecedented chaos. At this point, their help had not been requested but they knew it was just a matter of time.

They were watching a live split-screen of the events. On one side of the monitor was the feed from a local news station. The reporters and cameras had been cordoned far enough away from the school that they could not see anything. Their news helicopter, however, was flying overhead and the cameras were running.

The other side of the television monitor was a live feed from a Department of Homeland Security drone. It's cameras provided a much clearer picture than the news cameras. And what they were showing was America's worst nightmare.

The floor plan of the school filled the screen of one of the big computer monitors in the room. The men and Rebecca had been looking it over, trying to get a feel for what it was going to be like inside. They looked at entrances, rally points, and fall back areas inside the building. If they were called upon to assist the local police, they understood that they were going to be vastly outnumbered.

They would be going in to conduct rescue operations for those who were injured and for those who were hiding from the zombies. They would also be trying to eliminate as many of them as they could. With a school that large, though, there could be hundreds of infected by the time they arrived.

Rebecca's phone vibrated. The local police were now requesting federal help. That request had gone through the Department of Homeland Security. Several federal agencies were notified and would be involved but the CDC Response Teams were the first federal responders for anything related to the zombie virus.

She stepped out of the room to make a phone call as the men readied their equipment. For the first time, they would be wearing their heavy body armor. They also had their soft body armor on underneath their uniform polo shirts.

Even though there were no reports of shooting, their armor would add another layer of protection. Their chest rigs could hold six extra magazines for their suppressed M4s. Each officer also shoved a couple of extra mags into their cargo pockets.

"Are you sure you guys are feeling up to this?" Chuck asked Andy Fleming and Scotty Smith as they were slipping their body armor on.

They had both been shot in the attacks the week before. Fleming had gotten hit in the side by an AK-47 bullet fragment. The doctor had removed the fragment and patched him up. Smith had an AK-47 round rip across his left shoulder. It had taken out a chunk of flesh but didn't hit anything vital.

Both men laughed. "There's no way that we're going to miss this, Boss," said Smith. Scotty, a bearded former Army Ranger, turned firefighter/paramedic, turned federal law enforcement officer was a muscular six foot five and weighed about two hundred and fifty pounds.

"Plus, I hate teenagers," he said. "This will allow me to rid the world of a few."

"We're good to go, Chuck," said Fleming. He was a lean, wiry five foot eight. Andy had been a staff sergeant in the Marine Special Operations Command, the Marine Corps' version of special forces. "I think that we're going to need every gun that we can get on this one."

Smith pointed to Estrada. "And with Hollywood here killing a zombie with a knife, I believe that's just a bit of showmanship on his part. I'm going to try and kill one with a pencil once we get inside that school."

All the men were laughing as Rebecca walked back in. The serious look on her face lifted the levity from the room.

"Sorry, guys, to break the mood. We need to get going. The police over there are getting torn up. They lost contact with a four-man active shooter team. The SWAT Team finally got there and sent in a team to locate those officers. They found them but they were all dead, and then two of them woke up as zombies and attacked the SWAT guys.

SWAT put them down but had two guys get bit in the process.

"As SWAT was pulling back, they got overrun. It's sounding like they may have lost an entire eight man assault team. When I got off of the phone they were getting ready to send in another team. They're getting phone calls from inside classrooms from students who are trying to hide. It sounds like there are a lot of kids that need to be rescued but the number of infected is growing by the moment.

"Several kids have gotten out to the parking lot and then turned. Now, they're having to shoot some of these student zombies outside where the news chopper can film it. Two officers have gotten bit outside near the command post. What's making matters worse, is that now parents are showing up and rushing into the school. The police are trying to stop them but, you know, parents can get kind of crazy."

"Great, so we're looking at zombie teenagers, zombie teachers, zombie police officers, zombie SWAT officers, and now zombie parents. Did I miss anybody?" said Jimmy Jones.

Now Rebecca smiled. "No, Jimmy, that about covers it."

"And now that the locals have requested us, do they know what we're going to do?" asked McCain. "They do understand that we're going to shoot as many of those things in the head as we possibly can?"

Rebecca nodded. "I told them that our rules of

---

engagement were that we would shoot any aggressive, violent infected person that we came across. Non-aggressive, non-violent injured we would try and help. And, of course, we'll try and rescue as many as we can."

Eddie said, "Well, gang, its a long drive. We better get going."

"We aren't driving," said Rebecca. "A DHS Blackhawk will be landing on the roof any minute now. Let's go load up."

"A Blackhawk? I get to ride to work in a Blackhawk?" said Luis García. "And my ex-wives said that I wouldn't amount to anything."

As the teams filed out, Chuck hung back. Rebecca noticed and slowed down. Soon it was just the two of them in the briefing room.

"I guess this means I get a rain check for dinner if this thing takes all day?" she said.

McCain had finally gotten the nerve up the previous week to ask Johnson out for dinner. They were supposed to go out that night.

"Definitely. Do you have any plans for tomorrow night?"

She laughed. "You certainly are persistent. I'll have to check my calendar. I don't think I'm scheduled to kill any zombies tomorrow night."

"That's a relief," he said. "Well, let's go catch our ride."

Peachtree Meadow High School, Friday, 1100 hours

Jeffrey Bell understood fear. He was always scared before a football game. No one else knew it, but he threw up before every game. After the kickoff, he was OK, but the fear and stress right before the start almost paralyzed him. And this fear that he was feeling now was worse than anything he had felt before.

He still felt bad about throwing that kid into the wall. He was pretty sure that he'd killed him. He never wanted to hurt anybody. As the morning had progressed, though, he began to understand that the zombie virus had visited his school. A couple of times he had started to run for an exit. Get out. Get to where it was safe. Other kids had managed to do that. No one would criticize him for running away from what was happening inside the school.

Jeffrey felt guilty for running away while that teacher got attacked. He'd rushed to an exit but didn't go through it. Something inside of him, an inner voice, a sense of duty, something, told him that he needed to help his fellow students. The fear was still there but now there was something else. A feeling that he needed to try and protect those he could protect. Just like he had tried to protect that girl earlier.

As the numbers of infected grew, many groups of non-infected looked for places to hide. Many students had tried to escape but were caught by the zombies and killed before they could reach the exits. This latest strain of the zombie virus produced infected people who were quick, strong and deadly.

Jeffrey had heard the gunfire. There had been a lot of it from different directions. The police were there. Now, they just had to wait. He knew that they would be rescued. He was just worried about how long it would take and if they could remain undetected until then.

The screams of the victims had finally died down. There had been so many people screaming and yelling in the corridors. Those screams had been horrible and had imprinted themselves on Jeffrey's mind.

Periodically, he would see groups of five or ten or even fifteen infected walking by the doorway. If he could see them, he wondered if they could look in the same window and see him and the group he was with? What would he do if they tried to get in?

At the moment, he was with a group of around twenty students in a classroom. They were all lying on the floor trying to be quiet. Bell was holding an aluminum baseball bat. He had found the equipment bag discarded in the hallway.

Two other boys had armed themselves with the other two bats that were in the bag. They had then run off, in search of an exit. Jeffrey was the only one of his group who had some kind of a weapon.

The classroom that they were in was not the best hiding place but, at the moment, it had made sense. A large group of infected students and teachers had seen them from down an adjacent corridor. Bell herded the students into the classroom, closed the door, and motioned them onto the floor. The zombies came rushing by just seconds later.

This particular room was towards the middle of the school and not close to an exit. They had lain there on the floor of the classroom for over half an hour. There hadn't been any gunshots for a while. What should they do? How long should they wait?

Peachtree Meadow High School, Friday, 1115 hours

The Blackhawk touched down in the middle of the high school football field. A SWAT officer carrying an M4 rifle met the helicopter to escort the response teams to the command post. Sergeant Josh Matthews was devastated. He had lost twelve friends today and had come very close to losing his own life.

His police department took great pride in handling their own situations and their own crises. This was the first time that he knew of that they'd had to ask for outside help. He'd heard some stories about the CDC Enforcement Unit and seen some of the news coverage of them in action in the previous week's terror attacks. Well, he thought, let's see how good they are because this is the worst situation that I've ever seen.

The side door on the helicopter slid open. A giant of a man with a bushy beard stepped out. He was smiling and winked at Josh. Two black guys got out. One of them was muscular and had a shaved head. He was built like a linebacker. The second one was lean like a wide receiver. The next person out was a woman. A really beautiful woman. Josh caught himself staring at her and paid no attention to the other three men that got off the helicopter.

"What's the matter, Sergeant? Have you never seen such a handsome man before?"

Another big man stood in front of him. That voice sounded familiar.

"McCain? Is that you? The last I heard, you were getting shot at in Afghanistan. Good to see you."

The two men embraced.

"Good to see you, Josh. I'm sorry to hear about all your guys. Let me introduce you to the boss and you can take us to the CP. Josh Matthews, this is Rebecca Johnson. She has the honor of leading such a fine group of men."

Josh and Rebecca shook hands. He noticed that she was kitted out just like the men. They all had M4s hanging from their chests. They were all wearing heavy body armor, kevlar helmets, and had Glocks in tactical holsters. And they all looked like they meant business.

The command post was set up in the lower parking lot, about two hundred yards from the school. Chuck estimated that over a thousand students, teachers, and parents were milling around. Many of the students with cars had already left.

The school resource officers from several other schools had come to Peachtree Meadow to help out with crowd control. They were doing what they could to keep things somewhat organized. There were eight white sheet-covered figures lying scattered around the command post. All of the sheets had bloodstains on them. Other sheet-covered bodies were lying closer to the school.

Inside the CP, Major Hughes was the on-scene commander but there was plenty of other brass hanging around. The Chief of Police, two assistant chiefs, three other majors, three lieutenants, and two sergeants were also in the command post. Several of them were looking at a floor plan of the school and marking the locations for possible survivors. Two of the lieutenants and one of the sergeants were holding AR-15 rifles and keeping an eye on the crowd.

The SWAT Commander, another lieutenant, was standing off to the side, speaking into his police radio. An older man in a suit was talking on his cell phone. The major in charge identified him as the school principal and said that he was requesting school buses come and transport these students to a safer location.

McCain knew all of them and they knew him. He had been Josh's team leader on SWAT for several years. Now Josh was leading his own team. The SWAT commander and Chuck had also served together for years. They all shook hands and McCain introduced them to Rebecca.

"Thanks for coming. We hate having to ask for help, but we've gotten torn up today. Here's what we have," Major Hughes said. He recounted the events of the early morning.

"The first team of four officers that went into the school never came out. No radio contact, nothing. SWAT got here and sent in an eight-man team to try and locate them. They had to shoot several infected along the way.

"They finally found the four officers, dead. Two of them had been ripped to pieces by those things. While they were checking the bodies, the two of them that weren't as torn up woke up, or reanimated, or whatever you call it, as zombies and they had to shoot them.

"SWAT then radioed that they were getting attacked by another, larger group. There was gunfire and then nothing more from them. We lost contact. Sergeant Matthew's assault team of eight officers rushed in to try and help them. They never even got there.

"Their team got hit by a group of over thirty infected before they got fifty feet inside the school. They shot a bunch of them but we also lost another four guys. Josh and three others just managed to get back out. A few of the zombies followed them outside and we shot them over there by the front door.

"You can also see we had to shoot these that are covered in sheets," he said, pointing to the bodies near the CP. "They must've gotten bit or something inside and turned after they got outside. The Chief even had to shoot one of them. Those two lieutenants and that sergeant with rifles are providing security for the CP."

"What about the parents?" Rebecca asked. "The news reports are saying that a lot them managed to get through the perimeter and get inside the school."

"That's correct. We have a pretty good perimeter in place now. Earlier though, we were still trying to get a handle on things and I'd say at least fifty to seventy-five parents got inside the school. We've caught and detained a lot more. They can sue us later. The ones inside, though will either need to be shot or rescued."

"Do you think any injured and possibly infected people got away?"

"It's possible. They probably did. Like I said, it took us a little while to get a clear picture on what was happening. We didn't realize how big this was for almost twenty minutes. Then it took another ten or fifteen minutes to start getting more officers here. Some infected kids could have gotten out quick, got in their cars and left," the major said.

"The Department of Homeland Security told us that when you got here, you were in charge. I'm happy to release control of the scene to you, Ms. Johnson. Just tell me what you need."

"Major, for now, I think it's better if you keep doing what you're doing," Rebecca said. "The FBI and Emergency Management Personnel for the CDC are on their way. We also have our Clean Up Teams coming. They'll assist your crime scene people with evidence collection, processing the scene, and whatever else you need after we get things stabilized. Right now, I think the most important thing we can do is try and rescue some students and teachers."

"If you guys could make entry and start rescuing kids and teachers, that would be the greatest way to help us. We

---

have two other SWAT teams from other police departments on their way. I don't expect to see them for at least an hour, though."

"Do you have any SWAT officers that could go in with us?" Johnson asked. "I know they've had a rough day but it would be good to have the help."

"Josh, do you want to check with your guys?" asked the major.

"No need, sir. My three guys and I would love to help. I'll go let them know."

Chuck intercepted him before he could get away. "Hey, Josh, have you guys got any suppressed weapons?"

"I think we still have some suppressed MP5s in the SWAT truck. Why?"

"These things are drawn to sound and I anticipate that we're going to be doing a lot of shooting. The less noise we make the better."

Matthews nodded and hurried to prep his men.

Chapter Four

Peachtree Meadow High School, Friday, 1140 hours

"You guys notice that so much of this stuff happens right around lunch or dinner time?" Scotty asked, as they were checking their equipment.

"Tell you what, big guy," said Jimmy. "When we're done, let's get that helicopter driver to put us down at a nice restaurant and you can buy us all dinner."

Luis stepped up and said, "That's a good idea, amigo. My vote's for Mexican food."

Alejandro nodded at him and gave him a high five. "Fridays are for fajitas and cold cerveza."

Four paramedics walked up and joined the group. They had on their heavy fire turnout gear, including helmets with face guards, and were carrying medical bags. Normally, the police would have made some funny comments about their fire department brothers. Today, they were welcomed into the circle of officers with handshakes and pats on the back. These fire paramedics had volunteered to accompany the officers into the school. They were unarmed and knew the danger that lay before them. Josh and his other three SWAT officers also joined the group.

"All right you guys, listen up," said Eddie. "My name's Eddie Marshall and I'm one of the team leaders. That guy there," motioning at Chuck, "is our other team leader, Chuck McCain. For you SWAT guys, thanks for going in with us. We're really sorry about your friends. Maybe we'll get lucky and find some of them alive. Now, I want to introduce you to our commander, Rebecca Johnson."

She stepped forward and smiled at all the men. "I echo what Eddie said. We're all sorry that you lost friends today. I think that the most important thing we can do now is to try and rescue as many of these kids and teachers as we can and eliminate as many of the infected as possible.

"Our rules of engagement are simple. Any hostile, violent, or aggressive infected people are shot in the head. Center mass shots have no effect on them. You guys," she said, nodding at the four SWAT officers, "have been inside and know how dangerous it is in there.

"Any non-hostile injured people we come across, we'll try and help. Our main goal is to rescue people that are hiding. The principal thinks that there could still be a few hundred students and teachers in the school hiding from the zombies.

"We'll have two teams of six officers, each accompanied by two paramedics. Eddie and Chuck are the team leaders and once we get inside the school, they're in charge. I'm just an extra gun when the shooting starts.

"You paramedics, stay close to us and we'll protect you. Follow the commands of your team leader. There may be some people in there that we can't help. If the team leader says, 'Keep moving,' keep moving.

"Sergeant Matthews, you and your men will need to listen out for us on your radios. We don't have your frequency on ours. We'll need to know when those other SWAT teams get here so we don't have any blue on blue accidents. Questions? Okay, let's go."

The plan was for one team to enter from the rear on the far side of the school and the other team to enter through a side entrance of the school closest to the command post. That would hopefully prevent crossfire problems. The police dispatcher had the approximate locations for several groups of survivors. They had called 911 and the dispatcher had relayed that information to the SWAT officers.

These local officers also knew the layout of the school better than the CDC officers. Most SWAT teams train for worst-case scenarios and many of those involve schools. They had conducted an active shooter training scenario inside Peachtree Meadow just a couple of months earlier.

Both of the teams were in place and would enter at the same time. Team Two was at the rear entrance, furthest away from Team One. Jimmy was on point. A former Marine captain with two Iraq combat tours under his belt and a former Alabama State Trooper, he preferred to lead the way. A SWAT officer followed him and team leader, Eddie, was number three.

Eddie was a former Chicago Police sergeant turned Federal Marshal turned CDC team Leader. A paramedic was next, followed by Rebecca and then the other paramedic assigned to their team. Another SWAT officer followed and Alejandro brought up the rear. Estrada had been a military police officer in the army and then a LAPD officer, hence the nickname, "Hollywood."

Team One was stacked at a side entrance. Andy Fleming had the point. SWAT Sergeant Josh Matthews was second and team leader Chuck McCain was next. Next in the stack was a paramedic, the other SWAT officer, another paramedic and then Luis García. Luis was a former Miami Police Officer, a former Secret Service Agent, bouncer, and bodyguard. Bringing up the rear was Scotty Smith.

The officers were focused but felt the normal nervousness that accompanied every building entry. What was on the other side of the door waiting for them? They knew their training and experience would kick in as they moved and adrenaline would fuel them for whatever they would encounter.

"Team One in place and ready," said McCain into his radio headset.

"Team Two is ready," came Eddie's response.

The doors of most schools are kept locked. Josh had obtained two keys from the principal. He had one and one of the SWAT officers on Team Two had the other. They stepped up and quickly unlocked the doors.

"Entering now," Chuck said.

A few seconds later, Marshall said, "We're in."

Inside Peachtree Meadow High School, Friday, 1145 hours

They had lain quietly on the classroom floor for almost an hour. A few of the students were getting restless. One of the girls kept whispering loudly that she had to go to the bathroom.

One of the boys looked like he was in the beginning stages of a panic attack. He kept saying, "We have to get out of here," over and over. Jeffrey didn't know what a panic attack was by name but he recognized the fear that he saw in the sophomore's eyes.

Bell crawled over to him. "Listen, man, I understand but we have to stay quiet. The police are going to come get us but right now we can't make any noise. You have to stay calm. Try taking some deep breathes. That always helps me."

"Okay, I'll try," the boy said.

One of the girls was on the phone with her mother. She was whispering and telling her mom what was happening. One of the guys had managed to get through to 911. He whispered to the dispatcher, asking her to please hurry and send help. He didn't know the classroom number but he knew the approximate location in the school. Others tried to call out but didn't have any service on their phones.

Jeffrey crawled back over to his spot by the door. He knew that if the zombies made entry, he was going to have to be the one to try and stop them. He was starting to feel nauseous just like he did before a game. A figure walked slowly up the hallway to their classroom. He was wearing a button down shirt and a tie. His glasses were still on his face but were hanging at a funny angle.

One of the girls in the classroom said, "That's Mr. Taylor, the assistant principal. Maybe he's coming to rescue us."

Jeffrey motioned at her to be quiet but the damage was done. Mr. Taylor turned at the noise and slammed his arms into the window of the classroom door. The glass shattered and ripped his arms to shreds. He didn't even notice as he growled at the students in the room.

His eyes were glazed over and his mouth was opening and snapping shut. He had blood on his face and shirt. The reason his eyeglasses were askew was that his nose was missing. It appeared to have been chewed off and only a bloody hole remained in the middle of his face.

The door was still closed and the wooden lower part came up to just past Mr. Taylor's waist. He began to slam his body into the door and the sound of other zombie's growls filled the hallway as they responded to the noise. The students in the classroom began to lose it. The girls were crying and the guys seemed to have already gone into shock. No one seemed to know what to do. No one except

Jeffrey.

Bell jumped to his feet and swung the baseball bat at Mr. Taylor's head. It was a swing fueled by fear, adrenaline, and Jeffrey's powerful body. The bat swung through the broken window and caught the former assistant principal full in the forehead. A metal twang reverberated in the classroom and in the hallway. The blow was strong enough to fracture his skull and drop him to the floor.

Jeffrey glanced out into the hall. A group of at least twenty more zombies were coming from the right and another ten or so were coming from the left. The girl who needed to use the bathroom jumped up and ran to the door, screaming at the top of her lungs, "Help us! Please, please, somebody, help us!"

Bell pushed her out of the way. "You need to get back," he said, calmly. "There are more of them coming."

His wave of fear had passed and a calmness settled over him. It was just like after the football game started. After kickoff, he was always good to go. He looked around the classroom. There was nothing to use for weapons. Nothing.

A loud popping sound came from up the hallway to the right. And then another. And another. Some of the zombies collapsed to the floor with holes in their heads. It sounded like gunshots but not quite as loud.

A group of five of the infected reached the doorway and were growling and reaching in. Jeffrey recognized a familiar face in the group. Billy Allen. One of his best friends. They played on the offensive line together. Billy was one of the few players on the team who was bigger than Jeffrey. His glazed and bloodshot eyes didn't even register recognition for Bell. He was growling and his face was covered with blood and gore. He was wearing his green and white Peachtree Meadow letter jacket, just like Jeffrey was.

Shots continued to sound to the right and zombies continued to fall. The entire group of ten from the other direction were now shoving against the door. Billy was one of the biggest high school offensive linemen in the state of Georgia, weighing almost three hundred pounds. It was only a matter of minutes before the door was forced open.

Tears were streaming down Jeffrey's face as he swung the bat at Billy's head. It took two strikes before Allen fell, his skull shattered. His big body knocked three other zombies down as he collapsed to the floor. They immediately started trying to get to their feet.

Bell continued to swing the bat and continued to connect with zombie heads. They piled up around the doorway as he cried and swung the bat. There was more movement up to the right. Jeffrey's arms were getting tired. He wasn't sure how much longer he could keep it up.

"Police officers! We're coming in. Step back from the door and let us make sure the area is clear."

Andy Fleming led them deeper into the school. Josh guided him as to which hallways to take. A teenager and a police officer, both turned zombies rounded a corner in front of them. They were covered in blood and were growling the guttural growl that all zombies seemed to make. The student's face had been ripped apart and an eyeball was hanging out of its socket. Andy fired twice, dropping them both. He glanced at Josh and saw tears in his eyes.

"Sorry, man."

"Let's keep moving," was his only reply.

There were more shots from the rear of the team. Fleming stopped and glanced back. Scotty and Luis shot three zombie students that had run up behind them. Andy started moving again.

They passed body after body in the hallway. This was like nothing that any of them had ever seen or smelled before. The floor and walls were streaked in red and the smell was horrific where the bodies had been ripped open. They couldn't help but walk through infected blood.

They moved slowly as they got deeper into the school. The police dispatcher told Matthews that they had a group of twenty students nearby asking to be rescued. As they moved down the hallway, a loud metallic thud came from up ahead. A few seconds later, a girl screamed out, "Help us! Please, please, somebody, help us!"

"Oh, that's going to help," muttered McCain. "That should bring every zombie in the school straight to us."

The hallway they were on ended at a T intersection. It was clear to the right. To the left was a large group of infected converging on a classroom. Another big group was coming from the opposite side of the room. Fleming guessed there were twenty-five to thirty in total. The growls of the infected echoed down the hallway.

The former spec op Marine turned around and gave quick hand signals to the team. He motioned Josh and Chuck up with him and had everyone else guard their rear and the other side of the intersection that they were at. Fleming, Matthews, and McCain stepped into the hallway and started firing. The suppressed weapons were still loud inside the school and a few of the big group closest to them turned and started towards the officers.

Zombies started to drop. Over the sound of the gunfire was the distinctive metal twang of a baseball bat. Chuck and the other two officers squeezed off shot after shot to their heads. They shot students, teachers, and probably a few parents that had been infected. In less than two minutes the first group had been eliminated.

Now there were shots from the rear of the team. Scotty and Luis had killed four more teenage zombies that had tried to get to them. Andy motioned the team forward. Most of the second group of infected was now lying on the floor around the doorway with their skulls crushed. Another zombie teacher and student were almost to the classroom door. Fleming and Matthews made head shots on both of them. Everybody paused to reload their rifles.

"Police officers! We're coming in. Step back from the door and let us make sure the area is clear," Andy commanded.

Instead, the students rushed to the door and flung it

open. "Thank God you're here," one of the girls said between sobs.

"Is anybody hurt?" asked Andy.

No one answered him and all the students seemed intent on pushing their way into the hall. We need a plan, he thought. A group this big will be tough to protect all the way back to an exit. They were near the center of the school and not close to any of the outside doors.

Three of the male students pushed their way into the hallway, clearly in panic mode. Fleming and Josh shoved them back into the classroom.

"Everybody back inside," he ordered.

"We want to get out of here," a girl sobbed.

"Listen, we're going to get you all out. Keep your voices down and just hang on for a minute," said Josh.

Chuck waved the rest of the team into the room. He pointed at Luis, Scotty, and one of the SWAT officers and told them to watch the door and the hallway.

He saw a big, hulking teenager standing off to the side. He was holding a bloody baseball bat and was crying. He had blood splatter on his coat, hands, and face. McCain stepped slowly over to the young man.

"Are you OK? Did you get bit or injured?"

"No, sir," he said. "I just…I didn't want to hurt anybody but they were trying to get in. And I had to hit Billy. We were on the football team together. And I had to hit him."

Chuck put a hand on the boy's shoulder. "What's your name?"

"Jeffery Bell."

"Well, Jeffrey, you saved everybody in here. You did good. Now I'm going to have one of these paramedics come wipe the blood off of you so you don't get sick, OK?"

Bell nodded and McCain waved over a paramedic to clean him off with the new solution developed by the CDC scientists. Chuck stepped back to confer with his men. A shot came from the doorway from Scotty's rifle. Two more shots came from the SWAT officer's suppressed MP5. Three more infected had been eliminated. McCain glanced over. Smith smiled at him and gave him a thumbs up.

"I don't think it's a good idea to move such a big group. I counted nineteen heads. What do you guys think?" he asked Andy and Josh.

Fleming nodded. "Yeah, that's a lot of people to protect. What about we take ten and then nine? We can leave a few guys in here to protect everybody."

"What do you think, Josh?" Chuck asked.

"It's probably better to do it that way. It just seems dangerous splitting the team."

"Okay, that's what we'll do. Andy, grab ten of these kids to go with you. Me and Scotty will stay with the rest of them until you get back. That still leaves you guys with four shooters."

Andy nodded and started grabbing students to leave. He picked the nine girls. That left eleven boys. Chuck made eye contact with Andy and nodded at Jeffrey. Fleming stepped over to the big teenager.

76

"We need one more to go out with us. You've done your share today. Come on, let's get out of here."

Bell wiped his eyes with his now clean hands and shook his head. "Take one of them," he said, pointing at the other students. "I'll go out with the next group."

Chuck and Andy shrugged at each other. Fleming grabbed another one of the young men, picked one of the paramedics to stay behind, and then lined everybody up. Andy and SWAT Sergeant Josh were in the front. Luis and the other SWAT officer brought up the rear. The ten students and the other paramedic were in the middle. He briefed them about the importance of staying together and moving fast.

The ones that were getting left behind continued to protest but Chuck and Scotty told them that they were staying with them to protect them until the second trip. Fleming looked everybody over and then stepped out into the hallway. There were bodies sprawled all around the doorway and they had to be careful not to trip over them. McCain shut the classroom door and watched them leave.

The other side of the school, Friday, 1150 hours

Jimmy led Team Two through a back door on the far side of the school. After they were all inside, they started moving slowly and cautiously, deeper into the unknown. There were four mangled bodies lying just inside the doorway. They had to be careful not to slip in the blood.

77

The sound of footsteps came from up ahead. Suddenly, several students burst around the corner and came running down the hallway straight towards them. Jimmy raised his rifle, his finger on the trigger, not sure if these were zombies or not.

A skinny young black male was leading the group of thirteen other students. He raised his hands over his head and stopped. The rest of the teens followed his lead.

"Don't shoot. We've been hiding in a classroom but we haven't seen any of those things for the last five minutes so we decided to make a run for it."

Jimmy motioned him forward with his rifle. As the students got to the officers, Eddie waved them towards the exit.

Jones stopped their leader and said, "Do you know if there are any more students or teachers hiding in this part of the school?"

The young man shook his head. He was out of breath.

"We were hiding in a classroom back down the way we came. We didn't see anybody but the zombies," pointing behind him. "We kept seeing big groups of them going past us and down the hall. They were all moving towards the other side of the school, back to the right."

"Any idea how many you saw going that way?" asked Jimmy.

"A lot, man. Maybe sixty or seventy. Maybe more. We're all scared and just want to get out of here. There are still a lot of them in the school."

"And they're heading right towards Chuck's team,"

muttered Eddie.

He waved the student out the door, telling him to check in at the command post. Marshall pushed the transmit button on his radio.

"Team Two Alpha to Team One Alpha," he said quietly.

"Team One Alpha. Go ahead," came the reply.

"We just had contact with some students who had been hiding in a classroom. They said that a bunch of infected are heading in your direction. They said sixty or seventy or more."

"Okay, thanks. We came across a big group of students that were hiding in a classroom, too. Me and Scotty stayed with half and Andy took the other half, and the rest of the team to an exit. Maybe you guys could start this way? I'm really not sure where we're at but you'll probably hear us shooting."

"Eddie said that some kids told him a pack of sixty or seventy Zs are heading our way," Chuck said quietly to Scotty.

"Well, let's get this party started. I think I hear some growling out there now."

The big man stepped over to the doorway, where he could peer through the broken window back down the hallway. McCain looked at Jeffrey and the other students.

"There's another group of infected people coming towards us. You guys get in that corner over there. Jeffrey, make sure everybody stays back."

Chuck saw the fear in everyone's eyes. The paramedic was holding a serrated knife that he had pulled out of his medical bag. Better than nothing, he thought.

A shot came from Scotty's rifle and then another. McCain moved across the room and stood next to Smith, who shot a third one. The first three had rounded the corner one at a time, only twenty-five yards away.

Now, the infected started pouring into their hallway and moving quickly towards the classroom. Zombie teenagers and zombie adults were moving faster than Chuck had seen them move before. He and Scotty started shooting and dropping them one after another, but they kept coming.

They killed around twelve of them and the fallen bodies created an obstacle in the hallway. The next zombies began to trip over their dead comrades. By now there were at least thirty or forty pushing towards them, growling and snarling. McCain and Smith both knew that they would very likely be overrun. The infected kept getting closer to the classroom. It was just a matter of time.

Both men continued to make head shot after head shot but the crowd continued to surge forward. The only reason that they hadn't been overrun yet was that many of the infected kept falling over the bodies lying scattered on the floor.

"Reloading," said Smith.

His M4 had locked open. McCain continued to shoot. Scotty hit the magazine release button, dropped the empty mag, and quickly fed another thirty rounder into the rifle.

He hit the slide release and started shooting again.

Now, Chuck's rifle locked open. He said, "Reloading," dumped his empty mag, and deftly inserted a full one. He was quickly firing again, as well. As more and more zombies kept rounding the corner and moving forward, McCain realized that they were now less than ten yards from the door. There had to be at least another thirty or forty infected pushing towards them and intent on killing and eating Chuck, Scotty, and everyone else in the room.

McCain's EOTech sight filled with a face he knew. Paul Miller. He was dressed in full SWAT gear. Chuck hesitated when he saw the familiar face. A face now covered with gore. McCain had been his Field Training Officer many years before. He had later been on Chuck's SWAT assault team.

Miller's head snapped back and dark blood spurted out of a hole between his eyes. Scotty had made the shot. Chuck looked over and nodded at Smith and then turned his attention back the horde of infected trying to kill them.

Jeffrey Bell couldn't see everything from the angle that he was at but he could see the two big police officers shooting zombie after zombie. Neither man acted like he was the least bit afraid. They were shooting quickly but they didn't appear to be rushed. The bearded guy on the left actually looked like he was having a good time. How can they stay so calm? he thought.

The growling in the hallway sounded like it was coming from a large group of zombies. And it sounded like it was getting closer. Jeffrey could see them now almost at the classroom door. Suddenly, a woman he recognized as a math teacher lunged forward and slammed into the door. The police officer on the right who seemed to be in charge calmly shot her in the face.

The petite redheaded girl that Bell had saved earlier suddenly appeared at the door. She was so small the officers didn't even see her approach. As the officer on the right kept shooting through the broken window, the redhead jumped and got her teeth on his right forearm.

Jeffrey heard the officer gasp in pain and then lift her off her feet. She still had her teeth locked onto his arm and was pulling at it with both of her hands. The bearded officer looked on in concern but he had to keep shooting to keep the crowd back.

Oh, no, Jeffrey thought. What if that officer becomes one of those things? He saw him release his rifle and let it hang across his chest. He punched the girl in the head with his left hand, once, twice, three times.

The powerful punches destroyed what had been beautiful features on a beautiful face. The third punch by the big man caused her to release his arm and to collapse backwards. He quickly pointed his rifle down and shot her.

A male student with half of his face chewed off and missing one of his eyes, reached in the broken window and got his hands on the same officer's rifle. He drove the muzzle of the gun into the zombie's face and pulled the trigger. Another student reached in and grabbed at the bearded officer's right arm. He was unable to swing the long gun around. The officer on the right shot the zombie off of him.

Now there had to be at least thirty of them at the door, pressing against it and trying to get in. Others appeared behind them, the crowd continuing to grow.

"Back up," the officer on the right ordered. The two men backed as one, back-stepping and shooting as they moved about ten feet towards the middle of the classroom.

The weight of the mob was causing the door to shake. There was a cracking sound and it swung open. Other zombies seemed to replace those that the officers had shot. At least twenty-five infected surged into the classroom. McCain and Smith stepped to their right, putting themselves in front of the students and the paramedic. They would protect them even if it meant their own deaths. This isn't going to end well but at least we'll go down fighting, Chuck thought.

Both men fired until their rifles locked open. No time to reload, they released the long guns and let them hang from their slings. They drew their 9mm Glock pistols and kept shooting. Soon, the slide on Scotty's pistol locked back empty.

"Reloading," he said.

Chuck kept shooting to cover for him but his Glock locked open as well. There were still seven infected left and they reached for the two officers. McCain hit the magazine release button and dropped the empty pistol magazine. As he reached for another mag, he kicked the zombie that was closest to him with a front kick to the chest. The powerful blow propelled the student turned zombie back into his infected classmates and knocked them down like bowling pins. They scrambled to get back to their feet.

Smith reloaded his pistol and started shooting again. Chuck finished his own reload and shot the one that he had just kicked. A tall teenage girl managed to rush around McCain, growling towards the group of students that they were protecting. Even shooting the unsuppressed pistols, Chuck heard the loud metallic twang of Jeffrey's bat connecting with a head.

McCain and Smith shot the last two who had gotten into the classroom. The area was finally clear. For the moment. They quickly reloaded their pistols with full magazines, holstered them, and then did the same for their rifles.

Smith looked at McCain with concern. "Are you OK? Did you get bit?"

"Yeah, I'm going to have a nasty bruise. She really clamped down on my arm. Thank God for these kevlar jackets," he said.

Scotty nodded and stepped back up to the door to watch. Bodies were stacked in the doorway. He began dragging them to the side so he could shut the door.

Chuck turned to check on the students. They were all in shock. Bell was standing over the girl zombie holding his baseball bat. He smiled at the big teenager. He wasn't crying this time, McCain noticed.

"Sounds like more coming our way," commented Smith.

He joined Scotty by the door and heard footsteps coming from both directions. "This is turning into the Alamo, Scotty."

"At least they aren't shooting back at us."

"No, they just want to rip our throats out with their teeth and eat us."

McCain's radio crackled, "Team Two Alpha to Team One Alpha."

"Team Two Alpha, we could use some help over here."

Scotty's rifle barked once and then again as two more zombies came from the opposite end of the hall.

"That's why I'm calling," said Eddie. "We're almost there. Don't shoot us."

The sound of several suppressed shots came from down the hallway. Jimmy stepped around the corner from where the biggest group of infected had come from. They moved cautiously towards the classroom. Chuck's eyes went straight to Rebecca. She was in the middle of the stack and appeared to be fine.

Eddie's team surveyed the carnage. They had to work hard to get around all of the bodies in the hallway and the classroom. One enormous boy wearing a green and white letter jacket blocked half the hallway.

"You guys decide not to share?" asked Jimmy. "I think you two have cleaned out the school on your own."

"Team One Bravo to Team One Alpha," Fleming called over the radio.

"Go ahead," McCain answered. "Are you guys OK?"

"Yeah, I just wanted to let you know we're almost to you. We would've gotten back sooner but we ran into another group of Zs and had to deal with them."

A few minutes later, both teams were admiring the pile of dead zombies that littered the hallway. Rebecca snapped a few pictures on her cell phone.

"Not bad for a retired cop and a fireman," Andy quipped.

"The few, the proud, the firefighters," said Scotty, stealing the Marine's tag line.

"Let's get the rest of these kids out of here?" Chuck suggested.

Rebecca nodded. "Eddie and Chuck, let's stay together and get everybody out and then check in at the CP. Plus, Chuck and Scotty are gonna need to reload. I think we can all use a break."

Command Post, Peachtree Meadow High School, Friday, 1230 hours

By the time the two teams and the nine students had reached the side exit of the school, another twenty-three students and teachers had joined them. These had also been waiting for a chance to make an escape. In all, the two CDC teams rescued almost sixty students and teachers.

The other two police SWAT teams had just arrived and their team leaders were in the command post. Chuck,

Eddie, Rebecca, and Josh joined them to give them what intel they could. Major Hughes was about to send the new SWAT teams in.

"So, can you guys give them a quick briefing on what to expect?"

Rebecca nodded. "We were able to get around sixty students and teachers out safely. They were all hiding in classrooms. There are so many hiding places inside that school, it may take a while to locate everybody and completely clear the building. Chuck, how many zombies do you think we put down?"

"Probably between a hundred and twenty to one hundred and fifty. Does that sound right, Eddie?"

"I think it's over a hundred and fifty. You and Scotty killed close to a hundred, just between the two of you."

"Wow, that's a lot infected people," said one of the SWAT leaders. "Did any of your guys get hurt?"

"No, we were fortunate. Be careful, though. Me and that big guy over there," pointing at Scotty, who was regaling his teammates with a combat story from Iraq, "we almost got overrun. This virus seems to have changed in just a couple of weeks. These infected seem to move faster, to be stronger, and to have better motor skills than the ones we encountered last time."

The CDC teams drank some water and grabbed some sandwiches from a table set up next to the CP and reloaded their empty magazines. They had expended a lot of ammo, especially Chuck and Scotty. Rebecca was in the CP talking to the major, the Chief of Police, the principal, and several FBI agents. An Emergency Management Team from the CDC had just arrived to help the locals manage the incident.

Paramedics checked all the students that came out of the school and then turned their attention to the officers. Chuck and Scotty both had blood splatter on them from the close quarters fighting they had been involved in. The EMS personnel got them cleaned off.

McCain removed his kevlar lined jacket and wiped it down with the virus-killing solution. The girl who had bit him had left blood and saliva all over the right sleeve. He hung it across a chair to dry next to the CP. He put his body armor and web gear back on and slung his rifle over his chest.

After he had refilled his magazine pouches, Chuck noticed Jeffrey Bell standing by himself at the edge of the crowd in the parking lot. He was still holding the baseball bat. McCain walked over to him. "Jeffrey, right?"

"Yes, sir."

"My name's Chuck," he said, sticking his hand out.

Jeffrey shook it. "It's nice to meet you. Thanks for getting us out of there. You and that other guy, that was, well, I thought we were all going to die. But you guys were good. I was so scared but you were so cool and calm. How do you do that?"

"I'll tell you a little secret, Jeffrey. For a minute or two there, I thought we were all going to die, too. There were so many of those things and just the two of us shooting them. I really thought we were going to get overrun."

"But you didn't act like you were scared at all."

"Fear is an interesting thing. We all have it. God gave us a fear reaction to protect us. It's normal to feel afraid. In my line of work, though, I don't have the option of running away so I have to figure out a way to override the fear factor. We do that by training, training, and more training. The fear's still there but your training helps you keep fighting in spite of it.

"And that was what you did, as well," Chuck continued. "You were scared. Sure. Who wouldn't be scared when you have all those zombies coming at you? But you still stepped up and protected those other kids with your bat. I think you're braver than you realize, Jeffrey."

Bell hung his head. He'd never heard it put that way. Chuck's words took some of the weight off of his shoulders. It would be a long time before he got over this but he was starting to feel a little better.

"Thanks for telling me that, Chuck. I've never thought of it like that before."

"I see your jacket. You're a football player, right?"

Jeffrey nodded. "I'm an offensive lineman."

"You might want to think about trying out for the baseball team," Chuck said with a smile.

Rebecca saw Chuck talking to the big boy on the edge of the crowd and then watched him walk towards the CP. She had been as shocked as everyone else at how many zombies he and Scotty had managed to put down. She also had a quick feeling of fear at how close he'd come to dying.

Johnson had been with Marshall's team and they had had to shoot a number of infected students and teachers, also. They had only encountered a few at a time, though. It appeared that the zombies had converged on Smith and McCain. Thankfully, they were up to the challenge.

Chuck saw Rebecca looking at him and smiled. That was one of the things that she liked about him. Okay, two of the things she liked about him. His smile and the fact that nothing seemed to faze him.

"So, are we heading back in?" he asked.

"Not yet. Right now, we're just on standby. The word from the two SWAT teams inside is that they're not meeting many infected, just one or two, here and there. Maybe you and Scotty really did eliminate most of them."

"Just another day at the office," he quipped. "So, maybe we can still go out tonight after all?"

Her first reaction was to say, "No." After the tragedy and the carnage that they had encountered at the high school, she wasn't sure she felt like being sociable or that she would even be good company. Seeing so many dead teen-agers had left her feeling numb inside.

When she looked into his eyes, though, she heard herself say, "I'd really like that, Chuck."

He smiled and walked over to check on his men.

Flying over Atlanta, Friday, 1600 hours

Everyone was lost in their own thoughts as they flew back to the Centers for Disease Control Headquarters. Part of the reason that these men had been selected and offered jobs to work for the CDC was how they scored on the CIA's proprietary software that was used in their hiring process. Of course, the officers didn't know it was from the CIA. Each of the men was rated above average in how they handled stress and trauma.

Shooting infected teenagers could be one of those things that caused serious emotional stress for most people. Rebecca's teams, however, were able to process it quickly and move on. With the number and severity of the incidents increasing, there was no time to send their agents to counseling and therapy. The next call for help could be right around the corner.

The two other SWAT teams that had gone into the school after them had eliminated over fifty more zombies, but they were spread throughout the school. They had also located and rescued over a hundred more students and teachers. The high school would still need to be thoroughly cleared one more time before they could start the gruesome job of removing the bodies. And, of course, it was very likely that many of those bodies would reanimate because of the virus and would have to be put down. For the moment, however, the scene was secure.

Each of the CDC officers had given a recorded statement to an FBI Agent. There were ten FBI Agents and forty police detectives on the scene. They would all be working together, interviewing police officers, students, faculty, reviewing video, and documenting and examining evidence.

It would be days and weeks before federal and local police had answers. The FBI and the CDC Emergency Management Team would be assisting the locals in reconstructing the crime scene and trying to find out how the infection in the school had started. Rebecca directed both Clean Up Teams to respond. They would help the local CSI units and the FBI in processing the location and in securing the hundreds of bodies.

It would also be days before the school had a good idea of the number of casualties. They would get a body count from inside and outside the school but they had no idea how many infected students might have fled to their homes after the attacks had started. This was a tragedy that was going to resonate deeply in the community and throughout the country.

The Chief of Police and the other brass in the command post understood that Rebecca's two teams had turned the tide. They had rescued almost sixty students and faculty, but more importantly, they had eliminated the majority of the zombies. There was no doubt in anyone's minds that the death toll would have been much higher if the CDC teams had not made entry when they did.

Besides the students, teachers, and parents that the

response teams and SWAT officers rescued, at least another two hundred students and faculty had been able to escape out the front of the school because of the zombie hoard that Chuck and Scotty were fighting in the middle of the school. Those zombies were drawn to the sound of gunfire, which allowed many others to get out of the school safely.

The two teams would debrief when they got back to HQ and then head home for the weekend. Barring any other attacks like the one they had just left, they would be able to enjoy a weekend off. When the helicopter landed on the roof and discharged the officers, Rebecca handed out bottles of the anti-virus liquid so they could clean their boots before going inside.

The debriefing was finished and everyone was getting ready to leave.

Scotty spoke up, "So, who wants to go eat? I'm starving. Those little sandwiches that they had in the CP are long gone."

Andy and Eddie bowed out. They were the only married guys in the unit and they both decided to go home and be with their families. Chuck was in his office, making sure he didn't leave anything unfinished. Scotty stepped in, tapping on the open door as he did.

"Hey, Boss, you going out to eat with us?"

"Not this time. I have something else going on."

The bearded man nodded. "Rebecca said the same thing."

"You guys have a good time," Chuck said. "Try not to get arrested or end up on the news and I'll see you on Monday."

McCain stood and stepped towards his door, wanting to end the conversation. Rebecca was their boss and the men didn't need to know that the two of them were going out on a date. Plus, if they found out, he would never hear the end of it.

Smith gave him a knowing grin. "Have a good weekend."

"You too, Scotty. I'm glad you were there today."

"We put a lot of Zs down, didn't we? A few more and we might have both been going hand-to-hand. I saw you drill that girl who was chewing on your arm. It looked like you punched her so hard that you scrambled her brain and killed her. And the kick on that other one saved the day. Bad luck that we both ended up reloading at the same time."

Scotty knew first-hand how hard McCain punched and kicked, having asked to spar with his team leader a while back. That was a mistake he would not make again. Chuck held up right his arm so Smith could see the bruising he had on his forearm.

"Yeah, for future reference, if you find yourself in that situation, try and punch them in the forehead. That's where I hit her. It must have jarred her brain enough that she let me go. But, I think I still prefer shooting them to fighting them," he said.

Amir al-Razi sat in the one star hotel room and watched the television with delight. This attack at the infidel high school was an unprecedented success. The reporter on the local news channel did not have the exact numbers but estimated close to five hundred students and teachers had been infected and had died or had turned and then been killed by the responding police. That number was expected to rise. Sixteen police officers had also been killed with several others infected and not expected to live.

They were asking anyone who might have gotten bitten or injured by one of the zombies to report to a local hospital. The reporter stressed how dangerous this virus was and how easy it was to spread it to friends and loved ones. An official with the CDC stated that, so far, the virus had proven to be fatal in every case. They were still working on a vaccine and felt that they were very close to having something that could be distributed. The goal now, however, must be to prevent the bio-terror virus from spreading.

The news report then showed a clip of the local Chief of Police talking to the media. He praised the efforts of his officers and other first-responders. He pledged that they would find those who were responsible for the attack and that they would be dealt with. Al-Razi laughed at this. Then the Chief thanked a federal law enforcement team, "whose quick and decisive response turned the tide of this terrible attack. Without these unnamed warriors' help, this incident would've been much worse."

Amir sat back in his chair. He knew exactly who these 'unnamed warriors' were. The Centers for Disease Control Response Teams, while not stopping him, had at least interfered in all of his attacks. They had kept him from being as successful as some of the brothers who had been entrusted with targeting other cities around the United States.

One of the reasons that he had targeted this school was that it was forty-five minutes from their headquarters. How had they managed to get to the school in time to make a difference? He had lost his only asset inside the CDC the previous week so he had no eyes and ears in that agency.

Azar Kasra had been trained by the Iranian Ministry of Intelligence and Security and had been one of his agents. She had worked as an epidemiologist for the CDC and had provided him with some excellent intelligence over the last year. When he had received the order from his handler, Imam Ruhollah Ali Bukhari, to launch his attacks in Atlanta, he had passed the order on to Azar. She was to be his opening shot.

Kasra was given the green light to launch her attack inside of CDC Headquarters, infecting and killing as many as she could and then killing herself if the security officers or response teams did not kill her first. The goal was for her to inflict as much damage and cause as much confusion as she could. If successful, this would have pulled the CDC teams back to their HQ and his warriors would have only had to worry about the local police.

Al-Razi had no idea what had happened. There had been no mention on the news about any attacks or incidents inside of the CDC. Kasra had just disappeared. He assumed that she had been arrested.

Amir had no way of knowing that when McCain had arrested her, he had recovered a number of other loaded syringes from her pocket, along with her .38 Special revolver. During her interrogation by Rebecca and Chuck, Azar had broken quickly and given up most of what she knew. That information had assisted the teams in their response to the coordinated attacks on Atlanta. Azar had then been whisked away by the CIA for further interrogation by a professional team of agents.

The reports from other parts of the country showed a slow but steady increase in the number of infected. The attacks from the previous week had local and federal law enforcement and National Guard units scurrying to contain it. Entire neighborhoods in some of the big cities had been infected.

The goal of the government of Iran was to see America destroyed by this virus. The government of the United States had shown themselves weak and inept under the previous Presidential Administration. The Supreme Leader in Iran did not feel that the current President would be that much different.

Simultaneous attacks had been launched in Atlanta, New York, Washington, D.C., Los Angeles, Dallas, Houston, and New Orleans. The news reports were now showing that the virus was being spread beyond those cities as infected people fled for the false security of the suburbs. The attacks in the Atlanta area, while significant, had not had the impact that the other cities had experienced.

Today's attack at Peachtree Meadow High School might just change that. If enough infected were able to get home before the virus affected them, the damage would be spread throughout the surrounding neighborhoods. The United States Government was responding to the virus, but they were being very cautious because they did not want to violate anyone's rights. Eventually, Amir thought, rights would not matter because the only ones walking around in this infidel nation would be the zombies.

Chapter Five

Restaurant, Midtown Atlanta, Friday, 2030 hours

Rebecca selected a black dress that she hadn't worn in months. She was surprised at her own emotions. She hadn't felt this way since the captain of the football team asked her out in high school. Calm down, she told herself. We're just going out for dinner.

Chuck arrived at her apartment carrying a half-dozen roses. He was wearing a white button down shirt, a dark blazer, and jeans. He was nervous, too, but now that he was in the moment, his anxiety eased. For him, the hardest thing had been getting up the courage to ask Rebecca out. He handed her the flowers and said, "I hope you like roses."

She didn't get surprised by much but the gift of flowers surprised her. "They're beautiful, Chuck. Thank you so much. Come on in while I put them in a vase."

McCain watched her as she took the flowers out of their plastic wrapping, put water in a clear glass vase, cut the stems to fit, and then put the flowers in it. Her blonde hair was down and she looked amazing. She caught him staring at her.

"What?" she asked.

"You look really nice," he said, softly.

She suddenly felt self-conscious and looked away.

"Ready to go?" he asked. "And do you like steak?"

"Yes and yes." She picked up her purse off the counter and looked at him, with a smile. "You clean up pretty nice, too."

The restaurant that Chuck had selected was known for their steaks. He had eaten there once before and he was glad that he had called ahead to make a reservation. The line was out the door.

"Now, I know you like wine but do you have a preference?" he asked after they were seated.

"What's that supposed to mean?" Johnson asked, raising an eyebrow.

"Nothing. Nothing at all. I don't know very much about wine but I do enjoy it. I'm just not sure that I enjoy it quite as much as you."

They both laughed and she punched him on the arm. The week before, he had gone to her apartment to check on her after Marco Connolly had been killed. He had been attacked and killed by three infected people. The virus had then caused Marco to turn into a zombie, as well, and

Rebecca had had to make the head shot that put him down. When Chuck had arrived at Rebecca's apartment later in the evening, he'd found her a little tipsy after having consumed several glasses of wine.

"I'll have you know, Mr. McCain, I didn't drink that entire bottle of wine. Wait, let me rephrase that. I didn't drink the entire bottle that night. I only had half the bottle that night."

He held up his hands. "No judgment from me. I was just happy that you had that bottle of scotch so I had something to sip on, too. So, back to my question. What's your preference in wine?"

"How about a nice Cabernet Sauvignon?"

They settled on a Chilean Cabernet Sauvignon, a crab cake appetizer, and decided to share a salad. Chuck ordered a sixteen-ounce New York strip and Rebecca chose an eight-ounce Filet Mignon. The food was excellent and they talked about a little of everything.

They steered clear of talking about work, but Rebecca did tell Chuck how the CIA had recruited her while she was a senior studying Political Science at Virginia Tech. She had finally admitted to him the week before that she did, in line with his suspicions, work for the Central Intelligence Agency. She had been the field agent who had first alerted the US Government to the fact that the Iranians had developed the zombie virus and had been testing it on live victims in Afghanistan.

When it looked like the bio-terror virus would be

unleashed on the United States, the President had signed an Executive Order calling for the CDC to have an enforcement branch. The CIA was forbidden by law from working inside of America. It was very important, however, that they continue to try and stop the spread of the virus.

The CDC enforcement agents were legitimate federal police officers. What none of them knew except Chuck, however, was that they received much of their intelligence and most of their funding from the CIA. The CDC had response teams at all of their locations around the US and they were the tip of the spear in combating the zombie virus.

After they had finished their steaks, Rebecca and Chuck continued to sip their wine, the conversation becoming more personal. They were both enjoying their evening together and were in no rush to leave the restaurant.

"Tell me about your fighting career," Rebecca said. "Did you not get enough action with the police department that you had to go looking for more excitement?"

He smiled. "My police career was pretty exciting. I was involved in a lot of interesting cases and incidents over the years. And being on the SWAT Team was my dream job.

"But, I've been a martial artist and a fighter for most of my life. When Mixed Martial Arts came along, it was just a natural progression for me to want to test myself in the ring. I was pretty good, at least at the local level, and I had a little bit of success. I'd probably fight again if the opportunity came up. But, I do have to remind myself that I'm not as young as I used to be."

She looked at the scars around both of his eyes. "Did you ever get hurt in the ring, other than the scars on your face?"

"No, I was fortunate. I was never knocked out. Just the normal cuts and bruises of getting punched, kicked, elbowed, and kneed. I had ten wins and four losses. All four losses were by decision and they were all to heavyweights."

"Didn't you normally fight as a heavyweight?"

"No, I fought mostly as a light heavyweight, two hundred and five pounds, but I did have several fights at heavyweight, also," he answered. "I even won a few of my heavyweight fights. But I was undefeated as a light heavyweight. Believe it or not, I was a small heavyweight and a big light heavy."

"And your ex-wife, what did she think of you fighting?"

"I didn't turn pro until after we got divorced. I don't think she would've been a fan, though. She never really liked the violence of the martial arts."

"Can I ask what happened with your marriage? Or is that too personal?"

He looked down and was quiet.

"It's none of my business. I'm sorry I brought it up," she said, putting her hand on his forearm.

"No, it's OK. I guess I owe you a secret or two," he smiled. "I was young, selfish, and immature. I had no idea how to be a good husband.

"I was so involved with being a cop, lifting weights, shooting, and martial arts training that I just shut her out of my life. There were no other women. I was just a horrible husband. Honestly, I would have divorced me, too. Looking back, I'm surprised that she waited as long as she did."

"How long were you guys married?"

"Seven years. Melanie was three when we split up. That was hard. I've tried to be a good dad and her mom is a great mother. My ex got remarried to a nice guy a couple of years after our divorce. He's been good to them."

"That was a long time ago, Chuck. I'm surprised you haven't found someone else."

"Maybe one day she'll come along," he said, looking into Rebecca's eyes. "And I find it even more surprising that you've never found the right guy to settle down with."

Johnson laughed. "I haven't exactly had a normal career. Working for who I work for brings its own set of challenges. I don't think I even know how to have a normal relationship. I'm not sure what one of those looks like."

McCain nodded. "I can see that. And what we're doing now is definitely not normal."

Chuck pulled his Silverado into Rebecca's apartment complex and parked in front of her building. The good meal and the bottle of wine combined with the adrenaline dump of the day's events had them both yawning.

"Thank you for a very nice evening, Chuck."

"And thank you for saying 'yes,'" he said. "Maybe we could do this again sometime?"

"I'd like that," she said, quietly. "See you Monday."

He let himself out and walked around the truck and opened the door for her.

"I'll just walk you to your door," he said.

When they reached her apartment, Chuck said, "Thanks again, Rebecca. It was really nice spending time with you."

She unlocked her door and turned around and looked at the big man standing in front of her. The realization hit her full in the face. He loves me, she thought.

The woman could see it in his eyes. He really loves me. She froze because she had no idea what to do with that revelation.

Rebecca put her hand on Chuck's arm, reached up and kissed him on the cheek. He smiled at her and started to turn away. She then impulsively pulled him towards her and kissed him on the mouth. His surprise didn't last long as he wrapped his arms around her in a strong hug.

They broke the kiss and she gently pulled away. "Good night, handsome. See you Monday," she said, stepping into her apartment.

McCain did not realize that he was smiling broadly as he walked back to his truck.

CDC HQ, Monday, 1030 hours

Chuck and Eddie sat in Rebecca's office. She had had a busy weekend working at home and had several things to go over with her team leaders. She also still felt the emotion from Friday night. It wasn't far below the surface and it had been a long time since she had felt this way.

The rest of the men were at one of the local police department's driving courses, practicing evasive and pursuit driving. Scotty and Andy had taken out a team of terrorists on the interstate in the preliminary attacks. Smith had been driving and had used a modified Precision Immobilization Technique to disable the terrorists' van. They were all getting a PIT refresher today. Eddie and Chuck would join them later.

"I just got off the phone with the lead FBI Agent from the incident at the high school," she said. "They're still working on cleaning that scene up. Their casualty count at this point is four hundred and sixty-one students, fifty-three teachers and faculty, and twenty-seven parents for a total of five hundred and forty-one dead at the school.

"The casualty count for police officers is twenty one. Sixteen were killed in the initial incident. Five more died over the weekend who had gotten bit. Three of the five turned and had to be shot at the hospital.

"We still don't have an accurate count of how many infected might have gotten away and gone home. There have been several incidents in that area. The agent told me the locals had officers on the scene at three different neighborhoods where infected people had been reported. He said one officer responded to a sighting of an infected person in a subdivision and got bit before he was able to shoot the zombie. He said this one charged the police officer at a full sprint.

"Now these numbers of casualties are really high and this is an incredible tragedy but we also have to remember that this is a school with almost four thousand students so it could have been much worse. Of course, the concern now is whether or not this kind of attack could be repeated at another school. For the moment, until we determine how the virus got into the high school, all of the Metro-Atlanta schools are suspending classes."

"That makes sense," observed McCain, "but it could also play right into the terrorists' hands. Now we'll have thousands of unsupervised children and teenagers at home during the day while mom and dad are at work."

Both Eddie and Rebecca nodded in agreement. "Well, there's nothing we can do about it. No school wants to be the next Peachtree Meadow," she said.

"Next thing," Rebecca continued. "Eddie, you remember Chris Rogers?"

"Oh, yeah," he said. "How could I forget him? That kid has a set of...I mean he's something. He really helped us out at that mall."

Chris Rogers was a Fulton County Police Officer. He had been off-duty and shopping in the Arbor Place Mall when the first terror attacks took place a week and a half before. Five Islamic terrorists had rushed into Arbor Place, armed with AK-47 rifles.

They had also just injected themselves with a syringe of the zombie virus. The terrorists shot and killed a number of people before the virus took effect on them. Then, they continued their attacks, infecting others through biting them.

Rogers had heard the gunfire, drawn his .40 caliber Glock 23 pistol, and pulled out his badge. He heard shots from several different locations in the mall. Even though he was off-duty and wasn't wearing any body armor, he instinctively moved towards the sound of the gunfire.

He saw a bearded gunman running towards him. The terrorist saw Chris and raised his rifle. Rogers fired three quick shots of .40 caliber hollow points that caught him in the chest and stopped him. Chris continued to move forward, but minutes later, he saw Eddie and Jimmy shoot two more of the terrorists near his location.

Chris identified himself to them as a police officer and pointed out the terrorist that he had just killed. At that moment, the man turned over and tried to get up, now as a zombie. Jimmy quickly shot him in the head with his M4 and it was then that Rogers understood how serious and how deadly the zombie virus really was.

The young officer agreed to help Eddie and Jimmy locate and neutralize the other two terrorists inside the mall. They were also attacked by two more groups of infected before they could get out of the mall. This was definitely not the outing that Rogers had pictured when he had gone shopping for running shoes that afternoon.

After Rebecca had arrived at the scene, Chris had gone back inside with her team, to help locate and rescue survivors and to clear the mall of zombies. He had left a good impression with Eddie, Jimmy, and Rebecca. She gave him her card and told him that if he was ever looking for a job to give her a call.

"He called me over the weekend and asked what he needed to do to come work with us," she said.

"That's great!" said Eddie. "So, what's next?'

"How about if he starts Wednesday?"

Eddie and Chuck both looked surprised.

"Does that mean he'll start his training Wednesday? That's pretty quick. Did he give a two week notice with the police department?" asked Chuck. "Also, I don't know the kid. I was killing zombies at Six Flags while you guys were killing them at that mall. If you both say he's good, that's enough for me. But what do we really know about him?"

Rebecca nodded. "Good questions. First, we need him now. Eddie's team has been running short-handed so I want to get him working as quickly as we can. I've it set up so that he'll be sworn in Wednesday as a federal police officer with the CDC. He'll then spend seven days with Roy working on his shooting skills.

"The other stuff, you guys can teach him as we go. He's already a police officer so we're going to bring him on and train him on the job. I'll get some of the curriculum that they taught you guys in your two-month training and let him go over it on his own.

"Your second question, Chuck. I called Fulton County PD and talked to them about him. From the Chief of Police on down, they told me what a great young officer he was. They were all sad to see him go. I was able to use the Department of Homeland Security card and get a waiver on him having to work out his two-week notice.

"And for your third question: 'What do we really know about him?' He only has five years on the job. The last two, though, he's been on their Criminal Response Team. Their Chief told me that CRT is the next level below SWAT. They're a tactical unit that focuses on armed robberies, gangs, and street level drug enforcement.

"Chris is on the list to go to SWAT when the next opening comes up. They've already sent him to the basic SWAT school. He doesn't have any military but he's been to SWAT training and is currently in a tactical unit. Plus, Eddie, Jimmy, and I saw him work and he impressed us.

"So, having said all that, Chris will join us here next Wednesday after his time with Roy. It'll be up to you guys to train him and help him to integrate with the teams. I think that he'll fit right in."

"Me, too," said Eddie. "Jimmy and I both liked what we saw. There aren't many people, even police officers, that will take on a terrorist with an AK while only holding a pistol."

"And speaking of new people," Rebecca continued, "I'm leaving as soon as we finish this meeting and will be gone until Wednesday or Thursday. I'm going to be traveling and meeting with the potential candidates that we talked about last week. I want to hire two more full teams so that Jimmy and Andy can both have their own. These teams will go through the full two-month training and I want to see that starting within the next month.

"Chuck, you'll be the Officer in Charge while I'm gone. Eddie, we'll rotate that around. Next time I travel, you'll be the OIC." The two men nodded.

As they got up to leave, Rebecca motioned for Chuck to stay. "I need to give you a contact list for while I'm gone."

She got up and closed the door and sat in the chair next to Chuck. They looked at each other. She still saw it in his eyes but knew that he would never say it. At least, not yet. Did he even understand what he was feeling? He was, however, the consummate professional.

"You good with being in charge?" she asked.

"No problem. You gonna leave your company credit card with me?"

"Not a chance," she laughed. "Hand me your phone and I'll put in a couple of numbers."

He unlocked his smartphone and handed it to her. She went to his contact list and created two new contacts and handed the phone back to him.

"Just call me if anything big happens and I'll make the notifications. I created a contact for Admiral Williams. He's my boss at the CIA and is the Assistant Director for Operations. If, for some reason you can't reach me, and it's a situation like we've been dealing with, call him. I told him that I've cleared you. Also, if you can't get me, let Doctor Martin here at the CDC know what's going on. I put his number in your phone, as well."

"But, now that that's out of the way," said Rebecca, "I mainly just wanted to get you alone with the door closed."

He raised his eyebrows. "That sounds like Inappropriate Workplace Behavior."

"Very inappropriate," she smiled.

Northeast of Atlanta, Tuesday, 1430 hours

For the last three days, there had been an increasing number of zombie sightings in the neighborhoods around Peachtree Meadow High School. By Tuesday morning, there were reports of infected people throughout the area that the high school serviced. The police were attempting to locate and to deal with these with limited success.

With the public's awareness of the zombie virus and the with the horrible tragedy at the school fresh in everyone's minds, people were calling 911 to report zombies upwards of a hundred times a day. Many of these calls were one neighbor calling on another neighbor who was just out walking their dog or getting some exercise. Others were legitimate calls but the zombies had disappeared by the time the police had gotten there. In some cases, the police did encounter an infected person walking around in one of the neighborhoods.

Contrary to popular belief, the average police officer is not a crack shot. Many police departments only require their officers to qualify once a year with their duty weapon. Police are trained to shoot center mass chest shots. These will work most of the time in normal situations.

With zombies, they don't work at all. Officers were now reporting that many of these infected were running in pursuit of their victims. Police were not having much success making head shots on these sprinting zombies.

More officers had been bitten and infected before they could make a close range head shot. Even officers armed with rifles or shotguns were not able to stop the zombies because they just didn't have the training to shoot fast-moving targets. Responding officers were becoming hesitant to even get out of their police cars. The SWAT Team had been decimated the previous week and the casualties in the ranks also continued to rise.

The Chief of Police requested that the CDC Response Teams respond and help them secure one of the bigger neighborhoods that appeared to be on the verge of being completely overtaken by the infected. The county government had also requested the National Guard be activated. Chuck had taken the call and had mobilized the two teams to respond. Getting the National Guard there would be a longer process. McCain had his men on the scene within an hour.

The CDC teams met with several police officers, their sergeant, and lieutenant near the high school. The command post was in a park that backed up to the subdivision with the largest number of reported zombie sightings. The sergeant and lieutenant had a map and showed Eddie and Chuck the layout of the neighborhood. McCain already knew the subdivision from serving as a local police officer in that area.

"Do you have any officers that want to go in with us?" Chuck asked.

"No," the LT replied. "Sorry, but our guys are pretty gun shy right now. We've had six officers get bit in the last couple of days and the funerals start tomorrow for all the guys that we've lost over the last week. There are several funerals every day this week. We just don't have the protective equipment you guys have," he said, nodding at their kevlar jackets.

Chuck had asked Rebecca to order those after their first zombie encounters a couple of weeks before. The kevlar jackets and pants were similar to those worn by motorcyclists. The kevlar was not thick enough to stop bullets but it had worked several times to protect the federal officers from getting bit. The kevlar-lined gloves they wore were common with police officers everywhere.

"I understand," said Chuck. "Do you have an extra radio that we can use in case we need to talk to you or your dispatcher?"

"That we have," said the sergeant, handing Chuck a radio. "I only have one extra but it's set to our channel. Any people that you guys rescue, try and get them back here and we'll get them somewhere safe. We'll transport them to friends or family in the area."

"Will do. Just tell your guys that if we call for help to please come running."

After checking the map, Chuck and Eddie decided to enter the back of the subdivision through the park. It would give them some cover and concealment as they approached. There were multiple reports of groups of zombies trying to force their way into occupied homes. The local police had a loose perimeter set up but were not responding to any 911 calls for help now that the CDC officers were on the scene. No one else wanted to get infected.

One of the officers who had gotten attacked the day before had had his police car surrounded by them. They had smashed out the driver's side window. He shot several but got bit in the process. He ended up using his police car as a weapon and ran three of the creatures over as he escaped. Other officers had to shoot him after he turned into a zombie himself.

The police were trying to cover a large area and just didn't have the manpower to be everywhere zombies were reported. As the 911 calls continued to come in, it became clear to Chuck and Eddie that this was going to be an intense rescue mission. They needed to get people to safety before the infected broke into the houses where they were hiding.

The men were suited up and ready to go. Chuck had alerted Rebecca by phone of what they were doing. Eddie had the guys in a circle and was briefing them about what the mission was going to be. Chuck stepped away from the CP and joined them.

"What else, Chuck?" asked Eddie.

"I asked them to get a van or small bus and have it standing by near the entrance to the subdivision. We're going to need a way to get the people out of there and to safety other than having them run for it. The lieutenant said he'd try and take care of that but he couldn't promise me anything. We'll probably have to walk them out to start with.

"Let's stay disciplined with our shooting. We're going to be surrounded by homes and we don't want any friendly fire incidents. We have eight addresses right now where people are in their homes and asking to be rescued. We may find more victims as we get going."

"Any of their officers going in with us?" asked Andy.

"No," answered Eddie. "The LT said they've had six more officers get bit and infected in the last two days to go with all of their other losses from last week at the school. They'll man the perimeter for us and will be our last hope if we get in trouble."

"Then we better not get into trouble, amigos," said Luis.

Northeast of Atlanta, Tuesday, 1500 hours

The federal officers slipped through the hundred yards

of woods between the park and the subdivision. The first address that the police dispatcher directed them to was in the rear of the neighborhood. They could see the house from the edge of the woods about seventy-five yards away. There were at least ten zombies in the yard and on the front porch. The rest of the area appeared to be clear.

McCain directed them up the street until they were hidden behind another house. They moved quickly but cautiously through several yards until they were across the street from the house with the zombies. A head count showed twelve infected crowding onto the front porch or on the steps leading to the porch. A few more were walking across the yard to the house.

The banging sound of the creatures slamming into the door echoed down the street. Soon, the sound of glass breaking was also heard as the infected smashed out the windows on the front porch. Yesterday, these infected were neighbors. Now, they were monsters intent only on killing.

Chuck called the police dispatcher and told her to have the residents go to a back room in the house. He didn't want any stray rounds to hurt anyone inside. The high velocity rifle rounds from their M4s could penetrate the heads of the zombies and keep going.

"Fleming, Smith, and Jones, start engaging targets. Start with the low ones in the yard and try and get those on the porch to come investigate. After we kill them all, let's see if we can get these victims back out the way we came in."

"What about the bus?" Eddie asked.

"I haven't heard back from the sergeant. And when it comes in from the front, it'll alert the zombies and may lead them to us. If we can get these guys out quietly on foot, let's do that. Everybody else watch our flanks while they shoot."

Andy, Scotty, and Jimmy stepped out from the behind the house across the street and started shooting zombies. Six quickly fell with bullets in their heads. The ones on the porch heard the suppressed shots and moved towards them. Three of them fell over the porch railing in their efforts to get at the officers and the other three fell down the six steps in a tangled heap of arms and legs. They weren't nearly as coordinated going down as they were going up.

The last six all managed to get to their feet but they were easy targets and quickly joined the others, sprawled in the yard with shots to the head. The team waited before approaching the house to see if any more infected would be drawn to the noise. The three shooters quickly reloaded with full magazines.

After almost two minutes, McCain gave the signal to approach. "Luis and Eddie, can you guys make contact with the residents and let's get them out of here? Everybody else, watch our backs."

García and Marshall climbed the steps to the front porch and knocked softly on the front door. They could see that the glass for the two front widows was smashed out. The window frames were still in place but it would not have been much longer before the zombies had forced their way into the home.

A young Asian woman came to the door. She was crying and holding a sleeping baby.

"Ma'am, we're here to get you to safety. Who else is with you?" Eddie asked.

"My mother and my father are also here. Where will we go?"

Eddie pointed to the wood line behind him. "We're going through that little patch of woods into the park. The other police are waiting there and they'll help you get to some place safe. We need to go. There are other people in your neighborhood who need help."

"I need to pack some things first," she said.

Eddie and Luis looked at each other. "We'll give you five minutes," Marshall said, "and then we're leaving you. You need to hurry."

She turned and rushed back into the house. Eddie went and located Chuck and told him what was going on. McCain nodded and called the police dispatcher. He told her to tell whoever else called for rescue that they needed to have whatever they were taking with them packed and ready to go. There was no time to wait while people packed up their possessions.

Shots rang out from the next street over. The shots were muffled like they were coming from inside a house. Gunshot after gunshot echoed down the street. Chuck counted fifteen shots. After the last one, there was a pause and then a piercing scream.

"Oh, that doesn't sound good," said Scotty.

"Eddie, the way behind us still looks clear," said Chuck. "Why don't you and your two guys get these people to the police. The rest of us will go check out the shooting."

Marshall nodded and stepped back up on the porch. Luis joined his teammates and said, "Let's go save some more people. Or shoot them."

The Asian girl, her baby, and her two elderly parents were ready to go, carrying several bags. Eddie, Jimmy, and Alejandro pointed to where they were going and started moving them that way. Chuck, Andy, Scotty, and Luis moved to the sound of the gunshots.

The same neighborhood, Tuesday, 1515 hours

Melissa Owen had called her husband, William, an hour earlier. She didn't work, choosing to stay home to look after their three-year old son, William Junior. She had heard all about the zombie virus from the news but thought that it was just another exaggerated story to get people to watch and to boost their ratings.

That morning, though, she had seen several strange people walking in the street in front of their house. The numbers kept increasing throughout the day. She had tried to call her neighbor, Brenda, who lived next door. There was no answer.

Finally, Melissa had called William at work. He was an electrician but was working a job this week that was close to home. He told her to stay in the house and that he would be right home.

As William pulled into his subdivision, he saw a police cruiser sitting near the entrance. The officer did not want to put his window down and only opened it a crack.

"Officer, my wife called and said there are a lot of those zombie things in the neighborhood. Have you heard anything?"

"There've been a lot of sightings and a few attacks in your subdivision. Be careful if you go in there. We can't protect you," the officer said.

"You can't come with me to my house?" William asked the officer, not believing what he had just heard.

The officer put his window back up and shook his head. Shaking his own head in disbelief, William got back into his van and drove to the rear of the neighborhood where their home was located. He had to dodge seven people walking out in the middle of the street, two of whom he recognized as living near him.

They all appeared to have blood on their faces. He saw others standing on people's lawns and driveways. In one yard, he saw three people bending over what appeared to be an elderly man. William was driving fast but he would swear that it looked like they were eating him. As he pulled up to his own house, he saw two people in the street and two standing in his front yard.

He pushed the button on the garage door opener as he turned into his driveway. He pulled into the garage and pushed the button again. The zombies in front of his house started running towards William's van. The garage closed just as two of them got to it. They started banging on the garage door.

William rushed into the house. "Melissa, William Junior?" he called.

Melissa rushed out of the bedroom she had been hiding in and ran into her husband's arms.

"Where's the baby?" he asked.

"He's fine," she said. "I have him watching cartoons in our bedroom. He doesn't know what's going on."

The banging on the outside of the garage door got louder. William looked at Melissa.

"There were some of them in front of the house. I got in and closed the garage just in time. Now they're banging on it. I need to get my gun," he said.

He opened the bedroom door and saw William Junior sitting on the bed watching television. "Daddy!" the little boy exclaimed.

"Hey, Junior, how's my little buddy?"

"Cartoons, Daddy, cartoons." He held his arms out for a hug. William gave his son a big hug and kissed him on top of the head.

"You keep watching cartoons and I'll come back and watch them with you later, OK?"

"Okay, Daddy."

William opened his closet and grabbed the gray plastic gun case off of the top shelf. He left Junior watching television and shut the bedroom door behind him. He carried the gun case back out to the dining room and sat down at the table. He pulled out his keys and found the one that unlocked the small lock on the case.

Owen had purchased the Ruger P85 9mm pistol several years earlier. There had been some break-ins in the area and he wanted to be able to protect his family. He had shot the pistol a few times at a local range but he was no gun expert.

He took the pistol out of the case and saw that there was already a magazine in it. He fumbled with it until he found the magazine release. The fifteen round mag was full of hollow point bullets. He slid it back into the gun until it clicked and then pulled the slide to the rear and let it go forward, chambering a bullet.

The guy at the gun store had gone over it with him but that was so long ago. He saw the second fifteen round magazine was also full of bullets and was laying in the box. He wasn't sure if the gun's safety was on or off. It was in the down position. He couldn't remember if down was for 'Fire' or for 'Safe.'

"Do you remember how to use it?" Melissa asked.

"I hope so," he said. "I think we're on our own. I saw a cop sitting at the entrance to the subdivision. I asked him to come with me but he just put the window up on his cop car and shook his head."

William decided not to tell Melissa about the three people he had seen eating another person a few streets over.

"I tried to call 911 after I called you, but I just kept getting a recording," she said. "I'm scared, William. I don't want those things to get us or to hurt William Junior."

The sound of footsteps came from their front porch. Melissa had shut the curtains earlier. It sounded like there were several people outside their house on their porch. Something or someone bumped into their front door. The banging on their garage door had stopped and the noises were now coming from the front of the house.

William looked at his wife and swallowed, lowering his voice. "I promise you that I'll protect you and William Junior. Now, you go back there in the bedroom with him. Pack up some clothes and stuff for us."

"But, what about you?"

"I'll be fine. I'm going to go have a peek out the curtains and see what they're doing. It might even be a neighbor checking on us."

"You aren't going to open the door?"

"No, I'm not going to open the door. I'm just going to look out the window. I'll keep watch out here while you get us packed and then we'll get in the van and get out of here, OK?"

Melissa nodded and kissed him. She had tears in her eyes and hurried down the hallway to the bedroom.

William stood and walked slowly to the front windows. He pulled the curtain back slightly and saw the face of his neighbor from across the street. William didn't know him. They were an Indian family.

The face had blood on it and the mouth was opening

124

and closing. One of his ears was hanging on by just a tiny piece of flesh. The Indian zombie saw William and slammed his face into the window breaking one of the panes of glass.

Startled, Owen stumbled backwards and dropped his pistol. It landed on the hardwood floor with a loud crash. He reached down and picked it up but the noise had let the infected know that someone was in the house. A second pane of glass was broken, and then another. The zombies kept striking at the windows. Another one slammed into the front door.

The broken glass cut their hands and arms but they kept trying to force their way in. William retreated back to the small dining area. Melissa stuck her head out of the bedroom to see what was happening. He rushed down the hallway to tell her what the noise was.

"I'll be done packing in just a few minutes," she said.

"They're trying to get in," he told her. "You have to stay in the bedroom. Push the bed or anything else you can find up against the door. I'll keep them from getting to you."

She was crying and William Junior tried to push past his mother to get to his father. He felt the fear coming from his parents. When Melissa picked him up and took him back into the bedroom, the toddler began to kick and scream, "Daddy, I want daddy!"

The slamming, banging, and noise of breaking glass continued from the front of the house. Extending his Ruger 9mm in front of him, he walked back down the hallway to keep guard. The sound of footsteps coming up the steps let him know that there were more of them just outside his front door. He had only seen the one when he had looked out the window, but it sounded like an even bigger group was on the porch now.

Another pane of glass shattered as a zombie slammed into it. He knew the two windows would not keep them out. William looked around the living room. There was nothing to push in front of the windows.

The fireplace. The metal fire poker. That would be another good weapon and not as loud, he thought. He grabbed it and slid the pistol into his waistband.

The wooden frame cracked on the window on the right. The curtains were still closed but he saw a figure climbing through the window. William swung the metal fire poker at what he thought was the zombie's head. A growl came from another one on the porch. The one that he hit kept coming so he hit it again. This time it collapsed, hanging halfway into the house.

A second infected started climbing over the one that William had just killed. It was growling loudly and he could hear its teeth snapping together. This one managed to get tangled up in the curtains and pulled them from the wall. Owen felt terror in the pit of his stomach as he saw the group of at least fifteen of them on his porch.

He swung the fire poker at the head of the zombie that had just pulled his curtains down. William recognized him as the guy who lived a few houses up. He was the neighbor who was always working on his cars late at night or early in the morning and revving the engines. It took three strikes to the head to drop him.

There was a loud crack as the frame on the other window broke under the weight of the zombies. Two other figures were trying to climb into the house. William stepped over to that window and started swinging his poker. The two zombies both collapsed inside the house, not moving. More were trying to get in that window and the curtains were ripped from it, as well.

There was a noise behind him. William turned and saw that his Indian zombie neighbor had climbed in through the first window and was reaching for him. He swung the fire poker and connected with his head, smashing his skull and killing him.

Another young zombie woman, whom William recognized as Betty from next door, had climbed in the other window. She was covered with gore and her neck was ripped open. She was close and lunged at him. He raised the poker in front of him and tried to shove her backwards. Betty ripped the fire poker out of his hands.

William remembered the pistol and pulled it out of his waistband. He pointed it at Betty's face and pulled the trigger. Nothing. The safety was on.

She grabbed his left arm and bit down hard on his forearm. He pushed the safety up and shot her in the face. Betty released his arm and collapsed to the floor. Owen glanced at his forearm and shook his head. Blood. Keep fighting, he told himself.

He swung the pistol around and shot another zombie

that was reaching for him. William backed up to the dining area. Another woman zombie was in the house and walking towards him. He fired and missed. He pulled the trigger and missed again. Deep breath, he told himself. The third shot hit her in the face and knocked her onto her back.

They were climbing over the top of each other now as they came through both windows. William wanted to run. He wanted to hide. Melissa and William Junior were in the back bedroom, though. He couldn't let these things get to his family. He took another deep breath.

Owen ran over and shot three of them in the head at point-blank range before they could get to their feet inside the house. He shot at another one coming in the window and missed. What is the matter with me? he thought. How can I miss a shot that's less than five feet away? His next shot caught the creature in the side of the head.

Another one climbed through a window and fell to the floor. This one was one of the teenagers who lived two houses up. He had flipped William off a couple of weeks before for interrupting their street basketball game by having the audacity to want to drive to his house. He growled and lunged for William's leg. He shot him in the head.

Something grabbed his ankle. The Hispanic lady that lived on the other side of him was about to bite his leg. William shot her and jerked his leg away.

Owen was now hot and sweating profusely and was starting to feel dizzy. He looked at his forearm again. Betty had put a pretty good bite on him. She had definitely ripped his skin open with her teeth. How long do I have? he wondered.

One of the other neighborhood teens fell to the floor under the window. She was dressed in black and had purple hair. William's first shot hit her in the chest. She pushed herself to her feet. His second shot missed and his third shot caught her in the top of the head, sending her back to the floor.

Hands grabbed at his left arm and leg. He jumped backwards and pointed the pistol at the two zombies. Nothing happened when he pulled the trigger. It was locked open. Empty. Where was that other magazine?

William rushed towards the dining room table. He fumbled with the magazine release trying to get the empty mag out. Four zombies closed in on him inside his house. Three more climbed through the windows and started towards their victim.

Owen got the empty magazine out of the pistol and grabbed the loaded one off of the table. He tried to get it into the gun but it wouldn't go. The growling and snapping of teeth were so loud. They were almost on top of him before he saw his problem. He had the magazine turned the wrong way. I wished I'd practiced more with my pistol, he thought.

Just as he turned the magazine the correct way and inserted it into the gun, four sets of hands grabbed him and pulled him towards the floor. Three other sets of hands and teeth closed in quickly to help with the kill. William swung the heavy pistol into one of the zombie's heads, fracturing its skull and knocking it backwards.

The others began to bite him and rip at his flesh. Owen screamed out in pain and fear and helplessness. In seconds, he was dead. The creatures enjoyed this new victim. Several others climbed into the house to partake of their fresh kill.

Chuck took point and led the team towards where they had heard the shots. It was easy to spot the house on the next street over. There were several zombies in the yard and others were climbing through the windows on the front porch into the house.

McCain, Fleming, and García shot the five that were standing in the yard. As they approached the front porch, they heard a woman's voice from inside the house, "William? William, are you OK?"

The unmistakable sound of zombie growling was also heard from the interior of the residence. Chuck turned to his men. "Luis and Scotty, watch our backs. Andy and I'll take a look."

García and Smith set up a watch at the bottom of the steps. McCain and Fleming rushed up onto the front porch. Chuck did a quick peek through one of the smashed out windows. He motioned for Fleming to do the same.

"I see a dead guy on the ground. A couple of Zs eating on him and I'm hearing growling from the back of the house," said Andy.

A woman's scream came, along with a crashing sound

from inside.

Chuck nodded. "I'll kick in the door and let's get in there before it's too late."

It took him two kicks before the doorframe shattered and the front door flew open. Andy was the first in and quickly shot the two zombies that were eating William's corpse. The growling and hissing were coming from just around the corner. A woman continued to scream. A baby was crying loudly.

Fleming and McCain swung around wide into the dining area to see down the hallway. They saw eight zombies trying to push their way into a bedroom. Both men raised their rifles and started shooting them in the head. Less then ten seconds later, all eight were dead.

"Police officers," Chuck called quietly. "We're here to get you to safety."

Chuck motioned for Andy to cover him as he moved down the hallway to the back bedroom.

"Hello? Police officers, we're here to help you."

"Are they gone? Where's William?"

"Ma'am, we've killed all the zombies. I don't know about William but we'll get you out of here. Can you open the door? It's safe now."

The sound of furniture being slid across the floor came from inside the bedroom. Melissa had pushed their bed, a shelf and a chair against the door. A shot from Andy's suppressed rifle echoed through the house. Chuck looked back. William had turned into a zombie himself and had tried to grab Fleming's leg. A shot to the head had stopped him.

Andy figured this was the woman's husband. From the looks of things, he had made a pretty good last stand before being overwhelmed. He counted fifteen dead Zs that the man had killed. Fleming grabbed a blanket off of the back of the couch and covered him up.

The bedroom door opened and the woman appeared. She was holding a toddler close to her. "Where's William?" she asked.

"What's your name?" Chuck asked.

"Melissa Owen. William sent us to the bedroom. He said he'd protect us. I heard shooting and growling and then he screamed." She started crying.

"My name's Chuck, ma'am. William did what he said. He protected you with his life. Now we need to get you and your baby to a safe place."

"Is he dead?" She was sobbing and squeezing William Junior who was crying, too. "Oh, my God, he can't be dead. I just talked to him. He was going to come watch cartoons with Junior."

"Melissa, there are a lot more zombies in the area. William killed a lot of them and we killed some more but the others will come looking for us. We need to get you guys out of here. Come on, let's go."

Melissa retrieved a small suitcase from the bedroom and allowed Chuck to guide her down the hallway. She saw the blanket covered body and the many dead zombies around him.

"I want to see him," she said.

Andy shook his head. "No, you don't, ma'am. They really tore him up. You don't want that to be your last image of him. He saved you guys. Just remember that. He loved you so much that he gave his life for you."

Chuck guided the weeping Melissa out of the house and down the front steps. William Junior was just whimpering now. Melissa stopped crying when they got outside but was clearly in shock.

"How are we looking?" McCain asked Scotty and Luis.

"Quiet for the moment," said Scotty.

"Team Two Alpha to Team One Alpha," came through McCain's earpiece.

"Go ahead, Team Two Alpha."

"We're back. Where are you guys? We're at that first house."

"Hang on there. We'll join you in just a couple. We have two more who need an escort."

Tuesday, 1800 hours

The federal officers rescued four more families from the neighborhood and walked all of them out on foot. On two of the escort trips they had to shoot a few infected but they got everyone out safely. In all, they rescued nineteen people and killed forty-five zombies.

The men were surprised that they did not encounter more zombies or find more people needing to be rescued. The last two people that the teams had "rescued" were a retired couple that lived near the front of the subdivision. Al and Carla were the kind of people that live in every neighborhood. They know everybody and they know everybody's business.

They did not seem flustered in the least by what was going on. Carla had offered the men some sweet tea. Al said that he had watched many of the infected wander by their house and out of the subdivision. Some had left walking up the street and others had just walked off into the woods.

"How many zombies did you see leave the neighborhood, Al?" Eddie asked as the older man finished packing his minivan.

"I counted thirty-three that I saw walking towards the front of the subdivision or into the woods. And that was just today. I saw, maybe twelve or fifteen late yesterday afternoon heading out of here. Any idea why yesterday and today we started having problems with zombies?"

Eddie shook his head. "No one really knows how this virus works. I'm sure it's related to the outbreak they had at the high school. But why yesterday or today? We don't know."

Al had come out onto his driveway and flagged the officers down as they were walking up the street. They had just gone to an address that the police dispatcher had given them and had found the house abandoned. There was a lot of blood splattered on the walls and floors. The ripped up body of a woman was sprawled on the kitchen floor. Whoever had killed her had apparently left in pursuit of another victim.

Carla and Al weren't sure that they wanted to leave their home. They had not had any problems and Al told them he had a shotgun and knew how to use it. As they sipped their sweet tea, Chuck and Eddie told them a few of the stories of what they had encountered in the rest of the neighborhood. When Carla heard how the zombies had broken into people's homes, she was ready to go.

The officers stayed until Al and Carla got into their minivan and drove out of the neighborhood. They had agreed to go to a hotel for a few days, "until things calmed down," said Al.

"I don't know if things are ever going to calm down," said Jimmy, as they watched Al and Carla drive away.

"Yeah, with close to fifty of those things wandering off to who knows where, this whole area could be in trouble," said Luis.

"And those are just the ones that Al saw," said Alejandro. "There could be a lot more than that."

Vehicle traffic had been increasing in the neighborhood over the last hour as people came home from work. It was hard to imagine what they were going to encounter at their houses. Chuck watched a black BMW drive by them at a high rate of speed.

"And don't forget," said McCain, "a lot of people were at work. The numbers may be a little lower because of that. Let's walk back through the subdivision. We may get some more action before we get back to our trucks."

"I'm surprised," commented Eddie, "that the police

aren't restricting access or even trying to quarantine neighborhoods like this."

"Well, you have to remember," said Chuck, "we are in the South. There are a lot of guns in a lot of homes and I doubt the police want to tell someone they can't leave or they can't return to their home. These local cops have had a rough time of it. Whenever the National Guard starts showing up in force, it might be a different story."

Chapter Six

Amir al-Razi and Mohamud Ahmed were seated in Amir's rental car, a brown Ford Focus. They were in the parking lot of the Georgia Square Mall in Athens. After delivering death to Peachtree Meadow High School, Mohamud had abandoned the Coca Cola van at his apartment complex and left in his silver Honda Accord.

Last night, Mohamud had seen his face on the news. He was now being listed as a person of interest in the Peachtree Meadow High School infection. The report had given his vehicle description and tag number. He had already swapped license plates with another silver Accord from his apartment complex on the day that he left. The Accords were such common cars that he was not worried about getting stopped. He had also quit shaving the day before the attack and now had the beginnings of a beard.

Amir congratulated Mohamud on the successful operation at the school. "You have done well, my brother. The infidels are reeling from that attack. Would you like to strike another blow for Allah?"

Ahmed smiled. "I've waited for this moment for many years. I'd be honored to be a part of another attack on these infidels and to gain even more vengeance for my family that the Americans killed."

As al-Razi shared his plan with him, Mohamud could not help but smile. This was such a simple strategy but had the potential to cripple another of America's cities. Amir did not tell Ahmed what his own role would be or of the other agent that was going to be involved but assured him that there were going to be other strikes in conjunction with his. If somehow Mohamud was arrested, the less he knew about what Amir was doing, the better.

"This will be another great victory against the Americans. But why must we wait an entire week before striking?" Mohamud asked.

"The timing is very important. You must trust me on this. If we wait a week, our combined attacks will be much more devastating."

As they started to go their separate ways, Amir handed Ahmed a small duffel bag.

"This contains everything that you'll need. There's a pistol with extra magazines and ammunition. There are three vials of the virus. If you can infect three different locations in the city near that university, it will give us maximum saturation.

"There's a new driver's license in there if you need to show your ID for anything. It's a forgery and won't fool the police but it will work for everything else. I also put three thousand dollars in the bag. That will cover a cheap hotel and your food. Whatever money that's left over is yours.

"After you complete this assignment, you should try and leave the state. Your work is finished, at least for the moment. There's also a disposable cell phone with one of my numbers in the contacts. Call me only in case of an extreme emergency. I will use that phone to contact you at a later time for the next phase of the Jihad."

What Amir did not tell Mohamud was that while he was spreading the zombie virus in downtown Atlanta, he and another accomplice would be doing the same thing in Athens. The home opener football game for the University of Georgia was on the following Saturday. He intended to infect this mall that they were parked at, as well as the university. There would be no interference this time from the CDC Response Teams. Of that, he was sure.

Thirty minutes later, al-Razi parked on the side of the building at the Waffle House just outside of Athens. Terrell Hill took off his apron, walked out from behind the grill, clocked out, and left the restaurant. He was tall and slim and wore his hair in long dreadlocks. He got in the passenger seat of Amir's car and the men drove away. They had met once before and Terrell would have an important role in this next attack.

Terrell glanced over at Amir. Average height, average weight. He could pass for an Indian, a Latino, or a Middle Easterner. At first glance, Terrell would have even considered him a victim, someone that he would have picked to rob before his time in prison. One of the things prison had taught Hill, however, was how to read people. If you read someone wrong in the joint, you could wind up dead.

Amir was clearly someone that you did not want to misjudge. There was death in his eyes and the bulge of the gun in his waistband just confirmed that. The person who misread al-Razi would also wind up dead.

Before the first meeting with the Iranian, his imam had spoken to Terrell cautiously, probing to find out the depth of his anger and hatred against America. He must have passed the test because he received a short, cryptic phone call that told him where to be for their first meeting a few weeks earlier. There, Amir had asked him questions and spoken to him about jihad. The questions that he had asked were about his time in prison and the injustices that he had suffered at the hands of a racist criminal justice system, as well as his devotion to Allah.

At that first meeting, Hill was not given any type of assignment. He was just told that he would be contacted when he was needed. He had received that phone call the day before, telling him he was now needed, and asking him what time he got off of work. Now, he was in the car with Amir driving into Athens.

"I understand you work in the stadium at the university when they have football games? You sell food to the infidels?" Amir asked.

"Yeah, Waffle House doesn't pay a lot and I'm trying to get enough money to buy a car. Working the games pays pretty good."

What Terrell didn't say was that he hated every second of it. Every time he worked a football game, it was like ripping a band-aid off of a fresh wound. Hill had been a promising high school football wide receiver. He had broken several state records during his senior year at Clarke Central High School and had accepted a full scholarship to play for the University of Georgia.

Getting arrested for Armed Robbery and Aggravated Assault ended that dream. They were the Crew. Terrell and three of his friends. They drove around on Friday and Saturday nights, looking for people to rob.

They preyed mostly on drunk Mexicans walking home from the bar. They always carried cash and seldom fought back. If they couldn't find any Mexicans, they would rob some white boys. They usually had cash and maybe a nice watch. The Crew could make several hundred dollars apiece on a good weekend.

That one Mexican guy, though, didn't want to give up his money and tried to fight, even with three Hi-Points pointed at him. He swung a fist and Terrell shot him in the leg. One of the other boys pistol-whipped him, busting his head open. They got a hundred and twenty dollars from him but the police came from nowhere. Five police cars and even an officer with a dog.

The Crew driver had no chance. They yanked him out of the car and handcuffed him. Hill and the other two guys started running.

They threw their guns down because they didn't want to get shot but Terrell knew he could outrun any cop. He couldn't outrun that German Shepherd, however, and ended up having to get twenty-seven stitches in his left leg and arm. The other two Crew members got tazed and arrested, as well.

The police were able to link them to several other robberies. In all, they were charged with twelve armed robberies and one aggravated assault for the guy they had shot and beat up. Terrell's white, court-appointed lawyer talked him into pleading guilty to one count of armed robbery and the agg assault in return for dropping the other cases. He served almost six years of a ten-year sentence in a state prison.

If anything good came out of his time in jail, it was his finding Islam. The Muslims in prison seemed like the coolest guys in there and no one messed with them. After he made friends with a couple of them and went to a few of their meetings, he started to hear about something called jihad. They all felt that they were victims of a rigged criminal justice system and were all looking for revenge. That sounded good to Terrell and he converted.

As he was leaving the prison on his last day, one of the brothers handed him the name and phone number of an imam in Athens.

"Call him and go to the meetings. Maybe he'll be able to give you an outlet for your anger against those who've wronged you."

Finally, two years later, he was with Amir waiting for his assignment. He had no idea what would be required of him but he'd been following the news and knew that the zombie virus was a product of Iran. It looked like the United States and Iran were about to go to war over the bio-terror attacks. Hill had already decided that he would do whatever Amir asked of him.

Terrell had nothing to hold him back. He didn't know who his father was. His mother had died of a drug overdose while he was in prison. His seven brothers and sisters were all by different fathers and he wasn't really close to any of them. Not a single one had even visited while he served his time.

"What do you need me to do?" Terrell asked Amir.

"How would you like to strike a blow for Allah against the infidels while you're working at the football game?"

"Man, I'd like that but what does my job at the stadium have to do with it?"

Amir gave him the hint of a smile. "It has everything to do with it."

Forty minutes later, al-Razi dropped Hill off in front of his run-down apartment building on the edge of town. He was carrying a small black duffel bag containing two vials of the virus, a gun, extra ammo, a fake ID, a disposable cell phone and three thousand dollars in cash. For the first time in a long while, Terrell had a smile on his face as he walked into his shabby apartment.

CDC HQ, Friday, 1600 hours

By Friday, the men were physically and emotionally spent. They had been involved in clearing neighborhoods for the last three days. They had been able to rescue over a hundred people from marauding zombie bands and had killed close to a hundred and fifty infected people. The National Guard had finally moved in and were also working to clean out neighborhoods of the infected. The Guard would help with the removal of the bodies and they would be implementing a quarantine of some areas at the direction of the CDC.

Today, the first order of business for the response teams had been to clean their weapons and to reload their magazines after firing hundreds of rounds of ammunition. They also double-checked all their equipment to make sure that they would be ready to go as soon as they were needed again. Chuck had already set aside equipment for their new officer, Chris Rogers, who would be joining them in a few days.

After dealing with their equipment and weapons, the men had all written after-action statements. With the zombie incidents becoming so prevalent, there was no way that the FBI or the police could investigate each officer-involved shooting. Chuck and Eddie each wrote a summary of what their teams had done over the last three days and the men wrote statements of what they had done on each day. These reports would be kept on file in case they were needed later.

The problem was that the incidents had all started running together.

"Was it yesterday or the day before that we had to shoot that grandmother zombie in her see-through nightgown?" Scotty asked over the wall of his cubicle.

"I think that was yesterday morning," Jimmy answered

with a grimace. "That picture of a see-through negligee on granny will be forever seared into my mind. And what about that big, fat, naked girl zombie that tried to chase down Luis?"

"Fat girls need love too," said Luis. "In her case, though, she needed a bullet in the head. I think she was more girl than even I could handle. Wasn't that on Wednesday afternoon?"

Eventually, the paperwork was done and they broke for lunch. When they got back to the office, they could hear the television in the briefing room. Chuck stepped inside to find Rebecca watching the big monitor on the wall.

She looked up at him. "It looks like the war has started," she said. "We've launched cruise missile strikes at key targets throughout Iran. We've been building up our ground forces in Iraq and Afghanistan for the last few months so a ground war is probably next on the schedule after we pound them for a while with Tomahawk missiles and establish air superiority."

The men all slipped into the room and watched the events unfolding on the news. They knew that war had been a very real possibility. If the President could build the case that Iran was behind these bio-terror attacks, he was duty-bound to respond.

With the increase of attacks and their own involvement in trying to contain the crisis, most of the men had not been following the national and international news very closely. They had just been focused on staying alive and winning the battles that they found themselves in. And for now, this news, while sobering, had no effect on their own work and mission.

By 1800 hours, everyone was heading for home. The guys were unusually quiet for a Friday afternoon. Alejandro mentioned that he had a date with flight attendant Isabella Rodriguez in an hour. Scotty let everybody know that he had a date on Saturday. He had finally convinced paramedic Emily Clark to go out with him. She had ridden in the back of the ambulance after he and Andy had both gotten shot a couple of weeks before.

"She has no idea what she's in for," laughed Chuck.

"I think the poor girl needs a chaperone," added Jimmy, as they all walked out the door, heading to their cars.

"Or a bodyguard," added Andy.

Chuck hung behind. His excuse was to see if Rebecca needed anything else before he left. She was typing something at her computer and did not see him standing in the doorway of her office. He watched her for a minute or two and then cleared his throat.

"I knew you were there," she said, with a smile, continuing to type.

"I must be losing my ninja skills."

"Well, you're a pretty big man. It's tough for you to be too stealthy."

"How'd the recruiting mission go?" he asked.

Johnson looked at him. "Not too bad. I must be losing a little of my charm, though. I was only able to convince six of the eight guys to sign up."

"The other two must've been gay," he said. "How could they have possibly resisted your sales pitch?"

"That's what I'm saying," she laughed. "No, I get it. Both of them were already negotiating private security contracts and weren't interested in working for the CDC. And let's face it. The CDC Enforcement Unit just doesn't sound as sexy as a Security Contractor for Triple Canopy."

"So, what about the six new guys?"

"They start training in a couple of weeks. They'll do the full two months of training and then join you guys. Three for you and three for Eddie.

"After you work together for a couple of weeks and get them up to speed, you and Eddie pick one of the new guys you want to keep. Then I'll give a team of two to Andy and a team of two to Jimmy. It isn't perfect but it'll allow us to be in more places at once."

McCain nodded. It made sense and Andy and Jimmy would be great team leads. They both had a lot of real world experience and were excellent leaders.

"Where'd these guys come from?"

"They're good." She held up her index finger. "An army SF guy. He had his twenty years in and his wife told him that he needed to retire and stay stateside."

She held up a second finger. "Another army MP turned police officer. He's been policing in Dallas, Texas for a few years."

She held up two more fingers. "Two Marines turned police officers with different departments. One had an app to go to the ATF and the other had an app to go to the

DEA."

She held up a fifth finger. "A SWAT officer with LAPD. He had applied to go to the FBI with his heart set on joining their Hostage Rescue Team."

"Wow, LAPD's SWAT Team is really good. And the FBI's HRT is world class. How'd you convince him to give up wanting to go work with them?"

"An extra fifty thousand dollars a year and the promise that after working with you guys, he'd forget the HRT ever existed."

Chuck laughed. "Nice. And what about the last one? That was just five."

"A Navy SEAL. He'd gotten busted up a bit on his last couple of deployments. His Humvee hit an IED and he was shot a couple of times. Now, those SEALs are tough and none of his injuries were enough to get him to take a medical discharge but after almost fifteen years as an active duty SEAL, he jumped at the opportunity to come work with us. And the pay raise helped. And guess what? He's also a sniper."

"That's excellent," said McCain. "I was thinking we need to invest in a sniper rifle for Scotty. I have a feeling a couple of snipers might be a big help in the near future."

Rebecca nodded. "You know what helped convince most of these guys to come work with us? I showed them some of the videos those news helicopters shot of Scotty, Andy, you, and me taking out those zombie terrorists on the interstate a couple of weeks ago. When they saw that footage, they were hooked."

"That's impressive. I think your charm is working just fine."

"Does that mean you're going to ask me out again?" she asked.

"I, well…I, of course. I just didn't want to be pushy."

Rebecca stood up and walked over to Chuck. She stopped just in front of him and looked up into his eyes.

"Do you remember last Friday night?" she asked softly.

"How could I forget?" he smiled.

"I kissed you, Chuck. I couldn't help myself. Now, I'm giving you permission to take the initiative. You…"

Before she could say anything else, he took her face in his hands and kissed her gently on the lips. She looked at him with surprised eyes. Then she closed them and let him kiss her again.

"How was that?" he asked.

Instead of answering, she wrapped her arms around his neck and their lips met a third time.

"How about tomorrow night?"

"I'd really like that," she answered.

Rebecca's apartment, Saturday night, 0030 hours

They had another wonderful evening together. This time, they went to a restaurant that specialized in fresh seafood cooked with a southern flair. They held hands and talked quietly as they ate. They both sensed that their relationship had gone to a new level and they didn't want to rush their time together.

"I have a confession to make," Chuck said, as they sipped their wine.

"Do tell. I'd love to hear it."

"I fell for you the first time I saw you, when you came to my house to recruit me. I didn't want a job. I wasn't even thinking about looking for a job. But when you showed up, I would've talked to you about anything. That was why I offered you coffee. I didn't want you to leave too quickly."

Rebecca smiled and looked down. "I have a confession to make, too."

McCain's eyebrows rose. "Oh, well let's have it."

He saw that she was blushing and smiled.

"Remember when I told you that I saw you in Afghanistan?"

He did. She had been a CIA case officer in Afghanistan and had worked closely with some of the Special Forces soldiers with whom Chuck was embedded as their police liaison. He had never met her there but she had seen him. The SF guys had to go by their house to pick something up. Johnson had stayed in the car and had seen Chuck lifting weights in their outdoor gym.

He nodded.

"I think I fell for you then," she confessed. "Is that bad? All you had on were a pair of gym shorts. You were sweaty and your muscles were all pumped up and bulging.

"When the SF guys got back in the Land Rover, I asked them who you were. They told me that you were a former cop now working with them for a year. The team sergeant told me that you were really an SF guy in a SWAT cop's body. The team leader caught me staring at you and told me he could set us up."

McCain laughed. "You should've let him. That would have made those two contracts in the sandbox go by so much faster."

"Well, anyway," Rebecca continued, "that day I came to your house to try and hire you, I was so nervous. And, of course, you had to come to the door half dressed."

"With my muscles all pumped up and bulging after working out. At least I was wearing jeans. I had just gotten out of the shower."

"I think I did a pretty good job of keeping my composure," Johnson smiled.

"You were a total professional," Chuck laughed. "I was the one who kept telling myself, 'Don't say anything stupid.'"

Rebecca linked her arm through his as Chuck walked her to her apartment. She turned to look at him and said, "Can you come in for a drink?"

"Of course. I never turn down drinks from beautiful women."

She had another glass of wine and he enjoyed a tumbler of her Glenlivet twelve-year old single malt scotch. They talked for a couple of hours about everything and about nothing. They were just enjoying being together.

"It's getting late," he finally said. "I need to go."

She nodded and slid closer to him on the couch. He put his arm around her and started to say something. It was obvious that he had something on his mind. She waited.

"Feel free to say 'no,' but next weekend, on Saturday, I'm driving over to Athens to spend the day with Melanie. She wants me to meet the boy that she's dating. I need to go and decide if I need to kill him or not. But, I was thinking, maybe you might want to come with me? I'd love for you to meet my daughter and you could give me a woman's insight into her boyfriend."

Rebecca laid her head on Chuck's shoulder. He wants me to meet his daughter, she thought. That's a good thing but are we really at that point in our relationship? We've only been out twice. On the other hand, I don't think it'll hurt anything and it would be good to meet her. And, it would give me a little more insight into this man that I think I've fallen in love with.

"Chuck, I'd love to meet Melanie. And I've never been to Athens. That would be fun."

McCain audibly exhaled.

He was so nervous asking me that, she thought. He's trying to be considerate and has been a complete gentleman with me. Plus, he really wants me to meet his daughter. That's so sweet.

She kissed him on the cheek and pulled his face towards her. They kissed passionately for several minutes before he pulled himself free. He kissed her on the forehead.

"I need to go," he said again. "As much as I hate to

leave such wonderful company, I need to get my beauty sleep."

They walked to the door and he kissed her again before she let him out. What have I gotten myself into, she thought. I think I've fallen in love and I have no idea how to do relationships. At least Chuck seems like the guy to learn with, she hoped.

Chapter Seven

CDC HQ, Wednesday, 1030 hours

There was a knock at the door of the Enforcement Division offices in the lower level of the CDC. Scotty happened to be in the hallway carrying his empty coffee mug for a refill and heard the knock. After the attack on Chuck a couple of weeks earlier inside of their secure area, they were much more cautious in whom they let in.

Smith opened the door slightly and saw a slim young man in the gray cargo pants and black polo shirt uniform of their unit. He knew they were expecting a new guy but he hadn't met Chris Rogers yet. Scotty swung the door open and said, "Well, hello, young man. Does your mother know where you are?"

Chris' eyes got wide at the sight of the huge man with the bushy beard filling the doorway. He recovered quickly, though.

"No, but when I left your mom this morning, she told me that if I saw you to have you call home."

Smith's face broke into a huge grin and he stuck his hand out. "Ha! Come on in. I'm Scotty and you're going to fit right in."

Eddie stepped out of his office and saw Chris. "Scotty, are you bothering our new officer? Who let you out of your cage, anyway?"

Smith continued laughing as he walked back down the hall. When he passed Eddie, Chris couldn't help but notice that Scotty even made Eddie look small. And Eddie was a big man. Rogers figured Marshall was at least six foot three and a solid two hundred and thirty pounds. Scotty had to be two inches taller and at least twenty or thirty pounds heavier.

Eddie shook Chris' hand and led him into his office where they could talk. He sat down at his desk and Chris sat across from him.

"So, how was your training? You were the first guy to get the abbreviated version."

"It was intense. I probably shot more in the last week than I've shot in my entire law enforcement career."

"And what did you think of Roy?"

"Yeah, Roy was really something. He wouldn't answer any questions about himself. What is he? Some kind of a spook?"

"Good question. We have a couple of spec ops guys on the teams here and they figure him for a Navy SEAL turned contract instructor."

Chris nodded. "He's good. And shooting those circles, that was a whole new level. Because of working with you guys at that mall, I figured out pretty quickly that he was training me to just focus on head shots. That's a pretty big shift for a cop, though, since we're so used to shooting center mass."

"Well, at least you had some context. When the rest of us trained with Roy, we had no idea what was going on. We just thought it was a drill to tighten our groups up.

"Then, when he took us to the shoot house and we started shooting people targets, the only thing he counted were head shots. And when the zombie virus kicked in, we all found that we were making the kill shots without any problem. Thanks, Roy."

There was a knock on the open door. Chris turned around and saw another really big man step into the office. He wasn't quite as tall as Eddie but was more muscular.

"Hey, Chuck, I want you to meet Chris Rogers. He's our new team member."

To Chris, Eddie said, "Chris, this is Chuck McCain. He's the other team leader. The other guy you met earlier, Scotty, is on his team. Chuck was in the middle of the incident at Six Flags while you were helping us at the mall."

"Nice to meet you, Chris," Chuck said, shaking Roger's hand. "I hear you bailed Eddie and Jimmy out at that mall. Thanks for taking care of them. Everybody knows that when you need something done right, call in a street cop."

They all laughed and Chuck took a seat in the empty chair next to Chris. Rogers found himself staring at Chuck.

"Can I ask you a random question, Mr. McCain?"

"Just call me 'Chuck,' and fire away."

"Were you ever an MMA fighter? I'm a huge MMA fan and I think I saw you fight live a couple of times at

Cowboys and Cowgirls Country Bar."

"That was me. I haven't had a fight in almost three years but I fought pretty regularly for a while. Did I win when you saw me?"

"I saw you fight twice. You knocked one guy out in like thirty seconds. And I think the other fight, you lost a close decision."

"Yep, one of my heavyweight fights. Most of my fights were at light heavyweight. I only lost four times. They were all by decision and they were all to heavyweights."

Eddie noticed the look of awe on Chris' face. Chuck had never fought for the UFC or one of the other big promotions, but he had had some success fighting on the local circuit in the southeast. It took a special kind of man to get into a cage with another man for the sole purpose of trying to beat that man senseless.

"Are you a martial artist?" Chuck asked.

"Not really, but I did wrestle all through high school."

"That's still pretty impressive. Wrestling is very practical for police officers. I wouldn't recommend wrestling with a zombie but for taking down live people, it's great."

"So, you got sworn in last week and Roy signed off on your shooting?" Marshall asked Rogers.

"Yes, sir. I guess I'm a legitimate CDC Enforcement Officer now, huh?"

"Sounds like it. We're glad to have you. We've been running a man short for a couple of weeks, since we lost Marco. You've been a cop for a few years so you know that this is a dangerous line of work.

"The stuff we're dealing with now, though, is even worse. You've seen it. You were with us when those terrorists hit that mall out in Douglasville. The reality is that we're running into similar kinds of situations much more regularly now."

"That was you guys at Peachtree Meadow High School last week, wasn't it?" Chris asked. "The news didn't identify you but it was pretty easy to read between the lines."

Eddie nodded and pointed at McCain.

"Chuck and Scotty killed around a hundred zombies just by themselves. They got separated from their team and were protecting some of the students. They almost got overrun."

Chuck laughed.

"At one point, I thought we were goners. There were just too many of them. And no matter what Scotty acts like or says, he's somebody you want standing next to you when things go south. That boy can fight."

Marshall let what Chuck had said sink in.

"'So, Chris, we're glad you've joined us and I know you're going to fit right in. I heard you busting Scotty's chops.

"We'll all be helping you get up to speed on the stuff you need to learn. Normally, our new guys go through a two-month training course. In your case, though, Rebecca knew we needed someone right now and we all feel that you're quick enough and bright enough to pick up what you need to know as we go."

"Thank you, sir. I really appreciate you putting in a good word for me with Ms. Johnson. I don't think I've ever seen a hiring process go more quickly or more smoothly."

"She does have the ability to pull some strings, doesn't she, Chuck?"

"That she does."

"What do we have planned for the next couple of days?" Eddie asked Chuck.

"Tomorrow, we'll spend the day at the shoot house unless something comes up. I think Rebecca wanted Chris to collect all of his equipment today and read some of the training curriculum for bio-terrorism and some other things. She wants to talk to him when she gets back. She's in one of those intel briefings with the FBI and the DHS and will be back after lunch."

CDC HQ, Wednesday, 1400 hours

After lunch, Rebecca called for a meeting with both teams in the briefing room. When everyone got settled in, she publicly welcomed Chris.

"Thanks for joining us, Chris. I'm sorry that you're going to have to pick up things on the run but we really needed someone and you showed us what you could do in the attack in Douglasville.

"I just got back from an intelligence briefing with our

friends from the FBI and the DHS. You guys have already heard that a Somali national, Mohamud Ahmed, has been identified as a person of interest by the FBI in connection with the incident at the high school last week."

She was holding a small remote and pushed a button on it. Ahmed's picture flashed up on the wall.

"The FBI's lab has been working around the clock trying to figure out how the infection started at that school. Their findings and what they saw on the video surveillance footage are the reasons that Ahmed is now a wanted man. Warrants were signed this morning.

"At the time, he was working for Coca Cola and was responsible for servicing the drink machines at that school. It looks like he planted bottled drinks which had been infected with the virus in the drink machines at the location. The scenario is that Mohamud placed a variety of tainted drinks in several machines at the school early that morning.

"Surveillance footage shows that he was there before the students started arriving, servicing the drink machines. And, of course, as the students showed up, many of them just had to have a Coke pick-me-up before class."

"How did the FBI make the link between the infection and the bottled drinks?" Chuck asked.

"Several of the infected students had partially consumed bottles of soft drinks or water in their backpacks. One of their sharp forensics experts decided to test one of the bottles and it came back positive for the zombie virus. Then, they went back to the school and checked every drink in every machine. There were still a few in the machines that contained the virus.

"Now, here's where it gets really good. They found fingerprints on a couple of the bottles for Amir al-Razi. It looks like he and Ahmed are working together. The terrorists opened the drinks breaking the seal, added a few drops of the virus, put a little glue on the underside of the bottle cap, and then screwed it back on. It wasn't perfect but it clearly fooled a lot of high school kids."

"What do we know about Ahmed?" asked Andy.

"I've been doing some digging on him, Andy. He came here as a refugee five years ago. He got the job as a route driver with Coca Cola and hasn't raised any red flags at all. His supervisors at Coke said he was a model employee.

"But, I found out that his father and his uncle were both killed in the Battle of Mogadishu in 1993. Remember the movie, *Black Hawk Down*? Mohamud's dad and uncle were probably killed by some of Scotty's people, the Army Rangers."

Smith quickly jumped to his feet and stood at attention. "Rangers lead the way, ma'am." He then sat back down.

Andy and Jimmy, both former Marines, rolled their eyes at their friend.

"Only when the Marines aren't around," Jones quipped.

Rebecca smiled. "And, it gets better. Ahmed's brother was a pirate who managed to get himself killed by some Navy SEALs when he tried to hijack the wrong ship."

"Sounds like Mohamud comes from one unlucky family," said Jimmy.

"It sure does. That happened two years before he came to America. So, we may have a guy looking for some revenge for his dad, brother, and uncle."

"And now, he and al-Razi are working together," added Eddie.

"That's right. Here's where we're at. A nationwide lookout has been issued for Ahmed's silver Honda Accord. Amir's rental car is now listed as stolen, also. That's a brown Ford Focus. Of course, they could have dumped both of them and stolen something new.

"The next thing that you guys need to know is that the national media has really helped us by not blasting the zombie virus story around the clock. But the reality is that it's spreading everyday. The other cities that got hit are having a tough time. Alejandro, have you talked to your family in LA?"

Estrada nodded. "They say that parts of the city are closed down. Entire neighborhoods are sealed off. They said that their neighborhood has only had some isolated incidents but they have friends in other parts of the city that have had to flee their homes because of the zombies."

Johnson nodded. "Dallas, Houston, and New Orleans are like ghost towns. Their downtown areas were hit really hard by the virus. New York's was originally confined mostly to Manhattan but in the last week, it has spread to Brooklyn, Queens, and even onto Long Island.

"Washington DC's attack may be the most devastating of them all. So many people were infected who then carried the virus to Maryland, Virginia, Pennsylvania, and

West Virginia. Like I said, the media, for once, is helping us by not creating a frenzy, but the DC attack has the potential to infect the entire East Coast. Especially, when you factor in the attacks here in Atlanta."

"Is there any progress on a vaccine or some kind of antidote for this thing?" Eddie asked.

"Nothing. A week or two ago, they thought they were making progress, but Azar Kasra sabotaged much of that research. I stopped by the lab upstairs earlier today and they said that this is one of the most complex viruses anyone has ever seen. They're working in three shifts, around the clock, but right now, it sounds like they aren't even close to solving it.

"While I was talking to Dr. Edwards and the other epidemiologists upstairs, one of them told me that one of the really scary things is how this virus seems to get stronger over time. In other words, what they have extracted from victims to test and run experiments with seems to have gotten stronger. I'm telling you guys this because with al-Razi and Ahmed running around, whatever of the zombie virus they have left is going to be even more dangerous."

"It already turns people into murderous, flesh-eating monsters," said Luis. "How can it be any worse?"

"For one thing, it looks like the speed of death to turning into a zombie is much faster. And, when they injected the stronger virus into laboratory rats, they became stronger and faster zombies in a much quicker time. In other words, we've seen the time of infections vary widely from minutes or maybe even days before turning people. It looks like from here on out, minutes is going to be the norm, rather than hours or days."

"Nice. I do love my job," said Scotty.

"One last thing," said Rebecca. "With the war between the United States and Iran just getting started, there's a real concern that there will be more attacks like the ones we've already seen involving the zombie virus. There's no way that Iran can beat us in a conventional war. With these bio-terror attacks, though, they've really hurt us. We need to try and find Amir and Mohamud. There may be more terrorists operating in Atlanta, but we know these guys and we need to find them as quickly as we can."

MARTA Station, City of Chamblee, Thursday, 1100 hours

Jimmy pulled the Ford Interceptor into the MARTA parking lot and parked behind the marked City of Chamblee police cruiser. The Metro Atlanta Rapid Transit Authority is Atlanta's rail system and covers the city thoroughly. Jimmy, Alejandro, and Chris got out to talk to the uniformed police officer, his vehicle parked near a silver Honda Accord. The CDC officers were all wearing their tactical equipment. They had been training at a shoot house and had come straight from there when Chamblee PD had called them.

A young Asian officer shook hands with the three federal officers. "I'm Corporal David Lee. Thanks for coming out."

"What have you got?" Jimmy asked.

"This silver Honda is the one that you guys have been looking for. It's registered to Mohamud Ahmed. He did a switcheroo with the license plate. The tag that's on it was stolen from another Honda Accord and he probably put his plates on that car. This tag isn't even reported as stolen yet."

"Good work," said Estrada, approvingly. "How'd you find it?"

"We got the look out you guys issued for his car and I was just checking the parking lot. I drive through here a few times a shift to keep an eye on things. This isn't the best part of town so we try to maintain high visibility in the area. I figured that since I was here anyway, I'd run the three silver Accords that were parked in the lot. This one wasn't here a couple of hours ago.

"I ran the tag and it came back to the same make car. Just for the heck of it, I compared the VIN on the car to the one on the tag return and it was different. I ran this car's VIN on the computer and got the hit."

The three federal officers nodded appreciatively. That was good police work. Most officers would have just run the tag and when it didn't return stolen, they would've kept driving.

Corporal Lee went the extra mile and compared the vehicle identification number for that tag to the VIN on the dashboard. That told him that the tag for the Accord was different. A computer check of that VIN showed that the car had a warning for law enforcement officers to use extreme caution with Ahmed.

"Have you searched it?" asked Jimmy.

"No. As soon as I realized what I had, I just waited on the dispatcher to call you guys. I figured you would want to process it."

"You're right, Corporal. I'll have one of our forensics teams do that. Would you mind calling us a tow truck?"

Jimmy looked at Alejandro. "Hollywood, can you call and have a Clean Up Team meet the wrecker at the impound lot and do a very thorough processing?"

"Will do."

Estrada stepped away to make the phone call.

"The next thing we need to do is go to the MARTA Police Headquarters and watch some security video and see if we can figure where Mohamud went," Jones told Rogers. "It's not much. But maybe we can at least figure out if he got on a train and where he went to."

Downtown Atlanta, Thursday, 1700 hours

Mohamud Ahmed must have walked two or three miles getting to know the downtown area around Georgia State

166

University. His instructions from Amir were simple. Use Thursday and Friday to find three coffee shops or restaurants around the university.

He was to stay off of the campus itself because Georgia State had their own police department. It was a fairly small campus so the possibility of running into the police was very real. Instead, he would focus on three businesses within a block or two of the school.

On Saturday, starting around 1100 hours, he was to enter each location and buy a coffee. As he added cream to his coffee, he was to pour a vial of the virus into the pitcher of cream. Then he was to leave the shop and walk to the next one and repeat the process.

After infecting the third coffee shop or restaurant, he could begin trying to make his escape. He had known that leaving his car in the parking lot of the MARTA station was a calculated risk. It had very likely been discovered by now, letting the authorities know that he had utilized the train. Then again, maybe it had not.

Even if they had found his car, though, he felt confident that there was no way that they could track him. There were too many places that he could have gone on the rail system. When Mohamud was finished with his mission, he would take a westbound MARTA train to get away from the downtown area. Then, he was confident that he could steal a car to make his escape out of the state.

He found several likely target locations as he explored the area around GSU but he only had three vials of the virus. Ahmed's reconnaissance for Friday would be to try and figure out which ones would have the most traffic. The goal was to infect as many people as possible at each business. Because the virus was so potent, he would only need a few people to get infected to start spreading zombie terror in the heart of the city. Within a couple of hours, the virus would be carried throughout Atlanta.

He found a nondescript hotel about half a mile from the university campus. The New Century Hotel was a haven for prostitutes and drug dealers. Mohamud was able to rent a room for two nights using cash and a false name on the registration card that he filled out. This was clearly one of those places where no questions would be asked.

MARTA Police Headquarters, Thursday, 1530 hours

Jimmy, Alejandro, and Chris were given total access to the digital recording banks of footage captured in each of the MARTA stations. A MARTA police lieutenant put them each in front of a computer and showed them how to pull up video from the different stations. Jimmy quickly found a man who looked like Mohamud Ahmed getting on the southbound train at the Chamblee Station where he had parked his car.

They were not a hundred percent sure that it was him but for now, it was the best that they had. It looked like he had started growing a beard. He was wearing an Atlanta Braves ball cap, sunglasses, a black t-shirt, and was carrying a duffel bag over his shoulder.

Jimmy captured several images from the recording and sent them to Eddie and Rebecca. He asked if they could forward them to the FBI for verification using their facial recognition software. Now the question was, "Where did he go?"

Thirty minutes later, Chris said, "I found him. He exited at the Georgia State University exit."

Jimmy and Alejandro crowded around his monitor. Ahmed exited the train and took the steps up to the street. He was still carrying his duffel bag.

"He doesn't strike me as the type who's taking night classes," commented Jimmy. "I think we're about to get hit again. If he was running away, I don't think he'd head into the heart of the city."

Jones felt his smart phone vibrate and saw that Eddie was calling him.

"What's up, Boss?"

"Hey, Jimmy. The FBI got back to us in record time and confirmed that the guy in those pictures is Ahmed. Any idea where he went?"

"Here's what we know. He took the train into the city and got off at the Georgia State University exit."

"That doesn't sound good. Can you guys head that way? I'll meet you down there. Maybe we'll get lucky and see him. If not, we'll at least be close when the zombies start showing up. And, I'll ask Rebecca to begin notifying the locals."

The officers changed into civilian attire. They always carried a change of clothes with them in their vehicle for situations just like this. Within twenty minutes, they were driving around the block where the Georgia State University MARTA station was located.

Jimmy cruised slowly through the surrounding area for almost an hour with no luck. The streets were packed with people walking. There was no telling where Mohamud had gone.

Jimmy parked on the street near the GSU campus. The three officers had talked on the way to the location about their strategy. Chris was the only one of the three who was familiar with the campus. He had been working on a Criminal Justice degree at GSU when he had gotten hired by the Fulton County Police Department.

The three men would split up and try and cover as much ground as they could looking for Ahmed. Chris looked the most like a student and even had an expired student ID card if challenged. He would make his way through the classroom and administration buildings. Each officer had several printouts of Ahmed's photo that they could pass on to the local police. Jimmy and Alejandro would walk around the campus and the surrounding areas trying to get an idea of what Mohamud's target might be.

As Chris walked out of one of the classroom buildings, he saw a campus police officer writing a parking ticket. He walked over to her and identified himself, holding out his CDC Enforcement badge and ID. The officer barely glanced up and continued to write the parking ticket.

"I'm sorry to bother you but I have some important intel for you to pass on to your other officers."

"That's fine but you're still getting a parking ticket."

It took a minute for what she had said to register. "What? That's not my car. I'm a federal police officer working on a case and I was wanting to give you a heads up on possible terrorist attack."

She looked at Chris and continued writing. When she finished, she placed the citation under the windshield wiper of the car.

"Maybe it would be better if you called your sergeant," Chris said. "I don't want to pull you away from something more important."

"What were you wanting to tell me? I'm finished now."

"Please call your sergeant. I think I'd rather talk to them."

Rogers had no patience with people like this girl. He knew he was probably getting her in trouble by calling her supervisor over but he didn't care. She was more focused on generating a forty-five dollar fine than in hearing about a dangerous terrorist that was possibly planning an attack in the area.

Officer LaTeesha Thompson didn't want to get her boss involved but now she didn't have a choice. The sergeant had been requested so she had to call him. Chris could hear part of the conversation.

"He just said he wanted to talk to you. I don't know. He said he was some kind of federal police officer or something. He wouldn't tell me anything."

A few minutes later, another police car pulled up and a huge hulk of man pried himself out of it. Chris walked over and offered him his credentials. His nametag showed a last name of "Roberts."

"Thanks for coming over, Sergeant Roberts. I tried to talk to your officer there but she was busy writing parking tickets. Even when I told her that I had information on a possible terror attack, she didn't seem very interested."

The sergeant glanced at Officer Thompson who had walked back to her own patrol car. He shook his head.

"Sorry about that, Agent Rogers. It's easier to write parking tickets than to do real police work. Did you work anywhere else before you got on with the CDC?"

"I worked for Fulton County PD for five years. I spent most of my time in South Fulton."

Sergeant Roberts grunted and looked at Chris with new respect.

"Well, then you understand. Some people just aren't cut out for this line of work but it's getting harder and harder to find good people. Now, how can I help you?"

Chris gave him one of the photos of Ahmed and gave him all the information that he had.

"He has warrants on him for that attack at the high school two weeks ago. He's probably close to being Number One on the FBI's Most Wanted List. This is a really bad guy and I don't think he's down here enrolling for the new semester. Now, maybe his target is somewhere else in the city but he got off of MARTA here. Can you pass this photo and his info on to your officers?"

"I sure will. Thanks for letting us know. I'm going talk to our Chief right now. How are you guys working this?

And what about the FBI?"

"My boss has contacted the FBI to give them what we know. They'll probably put some people in the area, too. Right now, there are just three of us from the CDC down here and our team leader is on his way. Other than knowing that he got off of the train here, we don't have anything.

"We recovered his car earlier today at the Chamblee Station and it's being processed. Maybe that'll give us some clues. My guess is that we'll probably be down here again tomorrow looking for him. Have you got a card?"

Roberts and Rogers swapped cards that had their phone numbers and email addresses.

"I'll contact you tomorrow and let you know if we're going to be on campus. It'd be great to catch this guy but please let all of your officers know that none of the terrorists involved in this have been taken alive and they need to use extreme caution if they run across him."

Chapter Eight

Near Georgia State University, Downtown Atlanta, Friday, 1400 hours

On Friday morning, Mohamud spent time in several cafes and small restaurants around the university. He watched the people go about their lives, oblivious to the African terrorist sitting in their midst. Mohamud was impressed with Amir's planning and foresight. Georgia State University was in the heart of downtown Atlanta. This attack would create panic and terror and would turn a large section of the city into a graveyard.

He had questioned al-Razi on why they were waiting until midmorning on Saturday to launch their attacks. It seemed to him that a Friday afternoon or even a Monday morning attack might be more deadly. Amir had explained to him that they were coordinating multiple attacks in different locations and the timing was very important. Amir had not told him what the other targets were, but with their previous meeting in Athens, Mohamud guessed that the large university there was going to be infected, as well.

The area around GSU was a target rich environment. Amir had asked him to spread his three infectious visits over a few hours, finishing up in the early afternoon.

Mohamud considered himself a good soldier of Allah. He might not understand Amir's plan for the timing of the attacks, but he trusted the man and would follow the orders that he had been given.

By 1400 hours on Friday, Ahmed had mapped out his plan for Saturday. He had consumed several cups of coffee and had had lunch in two different restaurants adjacent to the campus. He pictured in his mind the death and destruction that his actions were going to cause and couldn't help but smile as he exited Ricardo's Mexican Restaurant and began the walk back to his hotel. He didn't notice the two men who exited a black SUV and started following him down the crowded sidewalk.

Georgia State University, Downtown Atlanta, Friday, 1415 hours

Sergeant Roberts and Eddie Marshall hit it off right away. Both men had worked for big city police departments before ending up in their present jobs. Roberts had spent ten years with the City of Atlanta PD before going to work for the university police department. He was making more money and had gotten promoted much faster than he would have at APD.

Marshall had spent fifteen years working for the Chicago Police Department, becoming a road sergeant and then a detective sergeant in the narcotics unit. His dream, though, had always been to work for a federal law enforcement agency. When he went to work for the U.S.

Marshals Service, he thought that he had died and gone to Heaven. He had spent five years tracking dangerous fugitives who were on the run from the federal courts. He tracked down and caught cartel leaders, members of the mafia, bank robbers, and murderers.

When Rebecca Johnson approached him and offered him a job, Eddie wasn't sure that he wanted it. The big pay raise had helped convince him to switch agencies but now he couldn't imagine doing anything else. He was working with a great group of people, trying to stop one of the most serious threats that America had ever faced.

Roberts and Marshall placed the CDC agents in strategic locations around the university campus. Each federal officer was accompanied by a campus officer. They were hoping to catch Ahmed before he could launch any type of bio-terror attack.

Andy and Luis, from Team One, were also a part of the surveillance team on the campus. Chuck and Scotty were in their Suburban, conducting mobile surveillance further away from the university. There were plenty of targets in Downtown Atlanta. McCain and Smith were scanning the sidewalks as they drove around the center of the city.

Jimmy and Alejandro were also acting as rovers in their black SUV. They were driving on the streets right around the university campus, watching the sidewalks for any sign of Ahmed. The GSU police representative assigned to them was LaTeesha Thompson, the officer whom Chris had tried to talk to the day before. They were all wearing civilian clothes as they tried to blend in with the throngs of people on foot and in cars in the heart of the city.

"Who's that young white officer that works with y'all?" LaTeesha asked.

"You mean Chris?" Jimmy answered.

"Yeah, the one that looks like he's about sixteen years old."

"Don't let that baby face fool you. That boy is dangerous with a capital "D," said Jimmy. "He took down one of the terrorists who was shooting up that mall in Douglasville. Chris was just in there shopping, minding his own business.

"A bunch of Muslim tangos with AK-47s came in shooting people. All Chris had was a pistol but he took out one of the bad guys. Then, he stuck around and helped us clear out the mall of zombies. He's a dangerous dude."

"Well, he got me in trouble with my sergeant yesterday," she pouted.

Chris had told them about the incident when he saw that LaTeesha was going to be riding with his teammates.

"You must not be in too much trouble. They're letting you ride with us, looking for a terrorist," said Estrada.

"Maybe that's my punishment," she muttered.

"Or ours," commented Alejandro.

Estrada and Jones both laughed.

Jimmy said, "LaTeesha, you can get out any time you want and write parking tickets. Maybe you'll find Mohamud double-parked." The two men laughed again.

"What do you guys know? You're federal police officers," she replied, the disgust in her voice was evident.

"You don't have to deal with parking complaints and some of the other crap that comes with working for a university police department."

"I was an Alabama State Trooper for a while and he," said Jimmy, pointing at Alejandro, "worked for the Los Angeles Police Department. That's why we call him 'Hollywood.' We're both just street cops at heart. Now, we're tracking terrorists and shooting zombies."

"If you were a trooper," LaTeesha pressed, "you know all about writing tickets."

Jimmy nodded. "True story, but I was always looking beyond the ticket. I found hundreds of kilos of cocaine, meth, and marijuana over the years because of traffic stops. I caught all kinds of fugitives on pullovers.

"I never liked writing tickets just for the sake of writing tickets, though. For me, it was always a way to find criminals. Bad guys have to get from Point A to Point B and most of the time they drive."

"Unless they're walking down the sidewalk," observed Estrada. "Slow down. That guy up there in the black t-shirt and the Braves hat? He just came out of that restaurant and sure looks like our terrorist buddy."

The slim man had stepped out of the business and turned right on the sidewalk, slipping sunglasses onto his face. He appeared to be smiling as he walked.

"He's wearing the same clothes he was wearing yesterday," Estrada noticed.

"Well, no one said he was a very good terrorist," Jimmy observed.

There was an opening at the curb and Jones pulled the Interceptor to the side of the street. There was a parking meter but neither officer had any intention of worrying about it.

"LaTeesha can write us a ticket later," Jimmy told Alejandro.

She didn't think that was funny. "Don't we need to wait for backup?"

"Please call it in on your radio and give them our location. You can come with us or wait in the car," said Alejandro, getting out of the SUV.

Jimmy clicked the transmit button on his own radio. "Team Two Bravo to Team Two Alpha."

Eddie answered immediately. "Go ahead, Team Two Bravo."

"We've spotted him and we're tailing him on foot. He came out of Ricardo's Mexican Restaurant at the corner of Decatur Street and Central Avenue. We'll be heading south on Central Avenue. It might be good to have some officers get over there and make sure he hasn't spread any zombie love in that restaurant. I'll keep you posted."

"Team Two Alpha clear."

Jones and Estrada trailed Ahmed at a distance as they walked down Central Avenue. The terrorist didn't seem to be in a hurry. They turned left down Martin Luther King Junior Drive just before they got to the Fulton County Court Buildings.

LaTeesha was trailing them by fifty yards. She wasn't

sure if she should stay with the two male officers or if she should hang back. This was the most dangerous thing that she had ever done in her short law enforcement career.

The sidewalks were packed and the officers didn't want to attempt to take Mohamud down in a crowd. It was likely that he was armed and they did not want any innocents to get hurt. His direction was taking him back towards Interstate 85. They crossed Washington Street but stayed on MLK Drive, passing the Georgia State Capital, with its gleaming, golden dome.

Jimmy motioned for the female officer to join them. She increased her pace to catch up.

"What's that next street?"

"That's Piedmont Avenue," she answered.

"Let's try and take him down near MLK and Piedmont Avenue. It looks like the pedestrian traffic is thinning out."

"Sounds good to me," Estrada answered.

"Can you call in our location to your dispatcher?" Jimmy asked LaTeesha.

The officers were about fifty yards behind Ahmed. The red pedestrian light caught him at the crosswalk with Piedmont Avenue. Jones slowed down to call Eddie and to give him an update.

As Jones was talking to his team leader, he saw the terrorist turn around and look at him, seeing Jimmy talking into the hands-free microphone. Their eyes met. He saw the surprise in Ahmed's eyes as he suddenly realized that he was being followed.

The terrorist turned and started running. Cars slammed

on their brakes to avoid hitting him. Drivers pushed their horns and yelled at the running figure.

Jones and Estrada pulled their badges out from underneath their shirts and let them hang on their chests by their chain as they started pursuing. Jimmy had been a track and field star at the University of Alabama as a sprinter. He quickly began to close the distance on Ahmed. Alejandro wasn't far behind.

They continued running towards the interstate. MLK Drive would go underneath the highway. Jimmy was only twenty-five yards behind the terrorist and closing the distance fast.

"Stop! Police! Mohamud Ahmed, you're under arrest," Jimmy yelled as he ran, drawing his pistol.

Ahmed glanced a look over his shoulder and saw the black man getting closer. He heard him shout for him to stop. He even heard the man yell his name. How did they find him? he wondered. Mohamud reached into his right front pocket and withdrew the Makarov pistol that Amir had given him. He felt regret that he wouldn't be able to carry out his mission.

His lungs were burning and the adrenaline propelled him forward but he was not a runner. Another quick glance over his shoulder. The police officer was now only ten yards behind him. Another officer was quickly closing the distance as well.

This was it. He knew that he couldn't run anymore. Even if he could, these police were too fast. Ahmed began to slow down. He stepped sideways to his right and swung his pistol towards the closest police officer.

Jimmy saw that Mohamud was slowing down. Now, he was just fifteen feet behind him. Jones had seen him reach into his pocket but he couldn't see what he had pulled out. He assumed it was a gun but he didn't want to shoot a guy who had just been grabbing for his cell phone. He had to be sure.

The terrorist took a quick step to the right. Jimmy moved to his left to give himself a little more distance and to make himself a tougher target. Jones brought his Glock up to eye level.

When Ahmed turned with a gun in his hand, Jimmy fired three quick shots that caught him on the right side of his chest. Time slowed down as he saw the shots impact. The terrorist flinched but did not go down.

Estrada saw the man they were chasing swing around with a small pistol. He observed Jimmy shoot and watched the rounds strike him, the fabric of the black t-shirt moving with each impact. Alejandro pulled the trigger on his Glock twice, his bullets hitting Mohamud in the sternum. Ahmed staggered but continued to try and aim his pistol at Jones.

Jimmy and Alejandro both raised their sights slightly and fired again. Jones' shot hit Ahmed on the bridge of the nose and penetrated into his brain. Estrada's bullet punched into the terrorist's left eye. His head snapped back and he collapsed onto his back.

They both covered Ahmed with their pistols, making sure that he was no longer a threat.

"I'll handcuff him," Estrada said.

He holstered his gun and pulled his kevlar gloves out of his pocket and put them on. With Jimmy covering him, he moved in and rolled the terrorist onto his stomach and handcuffed him. Ahmed's pistol was laying on the pavement next to him.

Thompson came walking up slowly. She stared at the body, unable to say anything.

Jimmy performed a tactical reload of his pistol, inserting a full magazine into the gun. He reholstered and called Eddie.

LaTeesha had hung back when the two CDC officers started chasing the skinny, light-skinned man. She had heard Officer Jones challenge him to stop and had watched as the guy swung around with a pistol. She hadn't even seen him draw it but Jones and Estrada had and calmly shot him several times, including two final shots to the head. Now, she was standing and watching the terrorist's blood leak out of a number of bullet holes. Jones and Estrada didn't seem to be fazed in the least by the death of Ahmed.

She heard Jimmy say to Alejandro, "Yep, that boy came from one unlucky family."

The campus police officer knew that she needed to request an ambulance and to let Sergeant Roberts know what had happened. Her hand was shaking as she pushed the transmit button on her radio but felt vomit suddenly rising into her mouth. LaTeesha was just able to move to the side of the sidewalk so that her puke did not land on the body or the other two officers.

New Century Hotel, Atlanta, 1800 hours

Within minutes after the shooting, the street was a sea of blue lights from both marked and unmarked police cars and red lights from the fire truck and ambulance that had responded. Yellow crime scene tape cordoned the area off. Eddie and Chuck controlled the scene until Rebecca arrived. She requested that the FBI send a team to help with the investigation and that both of the CDC's Clean Up Teams respond.

The media also arrived quickly and in force. She let the FBI's media relation's agent deal with them. The FBI had been the ones who had taken out the warrants on Ahmed and he had just made Number One on their infamous Most Wanted List.

It was obvious that the terrorist was dead. The paramedics had verified it so his body would be left where it was until the scene was processed. After the crime scene photos had been taken, the lead FBI agent put on a pair of rubber gloves and went through Mohamud's pockets.

In his left front pocket was an extra magazine for his pistol. In his right rear pocket was a black leather wallet that contained a room key for the New Century Hotel, a few blocks away. The wallet also contained several hundred dollars in cash and a Georgia Driver's License in the name of Cumar Ali.

Supervisory Special Agent Thomas Burns held up the ID and commented loudly, "It looks like you guys shot the wrong man." He glanced over to Jimmy, who was standing with Eddie, Chuck, and Rebecca. "I guess you didn't bother to try and confirm his identity before you killed him?"

"Is this guy an idiot or what?" asked Scotty, as he walked up behind Burns.

The special agent turned to confront the person who had just insulted him. When he saw the big, muscular man in the CDC Enforcement uniform with a rifle slung across his chest, he checked what he was going to say.

Smith walked by Burns without even acknowledging his presence. "I mean, really? Are all FBI agents this stupid?" Scotty asked motioning over his shoulder at the red-faced agent.

Burns found his voice and said to Rebecca, "You can bet that I'm going to report those insulting and degrading comments to my superiors."

"Just do your job, Burns," Rebecca said, coldly. "Are you going to check that hotel room or do you want us to do it?"

"This is our investigation," the FBI agent answered, trying to sound indignant. "We identified Ahmed and took out the warrants for him. Now, it looks like your men have shot the wrong person."

"When a man points a gun at you, he's the right guy to shoot even if he's not the guy you're looking for," said

185

Jimmy. "But, this is the right guy. We'll get the Clean Up Team to fingerprint him and verify his identity."

Chuck walked over to Agent Burns. "Can I see that driver's license?"

After examining it for about ten seconds, he handed it back to the FBI agent and said, "It's a fake."

"How do you know that?" Burns demanded.

"Because I'm a police officer and being able to spot fake documents is an important job skill. That's not even a very good fake," Chuck told him.

"Back to my question, Burns," said Rebecca. "We need to get into that hotel room. For all we know, Amir al-Razi is waiting there for Ahmed to come back. Send a couple of your guys with us if you want, but we need to get over there now. I don't think you'd want your superiors to know that you let al-Razi get away."

The four officers of Team One, Chris Rogers, Rebecca, two young FBI agents and two City of Atlanta police officers moved quietly down the second floor hallway to room 210. They paused for a moment when they got to the room. Chuck scanned the hallway. There was no noise except a television from a few rooms down. A 'Do Not Disturb' sign hung from the door of room 210.

There was no telling what was on the other side of the door. The CDC officers were wearing their heavy body armor and had their rifles slung over their chests. The FBI agents had thrown soft body armor over their polo shirts and had their "FBI" windbreakers on. They were holding their pistols down by their legs.

Chuck nodded at Rebecca and she slipped the keycard into the door. When the light turned green, she turned the handle and stepped out of the way. McCain was in the door first, followed by Smith, Fleming, García, Rogers, Johnson, and the two FBI agents. The uniformed police officers provided security in the hallway.

Chuck and Scotty cleared the small room while Andy and Luis checked the bathroom. The hotel room was empty. The bed had been slept in and there was a black duffel bag laying on the small table next to the window. One of the FBI agents started to grab it.

"I wouldn't recommend that," said Rebecca, quietly.

He shot a glance at her. "And why not?" he challenged.

"It probably has some of the zombie virus in it, for one thing. The other reason is that it's part of the crime scene and needs to be processed correctly. I doubt you want to be known as the agent that messed up a crime scene involving one of the worst mass murderers in American History."

"They really are all that stupid," Scotty commented to Andy, but loud enough for everyone in the building to hear.

"Be nice, Scotty," said Rebecca as she called the Clean Up Team. They were parked below in the parking lot and came up to process the room.

The Clean Up Team photographed the hotel room and processed it for fingerprints and for DNA evidence. They searched the room thoroughly. The duffel bag did contain the zombie virus. At least, that's what it looked like. Three small, glass vials of a clear liquid were wrapped in bubble wrap.

The duffel bag also contained more cash, more bullets, some clothes, toiletries and Mohamud Ahmed's Georgia Driver's License. What it did not contain was any clue about what his target was in Downtown Atlanta. A cheap cell phone was laying on the table next to the bed. The phone would be given to the FBI to see what their forensics people could get off of it.

Mohamud Ahmed was dead. That was not a bad thing. They had recovered a quantity of the virus. They were also at a dead end in their investigation.

Amir was still out there but they had no idea where. Was he in Downtown Atlanta as well? Rebecca and her men had no clue where to look next.

Sports Bar, Athens, Georgia, Friday, 1830 hours

Amir had been doing his own research and reconnaissance around Athens. He also had three vials of the virus. His first stop on Saturday morning was going to be the Georgia Square Mall. It wasn't a very large mall but it had a coffee shop just off of the food court.

The mall was about six miles from the university. When people started turning into zombies in the mall, it would pull police away from the campus. A breakout of the infection there would serve as a distraction for the police and for the emergency responders. An attack on the mall would ultimately be an attack on the university as well because so many of the students worked there and shopped there.

The main reason that al-Razi had chosen tomorrow to launch their attacks was because it was the first home football game of the season for the University of Georgia. Eighty thousand people or more would be packed into Sanford Stadium to cheer for the Bulldogs. Terrell Hill would be working at one of the concession booths inside. Amir had already given him his instructions. Al-Razi's plan was going to turn that stadium and the surrounding area into a graveyard.

The start of the game, the 'kickoff' they called it, was scheduled for 2:05 in the afternoon. He would visit the mall and cause some chaos there and then drive back to the campus and cause even more chaos there. His only disappointment was that he didn't have more of the virus. He had not realized how big this university was until he had spent some time walking around it yesterday and today.

Amir found a sports bar in downtown Athens. He got a table near the back of the business to watch the crowd, ordering a cheeseburger, French fries and a Coke. A story caught his attention on one of the many televisions playing throughout the restaurant. He could not hear anything but the headline read, 'Suspected Terrorist Killed in Shootout with Police.' The screen showed live footage of an area near the Georgia State University roped off by yellow crime scene tape.

He quickly got to his feet and walked out of the restaurant. If they had identified Ahmed, the police had very likely linked the two of them and his own face could soon be appearing on the television again. They had identified him as suspect after the initial attacks and his picture had been shown regularly for a few days before other stories became more important. Amir walked to his car which was parked a couple of blocks away. He turned on a local news radio station in the car to hear more.

The police were not saying much except that they believed they had stopped a bio-terror attack in the heart of the city. An unnamed source had told one reporter that CDC enforcement agents had shot and killed Mohamud Ahmed. He was being named as the primary terrorist behind the Peachtree Meadow High School attack that had killed close to a thousand students, teachers, parents, and police officers.

Al-Razi slammed his hand into the steering wheel in anger. How did they do that? How did they find Ahmed in a city the size of Atlanta? Once again, Amir's plans were thwarted by the officers of the CDC.

He took a deep breath. At least Mohamud had not been arrested. Granted, he had not known where Amir was going to strike but his death left no loose ends. He had nothing to connect him with Amir. While disappointing, it did not matter. Tomorrow would be another blow to the infidels as al-Razi and Terrell Hill brought jihad to one of the largest universities in America.

Waffle House, Athens, Georgia, Friday, 1845 hours

Terrell only had another fifteen minutes before his shift ended. The Waffle House is one of the few restaurants that offers jobs to ex-convicts. His guidance counselor from the Department of Corrections had helped him get the position. He always hated serving the police when they came in, though, and on a couple of occasions, had managed to spit in their food as he prepared it. Today, however, would be his last shift at Waffle House.

A friend from high school had helped him secure the part-time job at Sanford Stadium with few questions asked. He had worked all the home games for the last two seasons but tomorrow would be his last shift there, as well. He would complete the mission that Amir had given him and then he would disappear. Well, not completely disappear. Amir had instructed him to head towards the Northern Virginia area and had given him the phone number of a contact in Washington D.C.

"If you don't hear from me within forty-eight hours of our attacks, assume the worst and call the phone number. He will have some more work for you if you want it," al-Razi had told him.

All he had to do tomorrow was show up at the stadium on time and follow the instructions that Amir had given him. As soon as he was done, he just had to get out of there without becoming a victim himself. He even had a plan for driving away instead of walking.

Chapter Nine

University Parkway, Saturday, 1030 hours

Chuck picked Rebecca up at 0930 hours. The hour and a half drive to Athens was beautiful and the couple enjoyed the ride, watching the beautiful scenery. They would meet Melanie and Brian for an early lunch and then spend some time walking around the UGA campus. The football home opener was this afternoon and would create a festive vibe in Athens. Traffic wasn't heavy yet but there were a lot of cars and SUVs displaying the University of Georgia Bulldog banners as they drove towards Athens for the afternoon game.

"I'm kind of nervous about meeting Melanie," Rebecca admitted. "What if she doesn't like me?"

"No need to be nervous," he reassured her. "She's going to love you. You guys will be best buddies before the day is out. I promise."

She looked out the window at the passing countryside.

"What makes you nervous, Chuck? I know it's nothing

from work. It's like you have ice water in your veins dealing with the stuff we have to deal with. I've never seen you get rattled, except when you asked me out that first time," she said, with a smile.

He looked at her sideways and tried to think of the best way to frame his answer. That memory of finally getting the courage to ask her out made him smile, as well.

"Really? Did my nerves show that much?"

She laughed and said, "You were scared, big man. But you did it. And, here we are. But, there has to be something else that rattles you?"

He took a deep breath and looked straight ahead as he drove.

"I'm nervous every time we're together like this that you'll tell me you don't think it's a good idea that we're dating. That you'll say you just want to be friends. That you'll say you're going back to your policy of not having a relationship with someone you work with."

She reached over and took his hand in hers, brought it to her mouth and kissed it. She looked at him until he looked over,

"I'm never going to say any of those things to you," she whispered.

McCain exhaled and grinned. "That's a relief. I'd hate to make you walk back to Atlanta."

Rebecca sensed that Chuck wanted to say more but he kept his thoughts to himself.

For the first time since his divorce, so many years before, McCain felt something. He had dated a few women over the years but had not connected with anyone like he had with Rebecca. He loved her. He wasn't just attracted to her because of her beauty or intelligence or personality. It was even deeper than that. He was totally and completely in love with her, and he knew that she was the one for him.

That was another thing that made him nervous, he admitted to himself. He was terrified to actually to say those words and to share his deepest feelings. Should he or shouldn't he? That might scare her off, but he was beginning to think that she might actually love him, too. Maybe on the drive back, he told himself. Let's have a nice day with Melanie and Brian and then later on, I can bare my soul to Rebecca.

Atlanta, Saturday, 1200 hours

Emily Clark parked her Nissan Versa and walked across the parking lot to the apartment building. This was their second date. She had been hesitant to go out with the big, bearded man.

She had thrown a few excuses at him but he kept calling back. He just wouldn't give up. Finally, she had agreed to meet him for pizza. He had sensed her hesitancy at his offer to pick her up so he suggested meeting her, even letting her pick the restaurant.

And, she'd had a great time. Scotty Smith had been a perfect gentleman. Emily hadn't known what to expect. When she met him, it had been in a professional capacity.

He and Andy Fleming had taken out a vanload of terrorists on the interstate. Both men had been shot during the firefight. Fortunately, neither man's wounds were serious.

Clark was the paramedic who had ridden in the back of the ambulance with them to the hospital. That was after she had gotten Chuck McCain to take their rifles from them. Both men were determined not to be disarmed. The compromise that they had reached was that McCain had kept their rifles, but the two officers were allowed to keep their pistols with them.

It had turned out to be a good thing that they were armed. Infected people started showing up at the hospital emergency room where they had shot several. Somehow on that chaotic afternoon, Smith had gotten Emily to give him her phone number. And, he was persistent.

On their first date, Scotty had been so sweet. He had asked her questions about her job, her family and her hobbies. When he found out that she did CrossFit several days a week, he nodded approvingly.

There was no question about whether or not he worked out. Emily had seen him without a shirt on. She pictured him in the gym as one of those guys grunting, lifting really heavy weights, and then dropping them on the floor with a loud crash.

She knew that he was involved in fighting the zombie virus but he didn't give her many specifics about his job on that first date. Today, she planned on learning more about him. He had made their first date all about her; today she wanted to make it all about the big bearded man.

When he had invited her to his apartment for lunch, she again felt a bit of hesitation. Scotty picked it up immediately and said, "Hey, if you'd feel better going out to a restaurant or a park or anywhere, that's fine with me. I'd just like to spend some more time with you."

She had never had a guy try so hard to make her feel comfortable.

"I'd love to come over," she finally said, "but there's one condition."

"You want to bring your mom as a chaperone? No problem," he said.

She laughed into the phone. "No, we just have to watch the Georgia game," she said.

"You like football?" he asked with amazement.

"Is the Pope Catholic?"

"Well, OK! I'll burn us some steaks and we'll watch the game. That sounds like a great afternoon."

Georgia Square Mall, Athens, Georgia, 1200 hours

Amir slept in his car next to the North Oconee River, just south of Athens. He found a dirt drive that led off the roadway to an area where it looked like people had been parking to fish, camp, and party. He backed into the secluded spot next to some trees where his car was concealed from the road.

At this point, he didn't want to take the chance on using

196

a hotel. Especially after Mohamud's death, he did not need a suspicious hotel clerk calling the police on him. He reclined the driver's seat and slept lightly in his car with the 9mm Beretta pistol in his hand.

When he woke up, just before sunrise, he got out of the car with his prayer rug and said his prayers. Amir had been lax for the last couple of weeks in his prayers but he knew that Allah understood. It had been a busy time as he had planned and initiated attacks against the enemies of Islam.

Today, though, he knew that he needed Allah's guidance and protection if he was going to be successful. He did not need his hatred for America to make him careless. His main concern now was a zealous local cop who recognized him from a wanted poster.

When he had first arrived in Athens on Thursday, Amir found a store selling Georgia Bulldogs clothing. He had purchased a hat and a t-shirt bearing the hideous image of a dog. He was offended to even be wearing the items but he knew that they would help him to blend in. He would be able to throw those offensive clothes away soon enough.

When his prayers were over, he found a spot on the bank of the river and spent an hour mentally rehearsing his attack. He thought through every part of his plan and the built-in contingencies. When he was finished, he ate a sandwich that he had purchased the evening before at a convenience store and drank some bottled water.

After his attacks today, al-Razi would start driving towards Washington, D.C. His orders were to contact his handler, Ruhollah Ali Bukhari, and see what his next mission was. He hoped for an even larger role in this continuing jihad against America. Imam Ruhollah had made it clear that their next meeting would be face-to-face.

Amir's first order of business when he got to the mall was to eat an early lunch. He ordered a Philly Cheesesteak at the food court and then sat near the coffee shop he had identified as his first target. He ate quickly and noticed with satisfaction that the mall and the food court were both busy. It would be a good day.

After finishing his lunch, al-Razi walked into the coffee shop and ordered a cup to go. The young girl behind the counter smiled at Amir's UGA clothing and said, "Go Dawgs!"

He managed to smile at her and say, "Yes, of course."

She handed him his coffee and he walked over to the small counter where the cream and sugar were kept. He prepped his drink and then set it to the side. He glanced around. No one was paying any attention to him in the crowded coffee shop. The line of customers ordering was now six deep as people wanted a midday caffeine boost. He felt his heart beating faster.

Amir reached into his pocket and carefully pulled out a small glass vial. He would have preferred to wear rubber gloves but that would have drawn attention. He saw that his hands were shaking slightly and told himself to be very careful.

Al-Razi acted like he was having trouble with the pitcher of cream and unscrewed the top. It was three quarters full. Perfect. He quickly tipped the clear contents of the vial into the container and screwed the top back on. The empty vial was dropped into the opening on the counter for trash.

The terrorist exited the coffee shop as a middle-aged man and woman, both wearing red and black UGA clothing, came to the counter to prepare their coffee. Amir paused in the doorway, glancing back to see her reaching for the pitcher of cream. He walked down the mall until he came to the stairs. He climbed to the upper level and continued until he was near the entrance.

The Iranian stood at the rail, waiting, and sipping his own coffee. He gazed back towards the food court and the coffee shop. As he swallowed the last of his drink, he heard a scream. It was followed by an even louder one. That was followed by yelling and several people running from the direction of the cafe. Al-Razi turned and hurried out the exit to his car, throwing his coffee cup in the trash.

Athens, Georgia, Saturday, 1200 hours

Chuck, Rebecca, Melanie and Brian met for lunch at the Bulldog Cafe. The game day atmosphere in the city had put them all in the mood for hamburgers and the Bulldog Cafe was known for great burgers. Chuck watched Melanie and Rebecca talking animatedly as they shared their university experiences. He was happy to see how the two of them had quickly become friends.

McCain was also impressed with Brian. He and

Melanie had been dating for almost two months. He, too, was studying to be a teacher with a goal of teaching high school math. One of the things that pleased Chuck was that Brian was very involved in his church as a youth leader.

Chuck had raised Melanie in church and was still as active as he could be, when he wasn't fighting zombie terrorists. He had been concerned that Melanie might drift away from her faith when she had gone away to university. She told him that she had visited a few of the local churches in Athens but had never found one like her home congregation, The Hope Church, that she and her dad had attended for years.

Now, Brian was picking her up every Sunday and taking her to church with him. In Chuck's mind, that spoke volumes about the young man. He could tell that the young couple really liked each other and that made him happy, too.

"Mr. McCain, I know you probably can't talk about your work stuff," Brian said, leaning towards Chuck with a lowered voice. "Melanie showed me all the news videos, though, of you and your guys dealing with some really bad situations."

McCain glanced over at the two women. They caught him looking at them and suddenly stopped talking. He guessed they had been talking about him because Rebecca looked embarrassed and Melanie had a big smile on her face.

Rebecca grabbed her purse. "We're going to the ladies room. I think you guys can survive without us for a few minutes."

Chuck looked back at Brian. He realized that this young man would be the one to protect his daughter. As much as he wanted to be there for her, he just was not able because of the distance and their very different lives.

"Brian, this is the most dangerous threat that America has ever faced. The news, for once, is downplaying it so that we don't have a nationwide panic. I told Mel a few weeks ago that I wanted her to start carrying her pistol at all times."

"She told me," Brian nodded. "And she's been carrying it. Whatever you said got her attention. It makes me nervous, just because I don't want to see her get in trouble for carrying a pistol on campus."

"I know. I'm a cop. I get it. But, I think in this case, it's worth the risk. You have a pistol permit, right?"

"I do. I was thinking about taking Melanie to get hers."

"That would be great. I told her I'd pay for it. I wanted to help her get it, but, as you mentioned, things have been kind of crazy at work."

"I saw on the news yesterday where one of the terrorists behind that attack on the high school was killed by the CDC police in Atlanta, near Georgia State."

Chuck nodded. "That's correct but I can't talk about it. I don't want to tell you what to do either, but I'd recommend carrying your pistol with you all the time. Mel said you have a Glock?"

"Yes, sir. I have a few Glocks. I like the .40 caliber. I have the Model 22, 23, and the 27. One for every occasion," he said, with a smile.

"Good choices. And, God forbid it happens, but if you're confronted by someone who's infected with this virus, take your time and make a head shot. Nothing else works."

"Do you think the virus will ever get out here? We're a long way from the big city. From what I've seen on the news, that seems to be where most of the attacks have taken place."

"I don't know," Chuck sighed. "Anything's possible. The high school that was attacked is forty-five minutes out of the city. I just think it's good to be prepared."

A uniformed police officer, a corporal, was eating on the other side of the restaurant. Chuck noticed approvingly that he had positioned himself where he could see the entire dining area and watch the front entrance while he ate his burger. He had an earpiece connected to his police radio.

The officer suddenly dropped his half-finished hamburger and pulled out his wallet. He left some money on the table, said something into the radio, and left the restaurant quickly. A minute later, with siren blaring and blue lights flashing, the police cruiser raced out of the parking lot.

Georgia Square Mall, Athens, Georgia, 1300 hours

The first 911 call from the mall was for a domestic

dispute in the food court. Moments later, another call came in reporting that a woman was assaulting a man near a cafe inside the mall. A few minutes after that, another citizen dialed 911 and said that there were multiple people fighting in the food court and it was spreading out into the rest of the mall. Other calls came in requesting ambulances and more police.

All of the police in the Athens-Clarke County area knew that game day brought out the best and the worst in people. With the first call of a domestic dispute, only two officers and a supervisor cleared to be enroute. As the other 911 complaints came in, three other officers cleared as well.

Officer Barry Adams was driving by the mall as the first call was dispatched. Adams was a four-year veteran of the force. He chuckled to himself as he pulled into the parking lot.

Domestic calls were always entertaining. This one sounded like a good call as it was quickly upgraded to a woman assaulting a man. Usually, it was the other way around. What had he done to make her attack him? This would be interesting, he thought.

He parked in the fire lane near the lower level entrance that opened into the food court. When Officer Adams told the dispatcher that he was there, his backup officer said that he was still about five minutes away. Barry considered waiting outside until the other officer arrived.

Adams knew how handle domestic calls, though, and he didn't feel like standing outside waiting for his partner.

203

There might not be anything to the call and, if not, he could cancel his backup. It was as the officer entered the mall that the dispatcher updated him that there was a large fight in progress in the food court. Barry stepped into a scene of complete chaos.

In front of him, next to the door, an older man clad in UGA fan gear was lying on his back. A younger man was on top of him biting at his neck and growling loudly. A large pool of blood had spread out from the victim. This same thing was being repeated throughout the food court.

Adams was a seasoned police officer, but for a moment, he experienced sensory overload. He stepped into the food court expecting a simple domestic call. Now, he didn't know whether he should reach for his pistol, his taser, or his radio. He decided on the radio but before he could transmit, someone slammed into him, knocking him into one of the fixed tables that were scattered around the open dining area.

The officer was surprised but his training kicked in. He pushed the attacker away with his left arm and reached for his pistol with his right. His attacker was a young black man wearing the white shirt of a mall security guard. His eyes were glazed over and a growl was coming from deep within his throat.

There was blood on the guard's left arm and blood on the front of his shirt. Adams knew this kid. He recognized him from a previous conversation about his desire to get on the police force. Now, he was acting crazy.

"Stop it!" Adams ordered. "What's the matter with

you?"

The security guard grabbed at Adams' left arm and bit down on his forearm. Barry hesitated to shoot the young man. He wasn't armed but he was really biting down on his arm. The police officer slammed the Glock 22 pistol against the security guard's head. It opened a large cut across his face but he didn't release his grip.

Someone else banged into Adams' right side. He glanced over and saw a petite middle-aged woman wearing a Herschel Walker jersey. Her face was covered with gore and she was also growling loudly. She probably didn't weigh any more than a hundred pounds but when the officer tried to shove her away with his forearm, she promptly bit down on his right arm.

Barry continued to fight but he suddenly felt a wave of nausea go through him, to go along with his feelings of fear and panic. Sudden dizziness hit him and he lost his balance. His pistol fell out of his hand and he found himself lying on his back. The security guard's face loomed over him and he felt teeth digging into his neck.

The dispatcher called Adams to see if he was OK but got no answer. Officers were required to check in with dispatch every couple of minutes. Four officers and a sergeant were now on their way to the scene. This mall was notorious for being a dead zone for the police radios so no one was really worried. They just figured that Adams couldn't get a signal to transmit inside the food court.

The sergeant and another patrol officer arrived at the

same time. They parked behind Adams' police car and rushed through the same entrance that he had entered. They were also stunned by the carnage that lay in front of them. The sergeant hit the transmit button on his radio and requested more help.

"Radio, we have multiple casualties. There's blood everywhere. We need…"

His transmission was cut off as he was grabbed by Officer Adams. Barry's head was hanging at an odd angle and a gaping, bloody wound was visible on his neck. He pulled his sergeant to the floor and started biting him. The supervisor took bites to his arms and face as he tried to push the crazed officer off of him.

A gunshot shattered the silence. The other patrolman shot the infected officer in the head. Blood and brain matter splattered all over the sergeant. At this point, though, it didn't matter. He was infected, too.

"Sarge, are you ok? We need to get out of here. I think this is the zombie virus."

The officer grunted as a large man hit him from behind. He tried to swing his pistol around to get a shot but the infected man had him in a bear hug and bit down on the side of his neck, ripping open his jugular. The newest victim felt his blood pumping out of his body as he fell to the floor.

In the space of five minutes, three police officers had been lost. Corporal Matt Parker was eating at the Bulldog Cafe when the call had come in. He rushed over to the mall with his lights and siren activated but with game day traffic, it took almost fifteen minutes. He'd heard his sergeant's last transmission over the radio and he heard the dispatcher calling him repeatedly since then.

With the sergeant out of the picture, at least for the moment, Matt was in charge. He directed responding units to enter the mall from the upper level on the opposite side. Without knowing what was going on, the corporal thought that maybe the other three officers had been ambushed when they entered the mall. Another possibility was that they were caught in the middle of the fight that had been reported in the food court.

Either way, he thought it more prudent to enter on the upper level and approach more stealthily than just running blindly right into the middle of who knows what. More officers were responding to the mall after the last message from the sergeant. Matt radioed one of them who had just arrived and told him to try and get information from some citizens who had been inside.

Two minutes later, Parker arrived and parked behind three other police cars. The officers were talking with several citizens. The patrolmen walked over to the corporal and told him what their witnesses had said.

"The lady I was talking to said she walked by the food court and heard what sounded like a loud argument from that little cafe. Then this older lady came out chasing a man, maybe her husband, and trying to bite him. She also heard this crazy growling sound from several people. She just thought maybe there were some drunk people celebrating early but then there was screaming and more people came running out of that cafe. She got the heck out of there and went to her car to call 911."

Another officer reported, "I spoke to the young girl working at the sandwich shop next to the cafe. She said she heard all that and then saw that first lady bite the man she was chasing on the arm. After a few minutes, he collapsed and fell down and she jumped on him, biting his neck. This girl saw a couple of other crazies come out of the coffee shop growling and biting people. One of them bit one of the security guards.

"My witness saw Adams come in and get attacked by two of them, the security guard and that little woman who seems to have started everything in the cafe. When Adams went down, my girl took off running. She said two of the crazies chased her but she got up the stairs and out of the mall without any problem. According to her, Barry went down with those two people biting him. She never saw him get back up."

The last officer nodded. "Ditto to all of that. My guy was on the upper level and couldn't see everything but he heard what the other witnesses have said. He didn't see Adams get attacked but he saw the sergeant and Cooper come in. The witness said Adams tackled Sarge and Cooper shot him in the head and then he got taken down, too. That was all my man could take and he took off for the exit."

Corporal Parker processed everything. This sounded much more serious than just a fight between drunk fans. He needed to call the lieutenant.

"We need to get to those officers. If you've got a rifle or shotgun, grab it. I'm going to call the brass and let them know what's going on."

Lieutenant Anderson was getting dressed in his Bulldog best to attend the home opener. When his cell phone rang, he noticed that Matt Parker was calling. He answered on the first ring.

"Hey, Corporal Parker, how're you doing this fine Saturday?"

"Sorry to bother you, LT, but we've got a situation."

Athens, Georgia, Saturday, 1300 hours

After lunch, the two couples walked around downtown Athens, letting their food settle and enjoying the sights. After walking for several blocks, Melanie took Chuck by the arm and said, "You look like you could use a cup of coffee."

"I can always use a cup of coffee."

Melanie led them inside a coffee shop on the main street. Chuck and Rebecca were both startled by the name of the business. Zombie Coffee and Doughnuts was one of the most popular cafes in Athens. Mel and Brian both laughed at the surprise on their faces.

"Sorry, Daddy, but I couldn't resist bringing you here. And their coffee and doughnuts are really good."

Rebecca and Chuck looked at each other, laughed, and stepped through the door of the café, hand-in-hand.

Melanie was right. The coffee was good and the doughnuts were excellent. After getting refills on their coffee, Mel led them out of the cafe and in the direction of the stadium. She clearly had something in mind.

"Let's head over to the stadium," she suggested. "I think Rebecca would like to see it."

Chuck hated crowds and knew that the area around Sanford Stadium would be packed. Melanie knew her dad and saw the look on his face.

"Better yet," she smiled, "let's go to the game."

McCain hated crowds but he loved college football so that got his attention.

"Because we don't have tickets?" he said.

In an instant, Melanie was holding four tickets.

"Yes, we do. Brian and I were able to get our tickets as students and then swap them with some other guys for four seats together. Surprise!"

"Oh, that sounds like fun!" exclaimed Rebecca.

"What a great surprise!" Chuck said, grabbing Melanie and kissing her. "Thanks for doing that, sweetheart."

University of Georgia Campus, Athens, Georgia, Saturday, 1330 hours

As he had driven back towards Athens, al-Razi had seen multiple police cars and ambulances rushing towards the mall with their lights and sirens activated. The more police and EMS personnel that went to Georgia Square would be that many that would not interfere with him and Terrell at the university. Amir had two vials of the virus left and he knew where he was going to use them.

Traffic became much heavier as he drove the six miles to the campus. The game would be starting soon and fans were pouring into the city. It took almost forty minutes to get back to the area of the football stadium. Now, his problem was finding a place to park.

There was a parking deck five blocks from the stadium but as he drove up to it, he saw the big sign in front of the entrance that indicated it was already full. The streets were packed with people walking towards Sanford Stadium. They were all clad in the bright red and white of UGA and many of them with the disgusting image of that bulldog displayed on their clothing.

Amir's second choice for parking was a Christian Church three blocks further away. He was able to get one of the last parking spaces for thirty dollars. The irony made him smile. He was launching another attack in the jihad against America and was using a church to park his vehicle in. Hopefully, today, many Christians would die and suffer the judgment of Allah for their unbelief.

He carried a small duffel bag with him from the car. It contained some clothes, money, ammo, water, food, his cell phone, and a few other things. If he was compromised and couldn't get back to his car, he had some necessities to keep him going.

Amir walked quickly towards the area of the stadium. After his two days of reconnaissance, he had settled on the

Tate Student Center as his primary target. Athens was a target-rich environment but this was, perhaps, the most ideal location for his attack, other than Sanford Stadium itself. While there were not many restaurants around the stadium, there was a food court with several fast food businesses inside the student center. What was even better was that it was directly across the street from the stadium.

The terrorist entered the large building and saw that it was packed with hundreds, perhaps thousands, of loud football fans. The lines spilled out from each restaurant. The wait was long in the Starbucks as well, but he had a plan. He reached into his duffel bag, pulling out an empty Starbucks cup.

It was time. He felt the butterflies in his stomach again and Amir glanced around nervously. What if someone saw him as he initiated the infection? He felt comfort in the weight of the Beretta tucked into his belt at the small of his back under his Bulldog t-shirt.

He walked to the counter where the cream and sugar were kept and acted as if he was preparing his coffee. He picked up the silver pitcher for cream. It felt empty. He unscrewed the top and confirmed it. Al-Razi walked to the main counter carrying the pitcher. One of the baristas saw him and walked over.

"Out of cream, sir? No problem, I'll take care of that for you."

"Thanks," Amir nodded.

A moment later, the young man handed him a full pitcher. As he walked back to the condiment counter, Amir pulled a glass vile out of his pocket and opened it. He looked around as he unscrewed the top on the pitcher and acted like he was looking inside the container. In the crowded environment, he just dropped the open vial of the virus inside and screwed the top back on. He picked up his empty cup and walked to the other side of the food court.

Atlanta, Georgia, 1330 hours

After lunch, Emily and Scotty moved to the couch, continuing their conversation. They were both on their second beer. He had carefully nursed his first one during their meal of steak, baked potatoes, and salad. She was surprised but happy at his moderation. For some reason, she had imagined him as a heavy drinker.

"Have you been a Bulldogs fan all your life?" he asked.

"Pretty much. I grew up watching football with my dad. I went to UGA for a year, but then transferred to a technical school to get my EMT and paramedic certifications.

"Even though it was only for a year, I still consider myself a Bulldog. What about you? Where'd you go to college?"

Scotty laughed. "I didn't. I barely graduated from high school. The only reason I didn't drop out was football and wrestling. I joined the army a week after graduation. That was an education, in and of itself. I became a Ranger and spent some time in the Middle East."

"The Rangers are kind of like Special Forces?" she

asked.

"Oh, no, we're much better than the Special Forces. The SF guys call the Rangers when they get in trouble and we go rescue them. Just to become a Ranger is one of the toughest processes in the world."

"Really? Tell me about it."

Scotty told her about the three phases of the rigorous Ranger Course that he had gone through to earn the coveted tab on his uniform. He normally didn't like to talk about himself but there was something about this girl that made him want to open up. And, she was genuinely interested.

"So, why'd you get out of the army? It's obvious that you really loved it."

He thought about it before answering and sighed.

"My humvee hit an IED, that's an improvised explosive device. It busted me up pretty good but it killed two of my best friends."

"Oh, I'm so sorry!" She put a comforting hand on his forearm. "That had to be a rough time."

"Yeah, it was and that was a good time for me get out and start over. I enjoyed the army and got to do a lot of fun things but I'd always wanted to be a fireman. I'm glad I did it and they trained me as a paramedic, too. I think that time with the FD let me heal up and it's a lot of fun to ride around on that big red truck."

Emily read between the lines and understood that the healing he was talking about was as much emotional as it was physical. After a few years, though, Smith told her that he had gotten bored as a firefighter and decided to do some security contracting in the Middle East.

"Then how'd you end up working for the CDC?" she queried.

The big man's eyes lit up.

"That's an interesting story."

His twenty-four hour shift over, Firefighter Smith was ready to get home. They had run calls all night long and he was exhausted. Walking across the parking lot to his Dodge Ram pickup, he noticed a gray Chevrolet Impala parked next to him. One of the prettiest women that he had ever seen got out of the car as he walked by.

"Sergeant Smith?"

His tiredness left him immediately.

"Not anymore, but I'll be anybody you want me to be," he said, with a big grin.

She held a badge and an ID card out to him.

"My name's Rebecca Johnson and I work for the Centers for Disease Control."

"Did you come to give me my flu shot?"

She smiled. "No, I came to talk to you about a job."

"Well, I'm not the head honcho around here but I'd be happy to show you around our fire station and let you sit in the fire truck. If you're nice, I'll even let you help us polish it. And, you look like you're in pretty good shape so the fire academy shouldn't be too hard for you."

The woman rolled her eyes at him.

"I came," she said deliberately, as if she was dealing

with a slow child, "to offer you a job."

Scotty stood in silence for a moment.

"Why would I want a job at the CDC? I don't know anything about malaria, or the flu, or much of anything about diseases."

"That's probably why you want to have a cup of coffee with me and listen to my offer."

"I don't think so," he said, continuing towards his truck. "I have some other things going on and I don't think I'd be interested. Nice talking to you, though."

"Does the fire department know that you've been offered a contract in Iraq? And, really, why do you want to go back over there? It can't be the money. What are they offering you, a hundred and twenty grand? That's it? I know the security companies aren't paying as much as they were a few years ago but I think a man with your skill set can do much better than that."

Smith realized that he had stopped walking and was staring at the pretty lady with his mouth open. He'd never been a very good poker player. How did this woman know all of that?

Ten minutes later, Rebecca and Scotty were seated across from each other in the back of a McDonald's, holding cups of coffee. They studied each other as they sipped their drink. Scotty changed his opinion and now thought Rebecca was the most beautiful woman that he had ever seen. She was definitely the best looking one that he had ever drank coffee with.

He also had the feeling that she was or could be a very

good poker player. Her eyes were intelligent and inquisitive but she guarded her emotions well. She also knew exactly what to say to get him to listen to her pitch.

As she talked to him about the CDC Enforcement Unit that they were creating, he found himself being swept along as she said all the right things. Smith had never been a police officer, but as Rebecca Johnson talked to him, all of a sudden, he couldn't see himself doing anything else. He was ready to sign the contract but when she told him the salary was thirty thousand dollars a year more than he would've been making in Iraq as a contractor, he was ready to beg her for a job.

"It sounds like you have a thing for this woman, Rebecca?" Emily wondered, crossing her arms.

"Oh, she's gorgeous and a great boss but not my type. Plus, I think she and my team leader have the hots for each other."

"And what's your type? You kind of strike me as a lady's man," she said, playfully. "You probably have a contact list full of girls."

He frowned. "No, I'm actually pretty boring. I haven't dated much in the last few years. But as for my type," he said, watching her closely, "I can't think of anyone that I'd rather be sitting and talking with or getting ready to watch football with."

Emily blushed and looked away from his stare.

"Do you like what you're doing for the CDC, Scotty?"

His face lit up. "This is the best job I've ever had. I'm

working with some of the top operators in the world and I'm not crawling through a swamp, jungle, or desert. Now, some of the people we meet do want to rip my throat out and eat my flesh, but, hey, we have to take the good with the bad, right?"

She laughed. The more that Emily learned about Scotty, the more she liked him. She was glad that she had come over and was even more excited about watching the Georgia game with him. AC/DC's "Back in Black" cut through her thoughts. It was coming from Smith's phone.

"Sorry," he said, "I have to take this call. It's my boss."

"Hey, Eddie, what's up?"

The expression on Scotty's face as he listened to the phone let Emily know that she would not be watching the game with him, after all.

Inside Sanford Stadium, Athens, Georgia, 1330 hours

"Come on! You guys need to speed it up. Get those pizzas ready. They're almost out up front."

The loud commands came from Richard, Terrell's supervisor. He was short, fat, and usually had the remnants of his lunch or snack on his shirt. He was always telling them to work faster. While he normally stayed in his office, he would come out several times an hour to check on his employees.

In fact, the only time Richard came out was to yell at the staff about something. He never offered to help and he never had a kind or encouraging word for anyone. He just issued a few orders and then retreated back to his office. Today was going to be the last time that Hill had to deal with Richard and his disrespect.

Terrell glanced at the clock on the wall and saw that it was time. He was working in one of the many concessions booths that were inside the stadium. Amir had instructed him to use the vials of the virus at 1330 hours and then make his escape. He had formulated his plan and knew exactly what he was going to do.

The two instruments of infection were going to be pizzas. A pepperoni and a cheese pizza would be responsible for so much pain and death. Hill was wearing plastic gloves as required by the health regulations. Today, he was glad to have them on.

He felt his heart start thumping in his chest as he removed the pepperoni pizza from the hot oven and set it on the counter to cut it. The vial was in his left hand and the pizza cutter was in his right. A quick glance around confirmed that no one was paying any attention to him as Hill poured the deadly liquid onto the hot pizza in a circular motion and then quickly and professionally cut it up to be sold by the slice to hungry fans.

Terrell repeated the procedure with the cheese pizza and handed it to Shantella to take its place next to the pepperoni. Richard made another appearance to walk around the small concessions area, making sure that his workers were taking care of their many customers. He barked at Shantella and Terrell to keep up with the pizzas.

After a few minutes, he disappeared back into his small office. I got something for you, Richard, Terrell thought.

Step one was complete. He had used up his two vials of the virus. Now, it was time to make his exit. Hill looked around and saw that everyone was busy, either preparing food or serving customers. Both of the two pizzas that he had just put prepared were half gone. He wasn't sure how long it took for the virus to take affect but it would probably be good to finish his business and leave.

Terrell casually walked over to Richard's office and tried the knob. Unlocked. He opened the door and slipped inside. The pregame ceremonies were showing on the television on the wall. The short man was scrolling through Facebook on his computer. He sensed movement and turned to see Hill pointing a small pistol at him.

Richard's eyes grew wide and he said loudly, "What do you think you are doing, Terrell?"

Terrell swung the gun and cracked him on the side of the head, stunning him.

"Shut up, Richard," he snarled. "Give me your car keys and your wallet."

He started to get up and said, "You can't do…"

His words were cut off by another strike to the face with the gun.

"Now, Richard. You disrespected me for the last time."

The manager was stunned and bloody. The second strike had ripped his right cheek open but he managed to pull out his keys and wallet and gave them to Terrell, who shoved them into his pockets.

"Turn around and put your head on the desk," Hill commanded.

There was no more fight left in the man and he complied. Terrell grabbed one of the cushions that Richard was sitting on to give him a boost and laid it against the little man's head. He pressed the Makarov pistol against the pillow and pulled the trigger, shooting him behind the right ear. The pillow muffled most of the noise and prevented any blood splatter. When he stepped away, the body fell to the floor underneath the desk.

Hill decocked his pistol and slid it back into his waistband. He was about to turn away when he saw a blue bank bag laying on Richard's desk. A quick check showed a stack of cash. This was what had already come in from the day's sales. Richard should have locked it up but he hadn't gotten around to it. Terrell shoved what looked like several hundred dollars into his pocket.

He left the office, closing and locking the door behind him. He recovered the backpack that he had left in the storage room. Terrell walked out of the food stand without saying anything to anyone, heading towards one of the side exits.

Chapter Ten

Georgia Square Mall, Athens, 1330 hours

Corporal Matt Parker readied his AR-15 rifle. He was preparing to lead a four-man team into the mall. One of the other officers also had a rifle while another was holding a pump shotgun. The fourth patrolman drew his sidearm, a Glock 22, and held it by his side. A second four-officer team would make entry, also on the upper level, on the far end of the mall and the two teams would converge on the food court. At least, that was their plan.

Lieutenant Anderson had cancelled his plans to attend the football game, thrown on his uniform, and was driving with blue lights and siren activated towards the mall. He called the Chief of Police, Tom Morgan, and told him that he thought they had three officers down and possibly dead. Everything he had heard so far sounded like a bio-terror attack with the zombie virus. The Chief, however, would have to be the one who requested help from the

Department of Homeland Security.

Chief Morgan considered himself cautious. His men considered him indecisive and more a politician than a cop. Either way, he wasn't about to call the feds until he had something concrete to tell them. He told Anderson to call him when they knew something more definitive. Even though three officers were reported to be down and possibly dead or seriously injured, the chief wanted that verified as well. He told Anderson that he would be enroute to the scene but he lived an hour away.

The lieutenant knew that no amount of arguing would change Chief Morgan's mind. He was the consummate politician who was slow to make a decision until he was sure about the outcome. The sooner Anderson got to the mall and confirmed what Parker had told him, the sooner they could get some help from the CDC. He had been following the news and knew that the enforcement teams from the Centers for Disease Control had stopped some bio-terror attacks and kept others from spreading.

There had been no further contact with any of the officers inside of the mall. Approximately two hundred citizens had managed to escape. Surprisingly, only a few of them had been bitten. Ambulances had transported seven possibly infected people to the closest hospital. There was no telling how many other shoppers were trapped inside or who had gotten too close to the action and were now zombies.

Parker looked at the other three officers. He had

ordered them to put on a jacket if they had it. They were going to need all the protection that they could get inside the mall. He had read all of the bulletins that the CDC, FBI, and the DHS had sent out. This situation sounded like the zombie virus. He found it hard to believe that terrorists would drive all the way out to Athens to launch an attack, but all the indicators pointed in that direction.

"If this is the zombie virus," Matt briefed his men, "we're going to have to shoot some people. If we get bit, it's over. There's no cure for this and I don't want to turn into a zombie. If anybody has a problem with shooting these things, you can stay outside.

"If we're attacked, let's try and challenge them but the main thing is to not get bit. Let's take our time and make head shots. I have point. Everybody stack on me. Let's try and get to our officers but remember, we may to have to shoot them if they've been infected."

Matt's team entered the mall and moved towards the rail where they could look down onto the lower level. It was strangely quiet inside. That is, until a mall security guard stepped around the corner and came running towards them. They could hear him growling and saw that his white shirt was covered with blood and gore. His mouth was opening and closing and chewed flesh hung from his chin. The security guard was closing the distance fast.

Corporal Parker challenged him, "Stop! Don't come any closer!"

Now, the zombie was less than ten feet away and not

slowing down. The gunshot was deafening inside the mall. Parker's shot caught him in the forehead, dropping him at the team's feet.

"Good shot, Corporal," one of the officers said.

They watched the body of the zombie, not sure what to do next.

Parker spoke up, "We need to keep moving. There are probably a lot more of these guys in here."

He told the dispatcher that they had shot a person who appeared to have been infected with the zombie virus. The team stepped around the body and started forward again. A collective sound of a group growling seemed to be getting closer. As the team got to where they could peer down to the lower level, they saw at least thirty infected people standing below them. Others were shuffling their way from the direction of the food court.

"Look, there's Cooper and Sarge," one of the officers exclaimed.

The two bloody, infected police officers were in the middle of the group of zombies. Everyone in the pack was growling with their mouths opening and snapping closed. They all had various open wounds on their arms, faces, and necks. Their heads all jerked upward when they heard the officer's comment and started moving towards the stairs. Some tripped as they tried to climb the steps but others had no trouble at all climbing to the upper level where police officers waited.

The stairs were thirty feet from Parker's team. He picked up movement out of the corner of his eye and started to swing his rifle over. It was the second police team. They had entered further down and were opposite of Matt's team, also on the upper level.

Parker's first thought was to start picking the infected off. His men held the tactical advantage and could start safely engaging the infected people. But, what if they weren't all infected? What if they could somehow help them, especially his fellow officers that were down there? What if they weren't all zombies? He didn't want to kill a bunch of people that didn't need to be killed. And, two of those guys were his friends.

He yelled over the side of the rail to the mass of bodies below him. "Police Department! Stop! Don't go any further. Everybody get down on the ground. Sarge, Cooper, can you hear me?"

His words, if anything, seemed to create more of a frenzy from the crowd. The growling intensified as they tried even harder to get up the stairs. Matt swallowed hard.

"Get ready to start shooting," he told his team. "When they get to the top of the steps, start picking them off."

He waved to the team on the other side.

"Start shooting down into the pack and try to thin them out," he yelled.

Gunshots rang out as the police began firing at the infected, ten of whom had managed to get to the top of the steps. Once they got to the top level, they all started towards the officers, with four of the zombies breaking into a run. They quickly began to drop as bullets and buckshot impacted their heads. Other infected pushed towards the police after negotiating the stairs.

The officer with the shotgun, Miguel Sanchez, fired his last shell of buckshot at a running zombie, Officer Cooper. The blast missed his head but caught him in the shoulder, only slowing him down momentarily. As the living officer fumbled with shotgun shells, trying to reload his weapon, the dead officer leapt on him knocking him to the ground. He missed his neck but sunk his teeth into Miguel's face.

Sanchez screamed and cursed loudly. One of the other team members kicked Cooper in the side, knocking him off of his friend. He then put two rounds into the zombie's head. Corporal Parker saw that Sanchez's face was bleeding profusely where the skin had been ripped open. He pulled the wounded man to his feet and shoved him towards the exit.

"Get out to one of the ambulances," he ordered.

The three remaining officers turned their attention to the growing swarm of infected people surging up the stairs. The team on the other side was still picking off a few, but they had to quit shooting because the zombies were getting closer to the police.

What had originally been around thirty zombies was now over fifty. The noise of the gunshots had them stepping on each other at they tried to get at the fresh victims on the upper level. The officers had shot at least twenty but now they were down to three shooters on their side of the mall.

The other team of four officers started running towards Parker and his team. There was a scream of pain from another one of Corporal Parker's men. Matt had paused to reload his empty rifle, but glanced over to see that Sanchez had not made it out of the mall. He had become infected after getting bit and had returned to bite Officer Jeff Patterson on the neck. Jeff continued to fight as he tried to push Miguel away but his teeth were digging deeper into the side of his neck.

Matt's remaining officer turned to look at what was happening with Sanchez and Patterson. Twenty more growling zombies had made it to the top of the stairs and were rushing towards them. Patterson collapsed to the ground and stopped moving as blood continued pouring out of the wounds on his neck. The corporal started for Patterson but there was nothing that he could do for him. He quickly shot Sanchez in the head as the large group was almost upon him and his remaining officer.

"Pull back!" Parker yelled.

The two officers started backing up but they had no chance. Parker's partner was knocked to the ground and quickly ripped apart. Matt was shooting them in the head as fast as he could pull the trigger.

More of the infected got to the top of the stairs and charged him. He was making good shots but there were just too many of them. Matt finally turned to run but was grabbed by his infected sergeant and a Hispanic man wearing a UGA sweatshirt and pulled to the floor. Within seconds, the corporal was dead.

The second team stood transfixed twenty feet behind the remains of their friends. They all began firing into the swarm. Now that the officers were down, they weren't worried about hitting one of them by mistake.

They were so focused on eliminating all of the infected in front of them and in getting some vengeance for their colleagues, they never saw the four infected men and the two infected women who came up from behind them. These zombies had come upstairs further down the mall, also drawn to the noise of the shots. The four officers never heard the growling because they were shooting so fast. The officers were overpowered within seconds.

In less than ten minutes, eight more police officers had been killed and infected by the virus.

Parking lot, Sanford Stadium, 1340 hours

Terrell found Richard's black Ford Explorer in the employee parking lot. His heart was still pounding inside his chest. Strangely, killing Richard and infecting two pizzas with the bio-terror virus had not bothered him. As he was leaving, though, he saw a middle-aged black man assaulting a black woman.

Both were clad in Bulldog fan gear. The couple was standing at one of the many high tables in the pavilion area at the top of the steps leading up from the mid-field seating area. Many people would stop here and eat the food they had just purchased before heading back to their seats.

As Hill was passing by, making his way to the exit, he heard a growl and watched the man grab the victim, probably his wife, and sink his teeth into her neck. She began screaming and flailing her arms, the blood spraying outward. One of her arms swept across the table, knocking a paper plate with a half-eaten piece of pizza towards him. The pizza landed at Terrell's feet.

Several fans jumped in to try to save the woman. The infected man quickly turned his attention to other victims and bit a young white man who was trying to help. It was all he could do to keep from running but Hill kept walking quickly towards the exit. The sound of growling and yelling increased behind him and he felt a powerful sense of relief when he finally got to the parking lot.

Not surprisingly, Richard's vehicle was a mirror of the man. There were empty fast-food wrappers, pizza boxes, and soft drink bottles scattered throughout the interior. It even smelled like Richard. Well, you can't argue with free, Terrell thought.

He put the key in the ignition and started it up. The gas gauge showed less than a quarter tank. Thanks, Richard. You stuck it to me one last time, he thought. Let's see how much money you have for me. Terrell flipped open the dead man's wallet and found a hundred and twenty-seven dollars and several credit cards. He would count the rest of the money later.

His first stop was a convenience store on the edge of town where pulled out one of Richard's visa cards and inserted it into the gas dispenser and filled the tank. The card worked without a hitch. After getting gas, he walked inside and bought a hundred dollars worth of food, water, and beer. The credit card worked again and Hill was soon heading out of Athens towards the interstate.

University of Georgia, near Sanford Stadium, 1345 hours

Chuck, Rebecca, Melanie and Brian paused for pictures in front of the stadium. Sanford Stadium is one of the most iconic stadiums in all of college football. It first opened in 1929 and, after many renovations over the years, it is one of the largest in America, seating almost one hundred thousand fans for the University of Georgia's home games.

This was a special day and they all sensed it. Chuck and Rebecca posed with their arms around each other as Melanie snapped the shot. Chuck got a picture of her and Brian. Melanie and Chuck posed for a photo together. Another Bulldog fan offered to take a group shot of the four of them.

Sanford Drive was packed with excited fans hanging out before they entered the stadium. The atmosphere was festive and everyone was excited to see their Bulldogs play. The Tate Student Center was directly across the street from the stadium and many of the faithful were going in to get something to eat or a cup of coffee before the kickoff. Some fans and students who didn't have tickets would watch the game on one of the many televisions inside the student center.

"I really like her, Daddy," Melanie told Chuck.

Rebecca and Brian had taken a few steps away and were talking. He was telling her a little about his family.

"And I think she," his daughter paused, making sure she wouldn't be overheard, "well, I think she loves you."

"That's good. I know I love her," Chuck acknowledged.

It felt good to say those words. Now, he just needed to gather the courage to say them to Rebecca.

"I think she's a keeper," he added. "And from what I've seen, so is Brian."

"I'm glad you like him. He reminds me of you in so many ways. You two are a lot alike."

"Really, how so?"

She never got a chance to answer. The unmistakable sound of a gunshot came from the student center. A moment later three more shots rang out as people started running out the door. Shouts and screams carried out into the street as well the bang of another gunshot.

Inside the Tate Student Center, UGA Campus, 1345 hours

After infecting the Starbucks, Amir decided to use his remaining vial of the virus at another restaurant inside the packed student center. This would be the best place for him to do the most damage. With Terrell launching another attack right across the street inside the stadium, they had the potential to infect many infidels and spread the virus across the campus.

He strolled into the Mexican Cafe. His earlier recon had

convinced him that this would be the place to leave his last bit of poison. The line was long but he was prepared again. Al-Razi pulled a used paper cup from his last visit out of his duffel bag and walked over to the drink fountains.

The soft-drink machines were on one side of the counter. On the other, was the large silver cylindrical container containing sweet tea. Without hesitation, he stepped up to the tea dispenser and placed his cup under it. He acted like he was having trouble with the handle. People were all around him but most of them were getting soft drinks.

He lifted the top of tea dispenser, acting like he was checking to see if it was full. He let the open glass vial drop inside and quickly replaced the top onto the dispenser. Picking up his empty cup and pretending that he had changed his mind about what he wanted to drink, Amir stepped over to the soft-drink dispenser and filled his cup with Coca-Cola. An obese man wearing a Bulldog t-shirt and a Bulldog ball cap stepped up to the sweet tea dispenser as Amir walked away.

As the terrorist moved towards the front of the building, sipping his drink, someone screamed from back behind him, near the Starbucks. In front of him, a scuffle broke out near the exit. A bearded man was straddling a hysterical girl and biting her as two other men tried to pull him off. A Starbucks cup lay on its side, coffee pooling on the floor. The bearded man turned and bit one of the others on the arm. Even with his forearm in the crazy man's mouth, the victim punched his attacker in the face with his other hand.

Amir stopped, fascinated by what he was seeing. He had no idea the virus would act so quickly. The second man tried to help his friend who was getting bit. He began slamming punches into the bearded man's face, as well. Their blows seemed to have no effect on the attacker as he suddenly released his victim, only to lunge and bite one of the other defenders on the face.

A crowd had formed near the exit. Al-Razi turned and started walking in the other direction. He would leave through another door. Behind him, though, a similar scene was being repeated near the Starbucks. Several infected people were attacking those around them. Voices were being raised in protest and many in the crowd started running, looking for a way out.

Amir walked until he was in front of the Mexican Cafe that he had just infected. He heard a loud growling noise to his left and saw the big man in Bulldog's clothes coming towards him. His eyes were now glazed over and his mouth was opening and closing. This was the closest that al-Razi had been to one of the infected people and he felt the terror that so many others had felt.

The terrorist suddenly felt trapped. He turned back towards the front entrance. The bearded man was still attacking people but now, the girl that he'd bitten appeared to have turned as well. She was struggling with another young woman, trying to sink her teeth into her victim's throat.

Al-Razi pulled the Beretta out of his pants. The fat man

from the Mexican Cafe was moving more quickly than Amir imagined. He just managed to get a shot off before the obese man could grab him. The 9mm round caught him just above his right eye, dropping him to the floor. The loud gunshot caused the crowd to panic even more.

Amir rushed towards the front door. The bearded zombie stepped in front of him with his arms extended, forcing Al-Razi to slam on the brakes. He fired and missed but his bullet struck a teen-age boy in the arm. A second shot hit the zombie in the forehead.

Amir felt hands clutching his leg and then pain. He tried to jerk it free but they were too strong. He looked down and saw the small, bloody face of a young girl biting his calf and ankle.

He shot her in the side of the head and pulled his leg free. His ankle was throbbing. Angry voices were screaming at him. More hands grabbed at him.

Al-Razi fired blindly at the people who tried to block his path and saw a muscular black man collapse. The crowd dived out of the way of the man with the gun and then he was at the door. He pushed through the exit and started running.

University of Georgia, near Sanford Stadium, 1350 hours

Rebecca had had a really nice day. She loved meeting Melanie and had especially enjoyed watching how she interacted with her dad. Her own feelings for Chuck were even stronger now. Brian had impressed her as a really good guy. He seemed like the real deal and it was clear that Melanie was in love.

Rebecca asked him some questions about his family. One of the best ways to find out about someone is to ask about their parents and siblings and then watch their reaction. What emotions came to the surface? As Brian spoke of his family, she sensed nothing but the genuine love and respect that he had for them.

As she and Brian talked in front of the big stadium, Johnson felt her phone vibrate in her pocket. She slipped it out and saw that she had a text from her contact at the Department of Homeland Security and two missed calls and a voicemail from Eddie. As she scanned the message, she felt the color drain from her face and saw Brian staring at her.

"Bad news?" he asked.

Before she could answer, a shot rang out from the building across the street. Rebecca watched as Chuck drew his pistol in a blur of movement and then pull his badge chain out from under his shirt. As she withdrew her own badge and gun from her purse, more gunfire came from the student center, a crowd of people bursting out the doors. Screams erupted from inside.

For a moment, there was a pause and no one else was exiting. Then, the door flew open and a single figure came rushing out holding a pistol. People were scurrying and scattering in both directions, forming a barrier between them and the gunman. Chuck pushed Melanie towards Brian.

"Get her some place safe and call 911," he ordered the young man.

When Rebecca got to Chuck, he said, "That's al-Razi."

She was still processing the text that she had gotten and then the sudden shattering of the calm afternoon by the gunshots. McCain was already moving towards the terrorist who was running up Sanford Drive. In an instant it became clear to her, too. The text about the bio-terror attack at the mall a few miles away. Amir al-Razi here.

What better target for the zombie virus than game day at the University of Georgia? And, of course, Chuck's near photographic memory. He had identified the terrorist as soon as he came out the door.

They didn't want to get into a shootout with him in this crowded environment. Amir turned left onto the walkway next to the student center. There were people here, too, but it wasn't nearly as crowded.

McCain closed the distance and was only ten yards behind him, with Rebecca only five yards behind Chuck, offset to the left. The terrorist was limping noticeably now. His right leg appeared to be injured and he was starting to slow down. A black duffel bag hung from his shoulder.

"Amir al-Razi, you're under arrest. Drop the gun and get down on the ground," McCain ordered.

Amir slowed to a stop, raising his left hand and starting to raise his right, as well. Suddenly, he crouched, stepped to the left and spun in that direction, firing the Beretta as he did so. He managed to get off two shots before Chuck adjusted and shot him four times in the chest. A shot from behind him, it had to be Rebecca's gun, caught al-Razi in the pelvis.

The terrorist went down hard and landed on his back. McCain watched him to make sure that he was really down for good. He had shot center-mass because there was still some pedestrian traffic in the background and he didn't want to chance missing a head shot.

There was no movement. Al-Razi appeared to be dead. Chuck glanced back to see where Rebecca was. He didn't see her and then, all at once, he did see her.

She was down on the pavement, lying on her back. A sense of panic propelled him towards her. He saw the blood pooling on the ground. McCain dropped beside her.

"Rebecca, I'm here. I've got you."

His left hand touched her face, then her neck, feeling for a pulse. It was weak. His right hand attempted to stop the flow of blood pouring out of the wound just under her solar plexus. It had come from one of al-Razi's shots.

Her eyes opened and she looked into his eyes, the fear and pain evident. She tried to speak but coughed up blood instead.

Chuck felt a helplessness like he had never known. People were approaching. Melanie, Brian, others. Melanie was crying.

McCain yelled, "Call 911! Somebody please call 911! We need an ambulance here now!"

He felt for her pulse again and it was gone. She was

gone. The blood had stopped pumping out of her wound. He felt for her heartbeat with his other hand. Nothing. He stared at her beautiful face.

"Don't leave, Rebecca," his voice cracked. "It's gonna be OK."

His eyes were filled with tears and he was having trouble focusing but he knew that she was dead. The yelling, screaming, and chaos from the front of the student center continued to increase. As the infected multiplied inside and spilled outside, other innocents were attacked who became infected, too. Sirens drew closer as officers responded to the call of gunshots. Campus Police Officers, who had been on duty in and around the stadium, were just now getting to the student center and starting to confront zombies.

McCain heard a female voice yelling back from the direction that they had come. She yelled with authority, he thought. There were several more gunshots that sounded very close.

Chuck was just about to start CPR on Rebecca. It wouldn't work but he had to try something. She couldn't really be gone. He hadn't told her that he loved her.

"Daddy, Daddy, look up!" The tone in Melanie's voice snapped McCain's head up.

Amir had been infected by the bite on his ankle and had managed to get to his feet. He was less than ten feet away, shuffling towards them. Chuck jumped to his feet to confront him. He reached for his pistol but his holster was empty. He glanced behind him and saw it laying on the pavement next to Rebecca.

The growling terrorist-turned-zombie reached for him and McCain launched a front kick to the chest, knocking him off the sidewalk and into a metal light pole, where he slid to the pavement. Chuck followed him and waited until he started climbing to his feet again. He fired a sidekick into his right knee, the bones cracking loudly as it snapped.

The zombie again climbed to its feet. One misstep and Chuck could end up infected, too. Even with a shattered pelvis and a broken leg, Amir lunged for him. McCain sidestepped and kicked him in the back, knocking him into one of the many park benches that were scattered around the campus.

"Mr. McCain, here!" Brian yelled.

Brian ran towards him with his pistol. Chuck grabbed it and spun just as the infected terrorist managed to pull himself back to his feet using the bench. His shot hit him in the side of the head, putting him down for good. Chuck walked over to the terrorist who had caused so much pain and grief for so many people and fired one more round into his head, just to make sure that he was really dead.

People were running up the walkway towards them to escape the horror of what was going on around the student center and the stadium. He could hear a low growl over all the other noise of screaming, yelling, sirens, and gunshots from around the corner where the police were now fighting for their lives.

He pulled his keys out of his pocket and threw them to Brian.

"Take Melanie and get my truck. Come back for me."

Melanie looked at her father like he was crazy. She was still crying.

"No, you have to come with us."

She grabbed his arm and tried to pull him. He gently pried her fingers off, leaving some of Rebecca's blood on his daughter's hands.

"I'm not leaving her. Go with Brian and I'll see you in a few minutes."

Brian took her by the hand and said, "Come on, we need to run."

The two young people ran up the walkway in the direction of where they had parked. It was probably a half-mile away. McCain turned back to Rebecca.

A group of five zombies were almost to where she was lying. He started advancing and shooting, making head shots on all five. He picked up her Glock and tucked it into his waistband and picked up her purse.

More infected were coming his way, drawn to the sound of gunshots. Chuck scooped Rebecca up and started in the same direction Melanie and Brian had gone. He paused where al-Razi had dropped his pistol and bent down to grab it. He decocked the Beretta and stuck it into his waistband, also. He continued moving away from the chaos.

At least twenty zombies were following him. A few of them started running. Still carrying Rebecca, Chuck started running, too. He glanced over his shoulder and saw that they were gaining on him. He tried to lay her down gently but ended up dropping her. He drew his pistol and started shooting just as they got to him. The first zombie collapsed next to Rebecca.

McCain kept shooting and killing zombies until the slide on his pistol locked open. He dropped the empty magazine to the pavement and pulled his only backup mag out of his pocket and reloaded his gun. He shot another one that grabbed for him. He killed zombies until there were no more in close proximity. Another group turned the corner and started towards him but they were at least a hundred yards away.

Deep breath, assess your surroundings, he told himself. A quick scan of his area told him he was safe, for the moment. He popped the magazine out of his pistol and saw that it only held one round. With one in the gun, that gave him a total of two rounds. He holstered his Glock, picked up Rebecca, and kept moving up the walkway towards the next street.

Georgia Square Mall, Athens, 1400 hours

Lieutenant Anderson parked behind the other police cars near the upper level entrance. One of the officers on the scene reported multiple shots fired from within the mall just a few minutes earlier. Now, the dispatcher was unable to raise any of the police inside the location.

Four more officers had responded to the mall but had not gone inside. There was a general feeling of uncertainty.

242

A total of eleven police officers had gone in and none of them had been heard from since. There was a sense of relief when the lieutenant got there. He would know what to do.

Officer Pitts rushed up to Anderson. His voice got high when he was excited.

"It sounded like a war zone in there, LT, maybe a hundred shots, but it's been quiet for the last five or ten minutes."

Anderson nodded. "It sounds like we need to get SWAT rolling this way."

He called the dispatcher and requested that their SWAT Team be activated. He was aware that it would take a while to get them there. The dispatcher also alerted him of the reported attacks on the university campus. The Campus Police Chief was requesting help.

"Tell him we don't have anybody to send him right now. And see if you can find us another SWAT Team, maybe the GBI? We may need some extra help here or they may need them on campus."

Pitts heard the lieutenant's side of the conversation with dispatch and it didn't sound good. Pitts' official position was Administrative Aide to the Chief of Police. He had worked the road briefly and had gained a reputation as a below average police officer.

He was known as the guy who always got there after everything was over. If officers were fighting someone, Pitts showed up after the bad guy had been subdued and was in handcuffs. If there was an aggravated domestic call, he would make sure to get there after his backup officer. Sometimes, he would not even get to the call, making a traffic stop for some minor infraction instead.

When the administrative aide position became available, the attitude of most of Pitts' peers was, 'Good riddance.' It was no surprise that he got the position since Chief Morgan was his cousin. The only reason he was working today was because of the football game.

Off-duty officers made good money on game day, directing traffic and providing security, assisting the Campus Police Department. He had been forced into responding as a backup officer to the mall. The other officer he was working traffic with near the stadium had heard the calls at the mall and had said, "Come on, Pitts, let's go. I'll follow you."

Now, he was here and he was terrified. Lieutenant Anderson was not a carpet cop and that scared Pitts, too. Anderson wasn't going to sit back and wait on anybody to come help them. He would do something. Something dangerous.

"Let's do a little recon," Anderson ordered. "Pitts, come with me. I'm gonna to take a peek inside. We may be dealing with the zombie virus. Cover me and don't let anything out, even if they're in uniform. Nobody gets out, understand?"

Pitts swallowed. "Yes, sir."

Anderson pointed to the other three officers.

"Drive around to the food court entrance and see if you can look inside. Call me and let me know what you see."

The doors at the upper level entrance were tinted and not clear glass. Anderson was going to have to open one of them if he wanted to peer inside. Anderson and Pitts drew their pistols and walked towards the entrance.

The lieutenant paused at the door and put his ear up against it. Pitts stood a few feet behind him, holding his pistol in a low ready stance. He noticed that his hands were shaking.

Lieutenant Anderson made eye contact with Pitts and whispered, "I'm going open the door a little bit."

Officer Pitts nodded.

Anderson reached for the door handle and pulled it open slightly, moving his head towards the opening so that he could see inside. He saw movement and tried to bring his pistol up. Five zombies were standing just inside and rushed him, hitting the lieutenant and the door. He started shooting but all of his shots were low, hitting them in the legs and abdomens.

The collision knocked Anderson backwards. Pitts saw the door explode open as the infected attacked the senior officer. The lieutenant's shots startled Pitts and he started shooting, too.

His first shot hit the LT in the back. His kevlar vest stopped the bullet from penetrating but the impact staggered him, knocking the breath out of him. The five zombies tackled the lieutenant and began to bite him, ripping at his face and throat. One of them managed to sink his teeth into the officer's jugular, sending a spray of blood into the air.

Pitts continued shooting, mostly missing, and shattering the glass doors. He did manage to hit one of the infected in the head, killing him. The other four forgot about Anderson and lunged at the other officer. Pitts turned and started running back towards the parking lot. Fear drove him and he covered the fifty yards to his police car in record time.

"Unit 105 to dispatch!" he screamed over the radio as he ran. "The lieutenant is down. Zombies are attacking him and chasing me. We need more help!"

He grabbed at the key fob on his belt and managed to mash the unlock button. He jerked the driver's door open and dove inside. His hands were unsteady as he fumbled to get the key into the ignition. The four zombies slammed into the side of the car as their hands struck at the driver's window.

Pitts turned the key, put the car in drive, and accelerated away. In his rear view mirror, he saw the four zombies running after him. He drove around to the food court entrance to tell the other officers what had happened, minus the part about him shooting the lieutenant.

When Anderson went down, he fell in the doorway, blocking it open. Other zombies, drawn to the sound of the gunshots, converged on the open exit and began spilling out into the parking lot. Within fifteen minutes, over fifty infected people were walking across the mall parking lot to the other businesses that were nearby.

Officers continued to converge on the mall but no one had a clear idea of what to do. They saw groups of possible infected but were unsure of their next step. The loss of so many officers had everyone afraid to act.

Brian and Melanie didn't stop running until they got to her dad's truck. Melanie had stopped crying, but was probably close to going into shock, Brian observed.

He paused for a moment to catch his breath before starting Chuck's Silverado and heading back to pick him up. The problem was that this was game day in Athens and the streets were packed with pedestrians and vehicles. News of the incident was getting out because it had been mentioned by the pre-game sports shows on television and radio. Video was being shown from inside the stadium of infected people violently attacking and killing those around them. Many of them reanimated as zombies and continued the cycle.

"It's going to be OK, Mel. We're going right now to get your dad."

"She's dead, isn't she? Is Rebecca dead?"

"I don't know," he lied. "If we hurry, maybe we can get her to the hospital."

He was still trying to figure out what had happened. Everyone was having a good time and then somebody started shooting. And then the zombies showed up. How did that happen? Where did they come from? Was the Middle-Eastern looking guy that Mr. McCain killed involved in it? Had he turned into a zombie?

Mel's dad had kicked him so hard in the chest, Brian was stunned to see him get up. And that was after getting shot several times. Then, Mr. McCain had kicked him and broken his knee. Brian heard it crack and he still got up again. He didn't appear to be feeling anything until he had gotten shot in the head.

Brian knew that he had to get Melanie and himself somewhere far away. He sensed that the UGA campus wasn't safe anymore. There was no telling how far this thing had spread already.

Chuck ran up South Lumpkin Street. Pedestrians who hadn't heard about what was going on in the stadium were still streaming towards the game. He tried to warn them to turn around but the big, bloody man carrying a bloody woman looked scarier than anything that they could imagine. Several people called 911 about him. That was fine. Whatever it took to get some help here, he thought.

A woman screamed back from where he had just come from and then there were several more shouts. And the sound of zombies growling. Some of the fans had just run into the group of infected who had been pursuing him.

He needed to call his men and get them enroute but he needed to get Rebecca away from there first. But she was dead. She would want him to try and get the wheels turning. Just a little further, he thought.

His arms were burning from carrying her so far. He wasn't normally a runner but he was today. He had jogged block after block and a university building loomed up on his right. The sign identified it as Gilbert Hall, The Romance Languages Department.

McCain carefully laid Rebecca on a small brick ledge near the entrance and pulled out his cell phone. There was a missed call from Eddie and a voicemail. That would have to wait.

His first call was to Melanie. When she answered, he told her that he was OK and where to pick him up. He disconnected and called Eddie to get the teams moving. He answered on the first ring.

"Chuck! Where are you, man? I can't reach Rebecca and I left you a voicemail. Did you here about the attack in Athens?"

"Eddie, I'm in Athens. I'm with Rebecca but she's dead," he managed to say, his voice breaking.

McCain tried to tell Eddie what had happened but he wasn't sure any of it made any sense. Marshall couldn't understand everything that Chuck told him but he understood that Rebecca was dead, Amir al-Razi was dead, but that he had managed to shoot Rebecca before Chuck had killed him, and that they were on the University of Georgia campus.

If that was true, this must be a separate attack. He had never been to Athens but from looking at a map, the infected mall was several miles from the City of Athens and the university. And, what were Chuck and Rebecca doing there in the first place? Were they following al-Razi on their own?

Marshall could hear the pain in his friend's voice. He felt devastated when Chuck told him of Rebecca's death and he knew it was much worse for McCain. But now, they had to focus.

Eddie had already taken it on himself to mobilize the teams. Everyone was on their way to the office to get their SUVs and then they would be starting towards Athens. He figured it was a minimum of two hours before they could get to the mall.

"I'm sorry, Chuck, but let me tell you what's going on. I saw on the news that there was a possible infection at a mall in Athens. I tried to call Rebecca but couldn't reach her so I called the Athens-Clarke County Police. They think they've lost twelve officers. The infected were contained in the mall but now they're spilling outside and the police can't stop them."

"You guys get here as quick as you can, Eddie," resolve in McCain's voice. "I'll meet you at the mall and we can try and figure out what we need to do. It looks like it's spreading really fast over here at the UGA campus, too. I have to go, there's a couple more Zs coming after me."

A male and a female zombie were walking up Lumpkin Street. They were probably students and clad alike in UGA red and white. He saw blood on their faces but no other injuries. Chuck wondered if this was their first date.

Upon seeing him, their growling got louder and they increased their pace. He pulled Rebecca's Glock 19 out of his waistband and waited until they were inside ten feet. He made one head shot on each of them.

He glanced down the street and saw that it was clear for the moment. The gunshots made a few fans turn and hurry back the way that they had come. Chuck stepped over to Rebecca. He kept hoping she would wake up and speak to him. He touched her face but it was cold. Tears filled his eyes again.

Chuck held her hand. "I'm so sorry," he said, his voice breaking. "I'm sorry I couldn't protect you. I'm sorry I didn't tell you how much I love you." He sobbed and kissed her hand.

There was more growling coming from behind him and the sound of a vehicle coming from the other direction, down the closed street. Three more infected saw him and increased their pace. Two older women and an older man were opening and snapping their mouths closed.

Their eyes were glazed over and they all had visible wounds to either their legs or their arms. One of them also had a vicious wound to the face. Her cheek was ripped open to the bone. McCain made three quick head shots as Brian drove up. He jumped out to help Chuck.

There were more zombies coming, drawn to the gunfire. He scooped up Rebecca and carried her to the truck.

"Open the back door," he ordered.

Brian did and then ran around to the other side and got in the back to help Chuck lay her out on the back seat. McCain hurried around to the passenger side where Brian was standing and retrieved a small, black bag from under his passenger seat. He crawled into the back and let

Rebecca's head lay against him.

"You drive, Brian. Take us back to where you parked your car."

He opened the bag and pulled out several loaded Glock 17 magazines. He reloaded his pistol with a full mag and put two loaded magazines in his pocket. He opened a box of 9mm ammo and refilled the almost empty mag that had been in his gun. He also reloaded Rebecca's pistol.

"Melanie, are you alright?"

There was pain in his voice but he had to be strong so that he could help his daughter.

"No, is she…?"

"She's gone, Mel. There was nothing we could've done."

"What are we going to do?"

"I'm not sure. I'm meeting my guys in a while and we'll try and figure out our next steps. The Georgia Square Mall was infected. There are a lot of dead people and zombies there, too. It sounds like they lost twelve police officers there."

There was a stunned silence from both Melanie and Brian, as they digested this.

"This appears to be another coordinated attack that the four of us stumbled into. And it cost Rebecca her life. The guy that murdered her was one of the terrorists behind so much of this."

His eyes were watering again. Brian pulled into a small parking lot, several blocks north of the main downtown area. He had parked his Honda CRV there earlier when he and Melanie had met Chuck and Rebecca. The three of them got out of Chuck's truck.

"I need you guys to leave right now. Brian, you told me your family lives up near the South Carolina line?"

"Yes, sir, not far from Hartwell."

"Start driving. Don't worry about anything in your dorm rooms. I've never seen the infection spread so fast.

"We don't know if the guy I killed, al-Razi, was by himself or if he has other people spreading the virus in other parts of the city. People seem to be turning into zombies in just a few minutes and I'm not sure we're going to be able to do anything about it."

"But, Daddy," Melanie protested. "I don't have any clothes, my computer, or even the gun you gave me. Everything's in my dorm room."

"Brian, do you have a gun with you?"

"I have my Glock 23 in the car, in the glove box."

Chuck nodded. He pulled Rebecca's Glock 19 out of his waistband and handed it to Melanie. He reached into the truck and opened Johnson's purse. He found two more full fifteen round magazines and handed those to Melanie, along with a box of 9mm ammunition from his black bag.

McCain took all of the cash he had, a little over two hundred dollars, and handed it to his daughter. He checked Rebecca's purse and found another hundred and fifty dollars. He handed that to her as well.

"Here's Rebecca's gun and all the cash I have. Text me the address where you're going to be."

Turning to Brian and locking eyes with him, he said,

"Brian, can I trust you to get my daughter some place safe?"

"Yes, sir! We'll leave right now and be at my parent's place in about an hour. I'll take care of Melanie. I promise."

He patted the young man on the shoulder. He reached for his daughter as she started crying again.

"I'm so sorry, Daddy. She was such a great person. I love you and I'm praying for you."

"I love you. I'm sorry you guys got pulled into this. Brian's family sound like good people. They'll take care of you and we'll talk soon."

She was still crying as they drove away.

Chapter Eleven

Athens, Georgia, Saturday, 1430 hours

McCain drove towards the mall but he needed to make the phone call. Admiral Jonathan Williams was the Assistant Director for Operations at the Central Intelligence Agency. Rebecca had given him the Admiral's phone number to contact in an emergency.

He pulled into a convenience store parking lot between the university and the mall and stopped. He needed to concentrate. He dialed the number and it rang. There were a series of clicks and then it was answered.

"Yes?" the voice said.

"Admiral Williams?"

"Who is this?"

"Sir, this is Chuck McCain. I'm a team leader in Atlanta. I…"

"I know who you are Mr. McCain. What can I do for you? I'm assuming you're not calling from a secure line?"

"I'm calling from my government issued phone, sir. I don't know if it's secure or not but this is an emergency.

Rebecca has been killed and we're in the middle of two more coordinated attacks."

There was a stunned silence on the other end of the line.

"What happened to Rebecca?" the voice asked softly.

Chuck told him the story. He managed to do it this time without breaking down. He also gave Williams all the information that he had about both attacks, which was not very much at this point.

"Do we have al-Razi's body?"

"No, sir. I was being chased by zombies, carrying Rebecca. I know where it's at if you want us to try and recover it."

"If that's possible. I'd like to have his body or DNA and photos of the corpse."

"We'll try to take care of that, sir."

Again, there was silence as if the voice on the other end was thinking.

"Well, Mr. McCain, you're the man in charge now. Are you going to be able to function? I'm sorry to be so blunt, but this is…"

"Admiral, obviously I'm devastated but I'll grieve later. We may already be too late to stop this from spreading throughout the university and the city but when the rest of the guys get here, we'll do what we can."

"What do you need from me?"

Chuck gave the Admiral several requests and suggestions. He assured McCain that he would get everything he asked for.

His next call was to Eddie. He answered immediately. "Hey Chuck, we're about to leave. Everybody just got here."

"Hang tight, Eddie. That DHS Blackhawk is on its way to pick you guys up. It should be there in fifteen or twenty minutes."

"Excellent! That's so much better. Where are we going to meet you?"

"I'm heading towards the mall. Maybe he could set down there?"

While he was still stopped, Chuck got out and walked to the rear of his truck. He had a hard shell cover that enclosed the bed of the Silverado. He opened it up and pulled out a much larger duffel bag. It contained his uniform and all of his equipment. His Colt M4 rifle was in a hard plastic case.

He changed clothes on the side of the convenience store. He attracted a few stares but he wasn't really worried about what people thought. And, it wasn't like the police were going to be responding to a suspicious person call. They had much bigger issues to deal with.

Before starting for the mall, McCain made one last phone call. He notified Dr. Charles Martin of the CDC of Rebecca's death, the latest attacks, and the infected areas. He asked him to mobilize the CDC's resources and send their emergency management team to the Georgia Square Mall. They could stage there and then assist at the university whenever the location was secured.

McCain turned into the mall parking lot and saw that it was only partially full. He guessed that most people had fled when zombies started trying to eat them. It was tough to shop in that environment, he thought. He just hoped that none of them were infected when they fled or they would have to be dealt with later.

A group of police cars were clustered in the middle of the mall parking lot. That would be where he would set up a command post. The officers were all sitting in their cars, however.

Normally, in this kind of situation, they would be standing outside talking, with the officer in charge directing the action. It was hard to develop a plan if everyone was in their cars. Then he saw why.

Two infected were standing next to one of the police cruisers, slapping the passenger window. He could see their bloody faces, snarling at the officer just out of their reach. Chuck parked thirty feet away from the other officers and stepped out with his rifle. He could hear the zombies growling in unison. When they saw him, they started running in his direction.

He put a shot into each of their heads, their lifeless bodies crumpling to the pavement. Chuck scanned the area for any more infected, and then slowly walked over to the police cars. His badge was prominently displayed and he let the rifle hang over his chest. McCain realized he still had Rebecca's blood on his hands and arms. Later, he thought.

Two officers jumped out of their cars, pointing their pistols at him.

"Get down on the ground," they yelled.

"I'm with the CDC Enforcement Unit," Chuck said, calmly with his hands raised.

He slowly eased himself down to his knees. They stepped closer, seeing the badge.

"My ID packet is in my breast pocket if you want to take a look."

He kept his hands up until one of the officers holstered his pistol and retrieved Chuck's ID.

"I'm sorry, Mr. McCain," he said, handing the packet back.

"No problem. It's been a rough day for all of us," he said, getting back to his feet. "Why didn't you guys shoot those two zombies? They would have eventually smashed out those windows."

"Our chief told us not to. He said he's not really sure on the use of deadly force on zombies."

"Is he an idiot? If any of you guys get bitten, the best you can hope for is a quick death. Worst case scenario, you'll get bit, die, turn into a zombie, and then attack your friends."

One of the officers motioned at the blood on McCain. "Are you OK, sir? That's a lot of blood."

Chuck looked at his hands and arms and sighed, closing

his eyes.

"It's my boss's blood. She was killed a little while ago near Sanford Stadium. We got caught in the middle of this thing when it broke out. It seems to have started at the student center across from Sanford."

"I'm sorry about the other officer. You were there? We're hearing terrible reports over the radio. There are supposedly zombies walking all over the campus and attacking people. We heard that there was an outbreak inside the stadium. Some of the officers inside radioed that people were turning into zombies and infecting other people in the stadium."

"It's bad, real bad," answered McCain. "The area around the student center and the stadium are covered with them. It's already an epidemic. I probably shot close to thirty Zs trying to get away and I didn't even make a dent. What about here? I heard you guys got hit really hard."

"Yeah, we've lost a lot of guys in the mall."

Other officers got out of their police cars and were staring at McCain. A short, pear-shaped man got out of an unmarked police car and approached them. He was built like a Weeble, Chuck thought. 'Weebles wobble but they don't fall down,' the jingle went but this guy looked like he was about to have a nervous breakdown. As he walked over, he used a hand towel to wipe his balding head. His face was pale and his eyes were glancing around nervously.

"This is our Chief. He can brief you," one of the officers said.

"I'm Chief Tom Morgan," he said, sticking out his hand.

McCain did not shake his hand.

"I haven't had time to clean up, Chief. I'm Chuck McCain with the CDC. I have more men on the way. What's your plan?"

Morgan looked up at the big man. He saw the dried blood on both of his hands and arms. He even had a little on his face.

He had watched the newcomer pull up and shoot the two infected people without challenging them or trying to arrest them. Was that even legal? Those two people may have been infected but they were not presenting any threat when the CDC officer shot them in the head. He realized McCain was waiting on an answer.

"I don't really have any good information. We think we've lost twelve officers. They went in…"

Chuck interrupted him. "What do you mean, 'we think we've lost twelve officers?' You have or you haven't."

"Well, they went into the mall and haven't come out. One witness said she saw the initial responding officer get jumped by a woman and a mall security guard. Another witness saw the next two officers come in and get tackled. He saw one of our guys get a round off but then the witness fled.

"Then we had two teams of four go in through a different entrance. Pitts, here," the chief nodded at another officer even shorter than him, "said he heard maybe a hundred shots when those two teams went in, and then nothing. One of our lieutenants arrived and he and Pitts tried to peek inside the front entrance.

"Some of the zombies dove out the door onto the LT and killed him. Pitts managed to shoot one of them and barely managed to get away. The lieutenant's body is blocking the door open, though, and let a lot of them escape."

"That's right," said Pitts, obviously trying to sound tough. "The LT managed to shoot a couple but it didn't stop them. I hit one in the head and he went right down. I tried to get them to come after me and draw them away from him so that he could escape but it was too late. They killed him really fast and started chasing me."

Chuck stared at the two men. He noticed the way that the other officers stood away from their chief, off to the side, not even looking at him. It was also clear to him that they held Pitts in contempt. No one had to say anything. He understood. Every police department has an Officer Pitts.

"So, what's your plan, Mr. McCain?" the chief asked. "It would be good if you and your men could secure the mall and retrieve our men's bodies. Now that you're here, I'm more than happy to release the scene to you. Of course, we'll provide perimeter security for you while you're inside."

I'm sure you are, Chuck thought. He looked around the parking lot. He saw a group of probable zombies on the edge of the mall property, several hundred yards away. His phone vibrated. He hit the talk app and saw that Eddie was calling him on the walkie-talkie setting. He pushed transmit.

"Team One Alpha to Team Two Alpha."

"Team Two Alpha. Hey, we're five minutes out. Where do you want us to put down?"

"Team Two Alpha, there's a group of police cars in the mall parking lot on the east side. There's plenty of clearance to land."

"10-4, I'll let the pilot know."

McCain turned back to Chief Morgan.

"I think you guys are going to be on your own here. They're going to pick me up and we're going to see if there is anything we can do at the university. It may be too late but we have to try."

"But, you can't expect me to send any more of my men in there," Morgan stammered. "It's too dangerous."

One of the officers standing off to the side said, "I told you before, Chief, I'm willing to go into the mall. There may be people in there that need to be rescued. Plus, we can't let this infection keep spreading. If there are any zombies still in the mall, we need to put them down."

The Chief glared at his officer.

"No! I told you, this is the fed's scene now. This is a national security issue and I'm not sending any more of our people in there," Morgan snapped, motioning towards McCain. "This is their jurisdiction and they're more equipped to deal with it."

The Department of Homeland Security Blackhawk flew over the mall and circled the officers, probably making sure they weren't zombies. The pilot landed fifty yards away. The door slid open and the heavily armed men climbed out and walked over to Chuck. They all crowded around him.

The Athens-Clarke County officers watched as the CDC officers walked over to the big man with dried blood on him and told him how sorry they were. Several of them appeared to be struggling to keep their emotions under control. Morgan noticed a giant of a man with a bushy beard, wiping tears from his eyes as he walked over to McCain and hugged him. They held each other for a couple of minutes. This continued until each of the federal police officers had said something to Chuck.

Two other men in black BDUs, the crewman and the co-pilot, exited the helicopter and approached the group. One of them spoke quietly to McCain. He nodded and walked with the two of them to his truck. The rest of the CDC officers followed at a respectful distance. The local police officers weren't sure what was going on but they saw that Chuck had become emotional with the arrival of his team.

One of the men with Chuck unfolded something and laid it on the ground. McCain took off his rifle and handed it to a muscular black man with a shaved head. Chuck opened the back door of his truck and reached inside, gently lifting something out.

Chief Morgan's mouth fell open when he realized it was the body of woman. The big man laid her in the body bag and knelt beside it. All of the other response team members came around and put their hands on Chuck's shoulder.

"Who is that?" asked the Chief. "Why does he have a body in his truck?"

"That must be who he was talking about," one of his officers answered quietly. "He told us when he got here that his boss was killed earlier when everything started on campus. He said they were near the stadium when the outbreak happened. He said the blood on him belonged to her."

After a few minutes, Chuck allowed the men in black BDUs to zip the bag up and carry Rebecca to the Blackhawk. They very gently laid her in the back. The local officers watched the CDC officers huddle up and could see that McCain was speaking to them.

Georgia Square Mall, Athens, 1510 hours

"I don't know what to say, guys," McCain started.

His men were grouped around him next to his truck. They were far enough away that none of the Athens-Clarke County officers could hear what was being said.

"Rebecca and I were hanging out with my daughter and her boyfriend. Melanie surprised me with tickets for the game and just as we were about to go into the stadium, everything went crazy. We heard shots coming from inside the student center, right across the street from where we were. The door flew open and Amir al-Razi came running out.

"I wanted to take him alive. We started chasing him and I yelled for him to stop. He swung around with a gun and Rebecca and I both made good shots. Somehow, he managed to fire as he was going down and hit her. She was gone within a minute."

Chuck paused to wipe the tears from his eyes. A couple of the other men did, as well.

"Al-Razi was infected and turned within seconds and I finished him off. It looks like he or another of his associates spread the virus at this mall and then the student center across from the stadium. I don't know if he has any other helpers on campus or not.

"From what the local cops are saying, there may have been another terrorist inside the stadium. What I saw, though, was the virus spreading faster than anything we've seen yet. People were getting bit and turning within a minute or two.

"These were also the first zombies that I've seen running at a full sprint. I was carrying Rebecca and had stop and engage them. I killed around thirty but there's no telling how far into the city and the rest of the campus this has spread.

"I called our contact at the Department of Homeland Security," he lied.

None of the other men knew that the CDC Response Teams were supported and funded by the CIA. They were legitimate federal police officers and their agency was created by a Presidential Executive Order. Chuck had put the puzzle together and shared with Rebecca his suspicions. She confirmed what he thought and told him the truth, but had sworn him to secrecy.

The CIA, of course, was forbidden to operate inside the United States. At the same time, no other federal agency had taken the zombie virus seriously until unified attacks had taken place in several other major cities. The CDC Enforcement Unit was a front that allowed the CIA to combat this serious terror threat.

"For the moment, he has placed me in charge until they decide who will take over for Rebecca. Andy, you're now 'Team One Alpha.' My new call sign will be 'CDC One.'"

Andy Fleming nodded grimly. "No problem, Chuck."

"Next, we need to figure out what we're going to do. The short, weeble looking guy over there is the police chief. He told me that this mall is now our jurisdiction and we need to get in there and retrieve his officer's bodies and rescue any survivors."

McCain saw a flash of anger in the eyes of his men. They were professionals, however, and kept their thoughts to themselves. Except Scotty.

"Weebles wobble but they don't fall down," Smith said quietly, eliciting a laugh from the federal officers.

"My plan is for you guys to talk to the local officers here and give them a few tips on killing zombies. Then, we're going to get on the helicopter and fly over to the university and see how we can help there. I'm not sure what we can do but I think we need to try. We also have orders to get a positive ID on al-Razi's body. I'll take some pics and get a DNA swab from him.

"We'll fly over the campus, especially the area around the stadium, and see how it looks. I'll have the pilot find a place to put down in that area and we'll deal with identifying the body. Of course, we'll kill as many zombies as we can and see if we can save anyone. We'll have a better idea from the air of how bad the situation on the ground is."

Everybody nodded. Now that they had a mission, they all felt the familiar rush of adrenaline. It was time to go to work.

McCain looked at Smith. "Scotty, did you do much sniping out of a helicopter?"

As an Army Ranger, Smith had been trained as a sniper. He didn't talk about it much but he had evidently been pretty good and had a number of confirmed kills in Iraq. His sniper skills had not been utilized since he had come to work for the CDC Enforcement Unit.

Smith nodded, picking up on what McCain was thinking. "I did some. There were certain environments where I didn't have time to get in and set up ahead of the team. The chopper provided a mobile over watch platform. It would be better if I had a real sniper rifle, but I can cover you guys with the M4 if that's what you're asking."

"I know it's not perfect," McCain said, "but if it's bad as I think it is on campus, we're going to need all the help we can get. I'll go talk to the Chief and tell him he's going to have to man up and deal with the mall. Scotty, why don't you go talk to the Blackhawk crew and figure out the best way to set up as a sniper?

"Can the rest of you guys talk to the cops and tell them our rules of engagement and give them some advice? When I got here, those two infected that are lying over there were standing next to that police car slapping the windows. The guys informed me that the Chief told them they couldn't use deadly force so they were huddling in their cars."

The CDC officers were a hard bunch to shock but this was the kind of terrible leadership that would get police officers killed.

"Got it, Chuck," acknowledged Eddie. "We'll go talk to the officers."

"Hey, Boss," said Scotty, "let me clean you off first." He pulled a bottle of water and some gauze out of his pack and cleaned Rebecca's blood off of McCain. When he was as clean as he was going to be, he walked back over to the police chief.

"Chief Morgan, my men are giving your officers some tips on killing the infected people they will encounter, both in and outside of the mall. If the door was left open, most of them probably escaped and your guys will need to try and find them before they infect anyone else. They'll also share with them our rules of engagement. After they finish, we're going to fly to UGA and see if we can rescue some students."

"McCain, I've asked you to help us. I need you and your men to secure this mall," the Chief said, angrily. "My men aren't equipped to deal with this. I've already lost twelve officers. Isn't this what your department was created for?"

"There's a university with around thirty-five thousand students six miles away," McCain answered him. "I was there. That woman we just loaded onto the helicopter was killed by one of the terrorists who has been spreading this virus. I'm sorry for your losses but these are all the men I have and we're going to try and save as many university students as we can. Good luck."

Chuck turned and walked to to his truck to put the rest of his equipment on. He slipped his kevlar lined jacket on over his black polo shirt and then put his heavy body armor over it. His web gear and his rifle went on next. Lastly, McCain grabbed his kevlar helmet and carried it to the helicopter.

Fifteen other officers were now on the scene and were listening attentively as the CDC officers told them what they needed to know to combat and to kill the infected. Many others were on their way to the mall or to the university. The latter were having trouble finding someone who had a clue about what was happening and who could give them some direction.

McCain tried to telephone the campus police department to find out if there was a command post set up. His calls kept getting the recorded message, 'All of our operators are busy at this time. Your call is important to us. Please stay on the line and someone will be with you shortly.' Unless I get eaten by a zombie first, he thought.

He looked over to where his men were finishing their briefing with the Athens-Clarke County officers. The Chief had retreated back to his car. Chuck made a circling motion with his hand above his head and within minutes, he and the other CDC officers were airborne.

University of Georgia, near Sanford Stadium, 1545 hours

The helicopter was over the stadium within minutes and the federal agents gazed out over the destruction below. The CDC officers had had so much contact with infected people that they could immediately recognize them, even at five hundred feet. There appeared to be thousands of them milling in the streets, parking lots, and other areas around Sanford Stadium.

Inside the stadium itself, however, they could see small battles going on throughout. From the field to the different levels, people were fighting for their lives as zombies attempted to get to them. Bodies were scattered on the playing field, sidelines, over seats, and in the aisles. Survivors saw the hovering helicopter as a sign of hope and were waving frantically at them.

Chuck, Eddie, and Andy wore headsets that allowed them to communicate with the crew of the Blackhawk. Each of the men also had their personal headsets that connected them to each other. McCain pointed out the area next to the Tate Student Center where he had killed Amir and where Rebecca had been murdered. There were bodies carpeting the entire area and he couldn't pick out al-Razi from the air. Infected were feeding on corpses lying on the sidewalks and in the roadway.

"There are so many of them," came Eddie's voice over the intercom, voicing what everyone else was thinking.

"Can you move to the northwest?" Chuck asked the pilot. "Not too far. If I remember correctly, there's a place we can put down right over there," pointing off to their left.

The helicopter swung towards where McCain was pointing. There it was, just in front of them now, a large, oval-shaped area in front of the Richard B. Russell Library for Political Research and Studies. This open space was one of the things that made the University of Georgia such a beautiful campus. These areas were spread across the university. This one was easily large enough for the Blackhawk to set down.

They could see some infected people in the area, but not the mass that were just half a kilometer away. Of course, the noise of the big machine would draw more in. The officers would need to dismount and get out of the immediate vicinity quickly.

"What do you think, Mr. McCain?" the pilot asked.

Chuck had already formulated a plan. Normally, he was very collaborative and liked to have input from his teammates. There was a wealth of real-world experience in these men and he used it whenever he could. Today, however, there was no time to have a discussion. He trusted his men to execute the mission and to think on the run.

"It looks like the spot. Make a big loop and come back around and drop us off there," McCain ordered. "I need to brief the guys real fast."

The Blackhawk banked and made a circle over the downtown area as Chuck gave some final instructions to his men. As he talked, they could see infected people swarming through the streets of downtown Athens. Suddenly, a figure stepped out of a business and started running down East Broad Street. The zombies began pursuing the young man.

It appeared that he was running blindly, trying to outdistance them. Another group was up ahead, coming towards him from the other direction. The running man was cut off on the main thoroughfare but turned up a side street putting some distance between him and them. Smith was in one of the outside seats and shouldered his rifle. The group of infected kept running but their victim disappeared.

Scotty looked through his EOTech scope trying to locate the runner. He flipped the magnifier into place to give him the magnification to make long-range shots. The EOTech is the perfect optic for engaging an enemy up close but it doesn't help for shots of any distance. Smith had the magnifier mounted in front of it. When he needed to make a long shot, he just pushed it into place.

"He must've gotten into a building. I don't see him," the large man said.

"Let's get this over with. Can you fly us back to the insertion point?" McCain asked the pilot.

"On the way," came the response.

Chuck tapped the Blackhawk crewman on the arm. "Do you have any extra firepower?"

The man in black BDUs smiled. "When we land to let you guys off, I'll get it out. Between your man, the sniper," he nodded at Smith, "and my little toy, we'll be able to support you from the air."

"Thirty seconds," the pilot advised.

The Blackhawk touched down in front of the library and the CDC officers were off immediately and moving. Chuck was leading the way because he had been there before and knew where Amir's body was. The crewman jumped out and opened a storage compartment in the rear of the helicopter. He pulled the mini-gun out and quickly installed it opposite of Scotty, on the left side. Smith was set up to fire out the right side. They were airborne again within three minutes.

Chuck led them across a parking lot and between a couple of buildings. They came out on South Lumpkin Street. A group of eight infected were standing on the street, thirty yards away. They immediately began running towards the officers.

The lead zombie's head exploded and he fell down, causing three others to trip over him. Scotty had made the shot from the hovering helicopter. Eddie, Jimmy, Andy, and Chris paused to fire killing the rest. The others were scanning all around them, making sure that they didn't get surprised.

They continued across South Lumpkin Street and ran around a large, older building. The sign identified it as the Department of Germanic and Slavic Studies. McCain was taking them on a roundabout route to get back to the Tate Student Center. By cutting between buildings, he was hoping to avoid the large groups of infected that they had seen from the air.

The English Department was on their left as they approached Baldwin Street. Chuck paused next to the brick building and did a quick peek around the wall, checking for zombies. The street was raised a few feet from where the team was.

McCain led them forward to the embankment that led up to the street. Now, they could all see the twenty or more infected, standing in the road at Sanford Drive and Baldwin Street. The zombies were about seventy yards away but the men could not cross the street without being seen.

"CDC One to Air One," Chuck transmitted quietly.

"Air One, go ahead."

McCain told the pilot what he wanted, gave them the location of the zombies, and told him where the officers were located.

"Roger, CDC One. Engaging in one minute. Keep your heads down. You're clear to engage, Gunner."

The Blackhawk crewman manning the mini-gun heard the conversation and waited until the pilot swung the helicopter into position. He looked through his sites at the large group of infected and pressed the firing button. The six barrels spun sending hundreds of rounds into the zombies. Every fifth bullet was a tracer and he was able to see exactly where he was hitting. Three short bursts eliminated the entire group.

"Let's go," Chuck said, jumping up and running across the street. He led them down a short driveway to a parking lot and another large brick building. The Miller Learning Center was one of the many modern classroom buildings on campus. The long east wing would allow the CDC team to cut through and come out near where al-Razi's body should be.

They did not encounter any more infected as they ran up to one of the back entrances. The glass door was locked when McCain pulled on it. Without hesitation, he slammed the muzzle of his M4 into the door, shattering the glass. When they were inside, everyone stopped and listened for any signs of zombies. The building had been locked up because it was game day and they didn't hear any signs of life.

Everyone took a moment to catch their breath and have a drink of water from their CamelBaks. At the other end of the hallway was another exit. When they went out that door, they would be near where Chuck had left the dead terrorist. They would find Amir's body, get a few photos, some DNA swabs, and then make their way, or more likely, fight their way back to the exfiltration point.

So far, they had not seen anyone that they could rescue.

They had only encountered infected people. From the air, it looked like there were plenty of living people trapped inside the stadium but there were also hundreds and probably thousands of zombies as well. They all wanted to help the victims but they would need to figure out another way to do it. At this point, Chuck and Eddie had agreed that sacrificing their lives for a mission that had a minimal chance for success did not make any sense.

After a quick weapons check and reloads, Chuck led the men down the hallway. When they got to the other end, he looked out the glass door, back towards the student center. Bodies littered the sidewalk. Several zombies were crouching over corpses, the dead feeding on the dead.

There was al-Razi's body, lying about forty yards back to the left, still next to the bench. His memory was flooded from earlier. Amir turning with a gun and shooting. Chuck and Rebecca firing back. The terrorist going down. Seeing Rebecca lying on the pavement. The blood pooling around her. McCain's eyes filled with tears.

"I can see his body from here," he told the team.

Eddie sensed his emotion and saw the tears running down his friend's face. His put his hand on Chuck's shoulder.

"You need another minute?" he asked softly.

Chuck cleared his throat and wiped his eyes on his sleeve.

"No, I'm good. Let's get this over with."

Eddie turned to the rest of the men. "Amir's body is right over there," he said, pointing. "Maybe forty or fifty yards. Let's get over there quick. You guys form a perimeter. Chuck will get what he needs and then we'll try and go back the way we came. Let's leave this door propped open so we can get back in."

There was a rubber mat just inside the door. Marshall pushed the door open and wedged the mat inside it. With the door open slightly, they could hear the sounds of yelling, growling, and they could see forty or fifty more infected at the end of the walkway, near the front of the student center. That group of zombies would see the officers as soon as they stepped outside. They would have to be dealt with.

"Why don't we get the helicopter over here?" Eddie suggested. "They could thin them out a little."

McCain nodded and pushed his transmit button. At that moment, gunshots and screams echoed from the direction of the stadium. From their vantage point, Chuck and Eddie couldn't see what was happening but the shots were steady and sounded like the shooter was coming their way.

"CDC One to Air One," McCain spoke into the radio.

"Air One to CDC One, wait one," came the answer.

Chuck stared at the radio in disbelief and looked at the men. He and his team were on the ground with thousands of zombies all around him and their air support was telling him to wait.

"Team One Charlie to CDC One," came Scotty's voice over the other radio.

University of Georgia, near Sanford Stadium, Saturday, 1615 hours

Officer Grace Cunningham, University of Georgia Campus Police Officer, had been working security just inside one of the main gates at Sanford Stadium. Fans were pouring in to watch the pre-game warm-ups and the opening game festivities. The call over her police radio indicated that there was a fight in the Tate Student Center. She wasn't supposed to leave her post but no one would ever question her for going to a fight call that was right across the street from her location.

As she was walking out of the gate, one of the private security officers was arguing with a middle age couple dressed from head-to-toe in Bulldog clothes. They were both holding Starbucks cups but either did not know or had forgotten that there were no outside food or drinks allowed inside the stadium. The female security guard was trying to explain this to them but they weren't happy about it.

Grace wanted to get across the street to the fight before it was over but she stopped next to the security officer. She smiled at the fans sympathetically and said, "Sorry, sir and ma'am, you'll just have to drink all that coffee before you go in."

The dispatcher updated the call at the student center. Now, a bearded man was on top of a woman and biting her throat and neck near the front entrance. At this Grace, began to run. As she approached Sanford Drive, the unmistakable sound of gunfire erupted from inside the Tate Center. That slowed her down as she drew her pistol.

She keyed up her radio. "Badge 985 to dispatch. Shots fired inside the student center. I repeat, shots fired!"

Other units cleared immediately, which meant she would have plenty of help with her soon. She held her Glock 17 in a low ready position, continuing towards the gunfire. Suddenly, the front door flew open and a male wearing a UGA hat and t-shirt, holding a gun, ran outside. He turned left and started up the sidewalk that paralleled Sanford Drive. Grace was in the middle of the street and the Middle Eastern looking man had a large head start on her.

A big white man and a blonde woman, on the other side of the street and much closer to the student center, drew pistols of their own and started chasing the man. The three people turned and rushed down the walkway beside the Tate Center. The dispatcher let the responding officers know that several people had been shot inside and that the lookout was on a dark-skinned male, possibly of Middle Eastern origin.

Should she go to the victims or follow the people with guns? She didn't realize it at the time, but her choice to follow the people who were running probably saved her life. Other officers got to the scene and were immediately attacked and infected as they entered the student center.

Cunningham was about seventy-five yards behind the

three people that she was following when she heard someone yell, "Amir al-Razi, you're under arrest. Drop the gun and get down on the ground."

Seconds later, a string of gunshots exploded up ahead of her. She couldn't see anything yet but as soon as she turned the corner she'd be able to. Grace slowed down and did a quick peek around the side of the building.

The Middle Eastern man and the blonde woman were both on the pavement. The big man kept his pistol pointed at the downed man. He glanced over and saw that the woman was lying on her back as well.

Grace saw the fear and panic in his eyes as he ran to where she lay. The campus officer started towards them with her pistol pointed in their direction, but she moved slowly, having to cover a lot of open ground. Cunningham observed what appeared to be a badge hanging from the man's neck.

He yelled to the people who were gathering around him, "Call 911! Somebody, please call 911! We need an ambulance here."

At that moment, someone grabbed Grace's left arm. Instinctively, she jerked it away and stepped to her right, turning towards her attacker. A young man, probably a student, lunged for her again. His eyes were glazed over and her first thought was that he had ketchup all over his face. In half a second, however, Grace processed what she was seeing and took another step to her right.

"Stop! Get down on the ground!" she yelled, pointing her pistol at him.

The young man's left cheek was ripped open and the skin was hanging loose like a flap but his mouth was opening and closing. He made a noise that sounded like an animal's growl. Growling? A person growling? The FBI, CDC, and DHS bulletins she had read had told her that these were symptoms of the zombie virus. He kept coming forward, with his arms outstretched, and she continued backing up.

Another growl came from right behind her. Fear quickly settled in the pit of her stomach and she felt trapped.

"Please stop! Don't make me shoot you," she pleaded.

There was no evidence that he even heard what she was saying. Grace raised the pistol and put the front site between his eyes and squeezed the trigger. The impact of the 9mm bullet snapped his head back and he fell facedown onto the pavement, blood pouring out of the wound. The growling behind her was close. She took a couple of steps to her left and pivoted to face the next threat.

Two more of them were almost on her. A guy with a bloody arm and face and a girl with her necked ripped open changed directions and lunged for her. The guy was closer and she shot him in the forehead.

When he collapsed, the girl tripped over his body and fell down, tangled up in his legs. Her face smacked hard into the sidewalk. Grace covered the girl with the Glock. She looked so young, probably just a freshman.

"Don't do this," the officer said. "We can get you some

help. Just stay down on the ground."

Instead, the infected girl pushed herself to her feet and reached for Grace. She pulled the trigger again, shooting the girl in the face. Her body fell on top of her boyfriend's.

There were more yells from up ahead where the big man was now fighting the Middle Eastern guy that he'd shot. Hadn't he just been sprawled out on the pavement? What crazy world had Grace been transported to?

Several other growling, bloody, people were advancing towards Grace. They were after her. Somehow she knew that they wanted to kill her.

A quick glance back up the walkway and she saw the big man kick the man that he had shot. The powerful blow knocked him to the ground. The man with the badge hanging around his neck looked like he could take care of himself, whoever he was. At least, she hoped he could. Cunningham turned and ran back towards the stadium.

As she ran, the dispatcher alerted the officers that they now had reports of assaults inside the stadium. In one of them, a man had ripped a woman's throat out with his teeth. The dispatcher tried to raise one of the officers inside Sanford on the radio but got no answer.

"Badge 985 to dispatch," Grace said, as she ran. "I'm going back into the stadium. This appears to be the zombie virus. I've had to shoot three subjects and I have a group of possible infected people chasing me."

More infected people had left the student center, looking for fresh victims to attack. Some of them were moving towards the stadium. It was a race as to who would get there first. Cunningham had always been a fast runner and she outran the zombies who were pursuing her.

As she entered the gate that she had left from and slammed it shut behind her, Grace saw her friend the security guard lying on her back. The woman who had been arguing with her about the coffee was straddling her and appeared to be eating the flesh from her neck and face. A large pool of blood surrounded the security guard.

The zombie lady saw or heard Grace run up and turned towards her, bloody flesh hanging out of her mouth. The officer felt the vomit rising and she couldn't contain herself. The smell, the blood, the gore on the infected woman's face sent a wave of nausea through her.

She was able to hold it in until she fired a single shot into the woman's head. Then, Grace threw up her lunch, her breakfast, and everything else that she had inside of her. This was a bad place to be. She was vulnerable as she vomited and she knew it. She needed to keep her head on a swivel, even as she was bent over and heaving.

After a few minutes, Cunningham had nothing else to puke out. The fear, however, was still in the pit of her stomach. Her reasoning in coming back to the stadium was to protect people and she had done it without even really thinking about it. To Protect and Serve. That was what was on the side of her police car.

Now, she was having second thoughts. Could she really do anything? She didn't understand how those people had gotten infected but there were already a lot of them. In less than ten minutes, she had shot four people. Were they still people? she wondered.

Grace knew that she should leave and find a place to hide. No one would say anything. No one would question her.

Her father, however, had taught her to never run from things that you were scared of but to confront them head-on. Plus, were there any safe places? From what Cunningham had seen, the entire area was swarming with zombies.

As she was about to step back through the inner gate to go inside, she picked up movement out of her peripheral vision. The security guard was trying to climb to her feet. Her throat had been ripped out and her head hung at an awkward angle. She was a short, obese girl and she had trouble getting to her feet, but it was clear to Grace that she was witnessing the zombie virus reanimating someone who was dead. With tears in her eyes, she shot her friend in the back of the head.

The virus or infection or whatever they called it seemed to be spreading quickly through the stadium. Officers further inside were screaming for help over the radio. Gunshots rang out every few seconds. An officer transmitted, telling dispatch that he had gotten bit. Moments later, there was no answer from that officer when the dispatcher called him.

Grace didn't know where to start. She had to shoot five more infected near the concession areas. Many hundreds of people had managed to get to one of the exits and get out.

Many of these had even managed to get to their cars unscathed. Many others, though, had been bitten or ripped apart by the groups of zombies that seemed to now cover the area outside of the stadium.

A local reporter ran out of the gate that Grace had used to try and record the breaking news story. She and her cameraman set up in front of the student center. She had the microphone up to her mouth and was describing what was happening in Athens and what she had seen. The cameraman saw the big group of zombies coming up behind her and tried to get her to move.

"Just keep filming," she ordered. This story could be her big break, she thought.

It was one of her last thoughts as seven infected pulled her to the ground and ripped her apart. The cameraman dropped his camera and tried to run. They caught him before he could go ten feet and killed him, too.

A group of thirty survivors were about to flee out the same gate to try to get away. Grace stepped in front of them and held up her hand.

"It's not safe out there. There are big groups of those things killing people."

"It's not safe in here, either," said a tall, slim man in his twenties. "They're all over the stadium. I'm not going to stay in here. Out there, we can outrun them."

A girl and another couple all nodded in agreement. Cunningham could smell the alcohol on their breaths. Normally, that would be a citation. Some of them were probably underage and drinking in the stadium was a big no-no. Now, it didn't even register.

"I'm telling you, that's a really bad idea. I can try and protect you in here. Out there, you're on your own."

The tall kid laughed at her. "I don't need you to protect us. I can take care of myself."

The two girls in the group didn't look as confident now, as they were able to see some of what was going on between the stadium and the student center.

"Come on," he urged. "The car's only a few blocks away and then we're safe."

The officer didn't try to stop them as the group took off running across the street. A large pack of infected saw the four and started after them. Some of the zombies were running pretty fast. The four drunk students disappeared from sight with thirty or more zombies chasing them. The rest of the survivors looked at Grace with the hope that she would be able to keep them safe.

Now, they had been in the women's restroom for forty minutes. Grace had counted twenty-seven people, both men and women. It was mostly students but there were two faculty members, some parents, and a few concessions workers. The restroom could be locked from the inside so this was a secure location, at least for the moment.

Cunningham had shot three more infected as she was herding the group inside. Now, she took a moment to change magazines in her pistol. She had two full mags and another with five bullets in it.

Her backup pistol, a 9mm Glock 26 had eleven rounds

in it. She carried it inside a small holster in her ballistic vest. Grace leaned against the wall and wearily lowered her herself to a sitting position on the floor.

Everyone was trying to call out on their cell phones. Grace gave her dispatcher an update and told her where they were. The girl on the other end of the police radio did not tell Officer Cunningham that they had lost contact with all but three of their officers. There was no promise of rescue. No assurance that backup was on the way. Just an acknowledgement from dispatch that they knew where she was.

Grace wondered if her parents were OK. They lived on the edge of town and her father was the pastor of the Athens AME Church. Grace still sang in the choir if she was off on Sunday.

A year earlier, she had found her dad in his study working on his sermon when she decided she couldn't put it off any longer. She had to tell him. What was he going to say? Was he going to be angry with her?

"Hey, Daddy. Can I talk to you for a minute?"

"Baby, you know you can always talk to me. I knew something was on your mind but I didn't want to push it. What's troubling you?"

"I don't want you to be mad at me, but I have something to tell you."

"Grace, you can tell me anything. You know that."

She paused a moment and then said, "I'm going to be a police officer. I start the academy next week and I'll be working for the Campus Police Department."

Reverend Cunningham exhaled. "That's it? You had me worried, child. I didn't know what you were going to say."

"You aren't upset?"

"Upset about what? I think you'll do a great job. God's going to use you there. You know, police officers are to be God's agents of peace and justice and I think even your name is prophetic. You're going to bring grace to a lot of people who need it."

Grace wiped the tears from her eyes. "Thank you, Daddy. It's something I've always wanted to do. When I graduate from the police academy, I'd like for you to pin my badge on me."

Cunningham stood up and embraced his daughter. "I'd be honored to do that, Officer Cunningham."

"How long have you been with the police department?"

The question startled her. She looked up at the man. His blue eyes were clear and seemed to be free of fear. He was in good shape, probably in his forties, and he had easily lowered himself to the floor next to her.

"Just over a year," she answered.

He nodded. "You're doing a great job. This is a no-win situation but you got us in here where it's safe. You made good shots on those three you killed as you were herding us in here."

A woman came and sat next to the man. "This is my wife, Emily. I'm Kevin."

"I'm Grace. It's nice to meet you. And thank you for saying that. Are you military or law enforcement, by chance?"

Kevin's eyes sparkled. "I'm in the National Guard. I'm one of the full-time guys who helps run it. I'll stay out of your way, but if I can do anything to help you, let me know."

"I'll do that," she smiled.

University of Georgia, 1630 hours

From their vantage point, Chuck and Eddie couldn't see what was happening over at the stadium but the shots were steady and sounded like the shooter was moving towards them. Loud growls and yells also filled the air from the same direction.

"CDC One to Air One," McCain said into the radio.

"Air One to CDC One, wait one," came the answer.

Chuck stared at the radio and looked at the men. "Seems like we might have priority on whoever else he's talking to," Jimmy commented.

"Team One Charlie to CDC One," came Scotty's voice over the radio.

"CDC One," McCain answered.

"The pilot just made contact with the university police. There's an officer with a group of survivors that are trying to make their escape from the stadium. They're coming your way now. Estimated to be around thirty people being pursued by Zs. Try not to shoot the good guys."

"10-4, maybe you and your buddies up there can give us a little support and thin the herd out a little? And where are they escaping to? This area is covered in Zs."

"The pilot told the dispatcher to tell them to meet up with you guys and you'll get them to the extraction point. He said they'll make a few trips until they can get everybody out," Scotty answered.

"Okay. Give us some covering fire, Team One Charlie. We're about to go out and get pics and DNA of al-Razi."

Almost immediately they heard the Blackhawk hovering above them. The ripping sound of the mini-gun let them know that it was now or never. Chuck looked at Eddie and the rest of the team.

"Let's get what need from that body and then escort these survivors back to the extraction point."

"Then what?" Andy asked. "That helicopter can only take ten or twelve people at a time."

Chuck shrugged.

Eddie said, "That's why they pay us the big bucks. The main thing is to just get the people clear of here. He can set down a few miles away, off load, and then come back. In the meantime, we'll get to work on our marksmanship."

Andy grinned. "Sounds like a plan."

Chapter Twelve

University of Georgia, 1635 hours

The sounds from the stadium carried into the restroom where Grace was holed up with her group of survivors. There were screams, so many screams, growls, and the occasional gunshot. None of the gunshots were close but some of the growls and screams were. Every so often she would hear a helicopter. Were they a news chopper or people who could actually help?

There had been no answer the last several times that she had called her dispatcher. The battery in her radio was dead. She tried to call them on her cell phone but kept getting a recording. Cunningham could see that her phone battery was at ten percent. Finally, after twenty-something tries, someone answered.

"Dispatch, how can I help you?"

"Thank God! This is badge 985. We're still locked in the bathroom inside the stadium. What's going on out there?"

"Cunningham! I was hoping it was you. I've been trying to raise you on the radio."

"My battery's dead."

"Okay, I think I have some good news. Things are really bad and I've lost contact with everyone that was at the stadium but you and Fletcher. She's locked in one of the team rooms under the stadium with a few other survivors. I think she's on the other side from where you're at. She said there are zombies trying to break into their room."

"I thought you said you had some good news?" Grace asked.

"I do. CDC enforcement is on campus near you. They have a helicopter and will get you and your group out. It'll take a few trips by air but the alternative is, well, I don't want to think about it.

"They're near the Miller Learning Center, across from where you're at. They're at the exit closest to the student center and I've been told they're expecting you. They'll help get you to their extraction point. You just have to get over there to them."

All eyes were on Grace as she disconnected the phone call. She smiled at the people who looked at her expectantly. At the same time, she blinked away tears at the thought of so many of her friends and fellow officers who had been lost today.

She thought of Jennifer Fletcher, locked in a room

underneath the stadium. She was one of Grace's closest friends and she felt helpless that she couldn't get to her. For now, though, this group of people was her responsibility.

"We're getting out of here, " she told them.

She explained what her dispatcher had told her, including the fact that it looked like most of the officers who had been in the stadium were unaccounted for. There were mixed reactions from the group. Most of the people seemed inclined to stay where they were.

"At least we're safe in here."

"Should we really go out there?"

"Why don't we just stay here until someone comes to rescue us?"

"Isn't SWAT or the National Guard going to come and put a stop to this?"

Everyone was speaking at once and Grace wasn't sure how she was going to convince anyone to leave the restroom. An authoritative voice spoke from beside her, breaking through the buzz of the conversation.

"There's no one coming for us," Kevin said. "Not for a while, anyway. I'm in the National Guard and it'll be at least twenty-four hours before they get here.

"And then it might be hours after that before they actually start doing something. In the meantime, the police are just going to put a perimeter around this and wait. The cops have already taken heavy losses today and they aren't going to come rushing in.

"There was another attack earlier at the Georgia Square

Mall, not far from here. I just saw it on the news on my phone. They lost a lot of police officers there, too. All the police departments are going to be very cautious. We're on our own. Officer Cunningham has risked her life for us today and I'll follow her lead."

In the end, everyone said they would do whatever Grace suggested. The idea of being trapped for days in a restroom, hoping that they would be rescued, wasn't very appealing.

Grace handed Kevin her backup pistol. "Thanks for helping me out with the group. I hate to ask you to do this, but would you feel comfortable helping me get these people out of here?"

He smiled at her and took the gun. "Yes, ma'am. I'll feel better knowing that there are two of us providing security as we move. Just lead the way."

The pistol was a Glock 26 and held eleven rounds of 9mm hollow points. Kevin pointed the muzzle down, away from everyone, and did a quick press check of the slide to make sure a round was in the chamber. He slipped the pistol into his waistband and asked, "So, what's the plan?"

"The CDC teams are supposed to be across the street. There's a walkway that runs by the student center and they're down there, maybe two or three hundred yards. I'll go first, you bring up the rear?"

Kevin nodded at her. "Just like the good old days," he said, still smiling.

She listened with her ear to the bathroom door and

heard nothing. Maybe they had all wandered off to try to find some other people to eat. Grace nodded at Kevin and then unlocked the door, easing it open.

A senior citizen zombie, clad in UGA colors, was standing on the other side. His right arm had been ripped or chewed off at the elbow. He saw Cunningham, growled, raised his left arm, and reached for her. She shot him in the eye, spinning him around and sending him to the floor.

"Come on," she urged, stepping out into the stadium and moving in the direction of the gate. Two more infected came towards her. She rushed her first shot and missed, but her next two were good hits, dropping them.

As she ran through the gate, she could hear Kevin telling everyone to hurry, the authority evident in his voice. Two more were just outside the stadium. These were both young guys, probably students, and were covered in blood and gore. Grace shot the first one in the face. She fired at the second one, hitting him in throat, but not stopping him. He lunged at her and she pulled the trigger again, blasting a hole in his forehead.

Ahead, she saw a group of infected rush up Sanford Drive and turn left past the student center. Right where they were going. Great. For the moment, at least, her group was safe. The last six zombies, though, turned towards her at the sound of the shots and came shuffling on an interception course with the survivors.

She put herself between them and her group and started shooting when they were twenty feet away. Her first shot missed but she slowed down and started making good head shots. The last one fell right in front of her, an older man whom she recognized as a school administrator.

A helicopter appeared overhead, hovering. It was so low she could see the pilot and co-pilot, as well as the men leaning out of both sides. One of them held a rifle and the other was behind a machine gun. They both seemed to be looking for targets.

A gunshot came from just behind her. She waved the survivors on as another shot rang out. Grace saw that Kevin had put down two infected. He kept urging the people on. A few more zombies were following them but weren't close enough yet to worry about.

Cunningham noticed that the door to the Tate Student Center was propped open by a body. As they kept running, she watched as that body got to its feet and began walking towards her group. Three other zombies were also coming their way. She stepped up, calmed her breathing, sighted in on the closest, and made a head shot. Kevin came up to help her and shot the second one.

Kevin saw a running zombie charging towards the rear of the group of survivors. He left Grace to go deal with that threat, making a head shot as both he and the zombie were moving. Grace shot at the third one in the group she was dealing with but her bullet only grazed the side of his head, taking off the zombie's right ear. She adjusted her aim and the next round hit the creature just above the right eye. Cunningham saw the slide on her pistol locked open.

"Look out, officer!" someone yelled.

She turned just in time to see the guy who had been

lying in the doorway reaching for her. He was only five feet away as she swung her pistol around, dropped the empty magazine, and reached for her last full one. Grace knew she was about to get bit but the zombie's head suddenly exploded in a red mist and he fell to his back. Cunningham looked up at the helicopter. A man with a bushy beard was holding a rifle and gave her a thumbs up.

Grace and Kevin got the group running again. When they got to the corner of the student center and turned left, they saw at least fifty zombies in their path, directly between them and where they needed to go. Cunningham saw a group of men dressed in black burst out of the Miller Learning Center and start shooting into the crowd of infected.

The helicopter swung around so the man with the machine gun could get it into action. Cunningham realized that her people were in the line of fire and she directed them against the front wall of the Tate Center. The bricks would protect them from any stray shots.

The mini-gun began firing down into the crowd of zombies and hot, empty brass fell onto the sidewalk with a tinkling sound or landed on the survivors, burning their necks or arms. The CDC officers continued to add their own firepower as the zombies were dropping into piles on the sidewalk. Others, drawn to the sound, started to pour out of the stadium. The man with the beard began shooting these from the helicopter as fast as he could pull the trigger. They kept coming, however, and Grace and Kevin knew that they couldn't stay where they were.

When the machine gun fell silent, Cunningham peeked back around the wall. The large group of infected had been destroyed. She stepped forward so the federal officers could see her.

"Don't shoot!" she yelled. "I've got some survivors and was told to meet you guys here."

A muscular black man waved her on. The CDC officers had formed a wide perimeter around a dead body on the pavement and one of them was taking photos of it. The others were looking outward for threats. They all watched Grace and Kevin bring their group in.

Two running zombies rounded the corner the group had just come from. The CDC officers could not shoot for fear of hitting one of the survivors. They observed the man at the rear of the group raise a small pistol and make two perfect head shots. He turned and jogged back to where everyone else was.

University of Georgia, Saturday, 1645 hours

Chuck used his smart phone to snap photos of Amir's face and then swabbed the inside of his mouth to get DNA samples. The swab was placed inside of a doubled plastic evidence bag. That was sealed in another bag and secured in one of his cargo pockets.

He also searched the terrorist's clothes. A wallet and an extra magazine for the Beretta that he had recovered earlier also went into evidence bags. He carefully checked the small canvas duffel bag that al-Razi had been carrying. They could search it later; for now, he just wanted to make sure that it wasn't booby-trapped.

McCain noticed the group of survivors come running up but was focused on getting what the Assistant Director of Operations for the CIA had asked him to get. Al-Razi's death needed to be confirmed and McCain now had that proof. He straightened up and looked at the survivors.

A young, very attractive, black police officer was speaking with Eddie. Chuck observed that Jimmy eased over to be part of the conversation. Another man with an obvious military bearing stood nearby. He popped the magazine out of a small pistol and counted the rounds.

"You about empty?" Chuck asked him.

"Five rounds left. I don't suppose you're carrying a Glock nine?"

"As a matter of fact, I am," McCain answered, handing him a seventeen round magazine. One of the great features about the Glocks was that the bigger mags were designed to function in the smaller guns.

The relief was evident on the man's face. "Thank you. My name's Kevin, by the way. That's my wife, Emily, over there."

"I'm Chuck. Nice to meet you. When we start moving, try not to shoot unless they're right on top of us. These things are drawn to sound and our rifles are suppressed. It helps keep the noise down a little. Were you in the military?"

Kevin nodded. "I'm one of the full-time Georgia

National Guard guys. I've shot a little bit."

"Well, we're glad to have the help, Kevin. Hey, Eddie, I'm done," McCain said. "Let's get out of here."

Andy pointed up the walkway that Chuck had run up earlier carrying Rebecca's body. There was a large group of zombies about a hundred yards away coming towards them. Others continued to come from the other direction, leaving the stadium, drawn to the sound of gunshots.

"Let's go back the way we came."

"Sounds good, Andy. I had point coming, you want to lead us back? And this gentleman," motioning at Kevin, "seems to know what he's doing with his pistol. Maybe let him be close to the front, too?"

The former Marine Spec Ops warrior nodded and told Luis to join them in the front. Eddie, Chris, and Alejandro would stay towards the rear of the group. Chuck, Jimmy, and Grace would stay in the middle of the pack. McCain saw Jimmy hand Grace an extra pistol magazine. It was fortunate that the university police were carrying the same handguns as his men.

By the time they got back to the Miller Learning Center, the large group of Zs was only forty yards away. The officers quickly herded the survivors inside and secured the door. As they were leaving the building through the door at the other end of the hallway, they could hear the zombies banging on the closed front door.

The rest of the trip across campus to the Richard B. Russell Library for Political Research and Studies was fairly uneventful. They shot a total of twelve infected on their return and most importantly, they got all the survivors to the open field. The bad news was that they could see groups of zombies converging on them. Counting the CDC officers there were thirty-five people that needed to be airlifted out. That was three trips for the helicopter, which translated into a lot of time on the ground for everyone else, trying not to get eaten.

The Blackhawk covered the group all the way in and the pilot landed just as they got to the clearing. Scotty jumped off to give his place to one of the survivors. Of the twenty-seven people that Grace had rescued, fifteen were women. Chuck and Eddie picked the first twelve ladies, including Kevin's wife, Emily. She didn't want to leave without him but he kissed her and told her that he would see her soon.

The helicopter lifted off to carry the survivors away from the infected campus. McCain motioned to his men to move everyone up to the library. There was a large, flat area at the top of the stairs that they could defend. It wasn't perfect but it should work for a little while. From what the CDC officers knew, most zombies struggled with stairs and the team had a large, clear field of fire from which to engage targets.

The closest group of forty infected was now less than a hundred yards away and closing in on their location. Several of the zombies started to sprint. The men checked their weapons, got into prone shooting positions, and started engaging them. The optics on their rifles allowed them to make the long distance head shots.

The suppressed rifles spit out their rounds at over three thousand feet a second. Kevin stood with Grace behind the line of federal police officers lying prone on the pavement. They watched with respect as their bullets cut down the infected. So many of these were wearing the university colors of red, black, and white. Just an hour or two before, those people were anticipating watching their team play in the home opener. Now, they were dead but still functioning under the control of the hideous bio-terror virus.

In less than a minute, twenty-five of them had been terminated. Thirty seconds later, the last of the big group were sprawled on the pavement or the grass. The area was clear for the moment and the CDC officers stood and reloaded their weapons, keeping an eye downrange for the next attack. Scotty scanned the survivors, his face registering surprise when he saw Kevin.

"Is that Major Kevin Clark?"

Kevin looked at the bearded man and broke out into a grin. "Is that Sergeant Scotty Smith?"

The two men embraced, both talking at once. "The last I heard, you were putting out fires and posing for those buff fireman calendars," Kevin said.

Scotty laughed. "I was up until about a year ago when this fine organization realized that they couldn't function without me. They hired a couple of Marines," he said, nodding at Andy and Jimmy. "They're OK, but they quickly realized that they needed a Ranger to lead the way."

McCain, Marshall, and Fleming joined the two men. "Major Clark here was my CO on my last Iraqi tour," Smith told them. "He got promoted to major about the time I got blown up and decided to get out."

He introduced them and they all shook hands.

"I bet you have some stories you could tell us about this one," said Eddie, pointing at Scotty.

Kevin laughed. "We'll have to have a beer or three and I'll tell you some tales about Sergeant Scotty Smith."

"I thought I heard you say you were in the National Guard?" Chuck asked.

Clark smiled. "I am. I retired from the army a couple of years ago but accepted a promotion to light colonel to go full-time in the National Guard."

"I bet that was shock and awe for those weekend warriors. I doubt they've had many officers in the guard with a Ranger tab on their uniforms," said Scotty.

"Hey, amigos, we've got some more coming this way," said Luis.

The CDC officers immediately went back to their positions. A group of thirty came from the same direction as the first group. They came up the walkway that Chuck had run up earlier. It didn't appear that they had zeroed in on the police and the survivors yet. Another group of twenty, though, came from the left, the same direction the survivors had just come from.

"Is it just me or do these Zs act like they're smelling for us?" wondered Jimmy.

This closer pack seemed to be walking with their noses in the air, as if sniffing for their prey. The men started shooting them, cutting these down quickly. The second, larger group heard the shots and began moving directly towards them. The suppressors on their rifles did not completely eliminate the noise and these infected began growling and opening and closing their mouths, almost in unison.

The zombies began to run towards the library, anticipating an easy meal. The rifles turned towards them and kept firing. Making head shots on running targets was very difficult and they missed quite a few. Fortunately, these Zs were running right at them so that made it a little easier.

Some of the infected were only fifty yards away and closing fast. The men were aiming and firing as fast as they could. When their rifles locked open, their reloads were quick so that they could continue shooting. The last two zombies fell at the bottom of the library steps.

"Air One to CDC One, we're two minutes out," came the voice over Chuck's radio. "Is the LZ clear?"

"CDC One. The LZ's clear for the moment."

"Luis, Chris, and Jimmy, grab the next twelve passengers and escort them to the LZ. The rest of us will provide cover from here," Chuck ordered.

The Blackhawk lifted off with the second group of survivors. One more trip and they could all get out of there. Chuck thought briefly of Rebecca's body in a bag in the helicopter, and shoved the image out of his mind. Not now, he thought.

McCain watched the university officer, Grace, talking to Jimmy. He nodded at her and then shrugged his shoulders. The girl had a pleading look on her face. Jones said something to her and then walked over to Eddie.

Two more groups of infected were coming towards the library. Chuck estimated about fifty total. These also had their noses to the air, as if they were sniffing for victims. They were about a hundred and fifty yards away and didn't have a lock on the survivors yet.

The police officers and all the civilians went prone onto their chests to make themselves harder to see. The officers looked through the optics on their rifles, their fingers resting lightly on the triggers.

"Let's wait until they get a little closer," said Chuck.

Eddie was lying next to him. "Jimmy just told me that Grace is asking if we can go back into the stadium and rescue another police officer and some more survivors."

Both men kept looking forward, in the direction of the zombies. Chuck looked over at his friend but didn't speak.

"I told him I'd check with you," continued Eddie. "It's been a rough day. I'm ready to get out of here but I know if it was me trapped over there, I sure would appreciate somebody coming to get me."

McCain looked back through his scope. They hadn't moved any closer. The large group had stopped in the roadway, standing and sniffing the air.

He sighed. "I guess that's what our job is, Eddie.

Protecting and Serving. Let's get as much information as we can. And, let's make sure they're still alive. If we can get confirmation that this other officer and the other survivors are still there, we'll go get them. Or at least try."

Marshall nodded. "Sounds good to me. I'll go see what I can find out."

He crawled over to Jimmy and Grace and spoke softly to them. Chuck saw the relief on Grace's face. She slid backwards to get further back on the landing. She pulled out her cell phone and made a call. McCain heard her talking quietly to someone for about five minutes.

When Cunningham disconnected, she crawled back over to Eddie and Jimmy and spoke to them for several minutes. The group of zombies that the men were watching continued to stand motionless in the roadway as Marshall slid back over to McCain.

"Grace talked to her," he said, quietly. "She's still alive and has fourteen people with her. The zombies know they're there but haven't been able to break through.

"It's not gonna to be easy. Facing the stadium from here, she's on the left side, downstairs in one of the team's locker rooms. There's a field that the helicopter can drop us off at that's close to the gate. Grace said she'll go with us and show us the way."

"Let me call the Blackhawk," Chuck said, reaching for his walkie-talkie.

"CDC One to Air One," he transmitted.

"Air One, go ahead. We'll be back with you in five minutes."

McCain told him what he wanted and gave their new mission to the pilot. He would pick everyone up and then drop the officers off near the stadium. After that, the helicopter would take the survivors to the drop-off point at the local airport. A command post had been set up there and the survivors would be taken care of. The Blackhawk would then return for their new passengers and the CDC officers.

A couple of minutes later, they heard the distinctive sound of the Blackhawk. It stopped over the group of infected that stared up at the machine hovering above them. A few of them reached upwards as if they could grab it. The door gunner aimed his mini-gun and loosed several long bursts, eliminating all of them. The helicopter then flared in for a soft landing in the field.

The police officers and the last of the survivors were already at the extraction point and loaded quickly. Chuck looked around to make sure that no one had been left behind. Satisfied, he climbed aboard and the Blackhawk lifted off. As the helicopter rose, they saw a large group of zombies moving to the sound of the gunfire. Well, the more that are over here, he thought, the fewer we will have to contend with over there.

Near Sanford Stadium, University of Georgia,
Saturday, 1730 hours

The officers checked their weapons, grabbed some

more loaded rifle magazines from the aircrew, and got ready to go back into Hell. Chuck had briefed them on the new mission: rescue another police officer and fourteen more survivors. There were no complaints or questions. The men knew that this was their job and their duty and were ready to do whatever they needed to do to help these people escape a certain death.

The flight was a short one but the pilot circled the landing zone to make sure it was clear, the door gunner looking over the top of his mini-gun. When he was satisfied, he landed in the grass near Reed Hall, a dormitory adjacent to the stadium. The CDC officers and UGA Officer Cunningham jumped off the Blackhawk and ran towards Sanford's gates.

Scotty paused to shake Kevin's hand and promised to stay in touch. The helicopter lifted off to take the remaining passengers to join the others who had been rescued. The pilot still had plenty of fuel and would be returning to provide air cover for the officers on the ground.

Twenty-five zombies, hearing the helicopter, charged towards the officers from the direction of the stadium. Over half of these were wearing the UGA marching band uniforms, black pants, red jackets, and the distinctive black and red hat with the black plume sticking up. There were also a few cheerleaders in the crowd.

A friend of the band members had snuck three Starbucks coffees in for her friends to have before the game started. A hefty tuba player had his girlfriend bring him two pieces of pizza. The coffee and the pizza were tainted and these students were infected almost immediately. They quickly began attacking other band members and bystanders.

Almost the entire group had been infected or killed outright. One of the marching band had grabbed a cheerleader and managed to bite her arm. She jerked it free and ran away but quickly became infected and turned on another cheerleader, who spread it on to others.

Now they were rushing towards Grace and the federal officers. They were only fifty yards away and closing fast. Grace wasn't sure if these were infected people or if they were trying to escape the slaughter that was taking place inside Sanford Stadium.

She challenged them. "Stop!" she yelled. "Are you infected or escaping?"

The federal officers could tell that they were infected by their growling and by their mannerisms. They quickly swung out into a skirmish line. Jimmy stepped in front of Cunningham and the men started shooting, cutting them down with head shots. Two of the zombies made it to the police line, a band member and a cheerleader, one of them reaching for Andy and the other trying to grab Jimmy. Without hesitation, they both slammed their rifles into the zombies, knocking them backwards and then shooting them in the face.

They paused momentarily to reload and then continued forward. As they started up the ramp to the gate of the stadium, hundreds of zombies began converging on them from both directions. The officers shot as they ran, dropping more of them, and following Grace.

The infected were surging in large groups towards the sound of gunshots. We are going to be surrounded soon, McCain thought. Thankfully, all of the infected were not runners, but they were all tracking on the police officers and moving their way.

Grace led them inside and looked at Chuck. "Stairs or elevator?" she asked.

"Stairs," he answered, raising his rifle to blast an infected football official, wearing the distinctive black and white striped shirt. The shirt was covered with blood, as was the man's face. McCain's bullet hit him in the nose and continued into his brain.

Another official was on top of a UGA cheerleader, chewing on her neck. Her face had been ripped apart leaving her unrecognizable. He saw the police officers and started getting to his feet. Andy put a shot into the side of his head, putting him down for good.

Cunningham ran down the walkway, further inside the stadium, pausing to shoot two zombie concession workers that were blocking her path, devouring a middle-aged man's body. The loud retort of her unsuppressed Glock drew even more infected towards them. Everyone was running and shooting. They had to keep moving and they had to stay together. An isolated officer would be quickly overwhelmed by the sheer numbers of the infected.

The UGA officer came to a door that was marked, "Private." She pulled out a key and unlocked it, disappearing inside. Two hundred or more zombies were closing in on them. The CDC officers followed her and as soon as they were all inside, she slammed the door and made sure that it was locked.

They were in a stairwell. A quiet, empty stairwell. They all took a moment to catch their breath, reload their weapons, and grab a drink of water. A moment later, there was a bump at the door the door they had just come through.

The growling and snarling outside their door continued to increase, and bodies began to slam against it. It was a heavy, solid metal door that was anchored in the concrete walls. It would not give way anytime soon.

Grace pulled her phone out and dialed a number. "Jennifer, are you still OK?" they heard her ask. "We're inside the stadium and in the stairwell above you."

She listened for a minute. "Have everybody get against the far wall and down on the floor. I don't want anyone to get hit by a stray bullet. See you in a few."

The CDC officers gathered around her.

"We go down two flights of stairs. When we open the door, they're in the first room on the right, maybe twenty feet from the stairwell. It's a physical therapy room for the players. She said it sounds like a really big group is outside of where they're at. They're growling and banging on the door."

"A big group behind us and a big group in front of us. It sounds like we're surrounded," commented Estrada with a smile. "At least we aren't lacking for targets."

"Sounds like a party to me," grinned Scotty.

Eddie looked at Chuck. "What do you think?"

"That doesn't give us much room to maneuver. As soon as we open that door down there, they're going to be right on top of us."

"What about a flash bang?" asked Andy. "We could open the door a little and toss one down the hall. That should get their attention and then we engage them from behind."

McCain shrugged. "Why not? Anybody got a better idea?"

No one said anything. "I'll throw mine down the hall and we'll see how they react. Eddie can throw another one if we need to. The grenade should get them away from that doorway where the survivors are at for a little while so we can thin them out. Lead on, Grace."

She nodded and led them down the stairs. Chuck liked the fact that she was willing to lead and didn't expect the federal officers to go first. They moved cautiously down the two flights of stairs and stopped at the door. They could all hear what sounded like a large number of infected people growling just on the other side of the door.

The men all knew what lay on the other side of that opening. They knew that their odds were not very good and that they were in a poor tactical situation. Yet, none of them questioned their orders or gave a second thought to obeying them.

McCain pulled his flash bang grenade out of his cargo pocket. He was left-handed but with the way the door opened, he would have to toss it with his right hand. He let his rifle hang across his chest and pulled the pin, keeping the lever depressed. Andy and Scotty stepped up to cover him while he threw the grenade.

He whispered to Cunningham, "Open it about a foot. Shut it after I throw. After the grenade goes off, open the door about a foot again and you two," nodding at Andy and Scotty, "shoot as many as you can."

She opened the door and he arced it over the heads of the infected, down the hall in the opposite direction of the room that the survivors were in. Grace quickly pushed it closed. There was a two second delay and then the grenade went off, shaking the door.

Grace pulled on the door handle again, opening it enough for the two officers to start shooting into the mass of zombies that were moving towards where the grenade had exploded. They dropped around fifteen before the rest started towards the door. She slammed it quickly.

"There are still a few them out there," Chuck said. He had been behind Fleming and Smith, watching them shoot.

The thud of bodies against the other side of the door confirmed his words.

"How many you think?" Eddie asked.

"Maybe sixty or so. Not too many."

The other men laughed quietly. Cunningham stared at them incredulously. Instant or near-instant death was on the other side of the door and these guys seemed to be having a good time. Andy and Scotty reloaded their rifles.

"What now?" asked Scotty.

"Grace, call your friend and get her to bang on their door to draw them away from us. Eddie, toss your flash bang and let Andy and Scotty shoot some more of them. Then, I think we're going to need to let them in."

"What?" the UGA officer asked, quietly, but with disbelief in her voice. "What are you talking about?

"We'll wait for them on the next landing and shoot them as they come in. Most zombies aren't coordinated enough to climb stairs so we should be able to kill them all as they trip over each other. If any manage to start climbing, we can retreat up to the next level."

"That sounds like a big risk, sir," she said.

"Do you have a better idea?" the edge in his voice was evident.

She was silent for a moment. "No, sir."

"We don't have a lot of choices," he said, softening his tone. "This big group isn't going away. They know we're here and they know the survivors are next door. If we don't kill all of these zombies, we aren't going to be able to rescue anybody."

Grace pulled out her phone and called Officer Fletcher. She spoke quietly telling her what was going on and what she needed to do. She disconnected and said, "They should be banging on the door right now."

The sound of a loud knocking reverberated in the stairwell. The sound of bodies against their own door stopped and they could hear movement in the hallway. Chuck nodded at Eddie who was holding his flash bang. McCain opened the door about a foot and Marshall tossed

315

it down the hall. His throw carried further than Chuck's and the explosion sounded further away.

Chuck waited a moment and then opened the door slightly again so that Fleming and Smith could shoot. This time they managed to shoot twelve before the zombies turned towards the partially open door. McCain tried to shut it as a bloody arm reached in. He couldn't close it with the arm wedged inside.

Other bodies slammed against the door and other arms reached in. Chuck knew, even as strong as he was, he couldn't hold this horde back much longer. Smith and Fleming both moved to help him hold the door closed.

He made an instant decision. "Everybody up to the next landing," he ordered, "and get ready to start shooting. And don't shoot me!"

Everyone leapt into motion as Chuck strained against the surge of bodies. Grace ran up the stairs with the other officers. She looked back down and saw the big man straining to keep the zombies out. She could see that he was starting to get pushed backwards and the door was slowly coming open. He's dead, she thought. He's not going to make it.

McCain waited as long as he could and then leapt backwards and up the stairs. The door flew open and zombies fell into the stairwell, charging after the man in front of them. Bullets began tearing into them, stacking them up on the floor, and the first couple of stairs.

Chuck crouched low and got to where everyone else was and started shooting, too. At least fifty infected UGA football players, coaches, trainers, and fans shoved their way into the stairwell, intent on getting to where their next victims were. High velocity rifle bullets and Grace's pistol bullets slammed into their heads and faces, putting them down for good. Some of the players even had their helmets on but the 5.56mm and 9mm bullets punched right through the plastic and into their skulls.

It was a brutal slaughter. The concentrated firepower stopped the mass of zombies. As Chuck had predicted, most of them tripped over the stairs and over the bodies that fell around them. Only a few managed to get up to where the officers were and they were shot in the face at point-blank range.

In less than five minutes, it was over. The adrenaline was pumping through everyone's bodies. Grace noticed that the slide on her pistol was locked back. She had fired both of her magazines and was empty again. Without saying a word, Jimmy handed her another full one.

Everyone reloaded and waited for any others to come through the door. It was quiet again except for their heavy breathing.

After a couple of minutes, Chuck said, "Let's drag some of these bodies out of the way so we can get back out of here."

Jimmy and Andy stepped cautiously into the hallway to provide security. Everyone else grabbed zombies by the legs and pulled them out of the way, creating a walkway for the survivors.

They followed Cunningham to the next room down

where she knocked lightly and said, "Jennifer, open up, it's safe now."

A minute later, the two happy, crying officers were embracing and everyone was in the room discussing how they were going to make their escape.

"We need a better way out of here. I don't want to run through that gauntlet upstairs again," said Eddie.

"Yeah," agreed Chuck. "There are probably two or three hundred waiting for us right outside the door we came in. Is there another way out of here, ladies?" he asked the two UGA officers.

"Let's try the lower parking lot," answered Jennifer. "It's down another flight of stairs. This is the parking area where the staff park and the visiting team drops its people off. It'll take us out the east side of the stadium. But then what?"

"There's a helicopter that'll pick us up. They dropped us off in that field next to Reed Hall," said Grace.

"The problem is that the Blackhawk can only carry twelve at a time," Chuck told them. "So, it's going to take two trips. Maybe we could wait in that dorm until the helicopter comes back?"

Among this group of fourteen survivors was a couple that appeared to be in their mid-seventies. Bob and Martha were alumni from the class of 1964. They had not missed a home opener in over forty years. They seemed to be in good shape but they wouldn't be able to move as fast as everyone else.

Alejandro and Chris were providing security at the

door, making sure nothing snuck up on them. Andy made eye contact with Chuck and motioned with his head for him to step aside from the group. They walked to the opposite side of the room.

"Luis is hurt," Andy said.

"What happened?"

"He twisted his ankle at some point on that run through the stadium. He's not even sure how he did it. He can walk but he's in a lot of pain. I'm not sure how he's going to walk or run all the way back to the extraction point. That's a long way to go on a bum foot."

"Maybe we could find some transportation in the parking area? I wonder if the other team's buses are down there? Bob and Martha over there aren't going to be able to move very fast, either. How would you feel about taking somebody with you and scouting that exfiltration route downstairs?"

"That's a good idea. I'll take Smith and we'll see what we can see."

Grace watched Chuck take his helmet off and drink some water. Then it hit her. He was the guy that she had seen earlier chasing the Middle Eastern man who had run out of the Tate Center. Him and that blonde woman. She remembered seeing her down on the sidewalk. I wonder if she made it? And who was that man that they were chasing?

The group was waiting on Andy and Scotty to come back from checking the parking area below. The officers were drinking some water, checking their weapons, talking quietly, and getting ready for the next phase of this rescue mission. Cunningham wanted to ask Chuck what had happened earlier but she sensed that this wasn't the time. She was good at reading people and he was a man who was feeling a lot of pain.

Grace stepped over to Jimmy, who was checking his magazines to see how much ammo he had left. He smiled when she approached.

"I wanted to thank you," she said, returning his smile. "Thanks for the ammo and thanks for helping convince them to come and rescue these guys."

"No problem. That's what we do. I'm just glad we were able to get here in time."

"I have a crazy question for you. Earlier today, I think I saw Chuck across from the stadium. He was with a woman and they were chasing a guy with a gun. I was responding to a fight call at the student center when everything broke loose with the zombies."

Jimmy nodded. "You probably did see him. That woman he was with, was she blonde?"

"Yeah, she was."

"That was Rebecca, our boss," he sighed. "She was shot and killed by the guy they were chasing. He was one of the key Iranian terrorists responsible for the zombie virus, at least in the Atlanta area. We've been after him for a long time. Chuck killed him but he managed to get a shot off that hit Rebecca."

"Oh, I'm so sorry. I saw her lying on the pavement and

heard Chuck asking someone to call an ambulance, but then I got attacked and had to start shooting zombies. I wasn't able to help him. The last I saw, that guy he had shot was back on his feet and looked like he'd been infected, too. Chuck was fighting him and I saw him kick the guy in the chest and knock him down. A big group of zombies were coming after me so I ran back to the stadium to see if I could do anything there."

Jimmy nodded slowly. "Yeah, Chuck was able to finish him off but it's been a bad day for all of us. I heard you guys lost a lot of officers in the stadium and at the student center?"

Grace's eyes filled with tears. "So many of my friends. That's why I'm grateful you guys were willing to come and rescue Jennifer and these other survivors."

Sanford Stadium, University of Georgia, Saturday, 1810 hours

Andy and Scotty led everyone down the final flight of stairs. García was limping, clearly hurting but trying not to let it show. Chuck had Luis towards the middle of the group so he could help him if he needed it.

Georgia's opponent for the day was to have been Appalachian State University. Fleming had found one of their buses with the keys in it, already pointing towards the exit. The big bus would provide transportation to the extraction point and, more importantly, protection from the hungry hordes of zombies.

On their reconnaissance, Fleming and Smith screwed the suppressors onto their pistols and killed eight zombies that were lingering in the parking area. The suppressed 9mm pistols did not have the range or the power of their rifles but they were also not as loud. Now, the two warriors were leading the group out through the zombie free parking area.

As a Special Operations Marine, Andy had learned to drive a variety of vehicles, including busses, because you never knew when that skill might come in handy. Like today. Grace and Jennifer sat right behind him to tell him how to get back around to the landing zone. The shooters all set up in open windows of the bus to eliminate any threats they might encounter.

The big vehicle turned left out of the parking lot onto East Campus Road. They would have to make another left onto Hooper Street but the intersection looked like it was completely blocked by an accident. Several cars had smashed into each other and infected people were walking around the vehicles.

Mangled bodies littered the roadway. A dead woman, wearing a bright tie-dye t-shirt, was lying half in and half out of the driver's door of a Toyota Corolla on the far side of the intersection. Two zombies were bent over her, chewing on her corpse. Fleming slowed down, observing the scene in front of him.

McCain walked forward and stood next to him. "We don't have to go far on Hooper Street. Can you shove that smaller car out of the way?"

Andy nodded. A Toyota Prius was blocking one lane of the intersection. A Ford Expedition and several other passenger cars were blocking the other lanes.

He turned the steering wheel and applied the gas, easily shoving the Prius out of the way. They also bumped into the Expedition, pushing it back enough so that they could get through. The officers on the right side of the bus shot five zombies that came shuffling their way.

Chuck had already called the helicopter and let them know where they were. Air One was hovering and covering their approach. The LZ was clear for the moment and Jennifer showed Andy where to stop on Hooper Street. There was a walkway that would take them the fifty yards to where the Blackhawk could set down.

Andy stayed on the bus with Jimmy, Luis, and the two UGA officers to protect it and the two male students who would be going on the next trip. They were both journalism majors and were taking photos and video of their ordeal. Joel and Trent were scared but they also realized that they had their senior project on their phones now, thanks to this adventure. They just had to keep from becoming victims themselves and these big men in black seemed pretty capable of protecting them.

After getting the first twelve on board the chopper, the CDC officers retreated to the bus to wait for their own extraction. They could see infected walking around the area but none were close and they did not want to attract anymore by shooting. Their goal now was to just get everyone on the helicopter and get out of there. They were all running low on ammo so they would have to make every shot count.

As they waited, Andy said, "So, Chris, what do you think? Are you still glad you made that career change?"

The young officer smiled. "I am," he answered. "This is intense, but I know I made the right decision. I still have a lot to learn but you guys are great teachers."

Fleming grunted, still looking out his window. Chris was only twenty-eight but he carried himself like a seasoned warrior. Andy didn't give out compliments quickly so when he said, "We're glad you're part of the team," Rogers knew it was high praise.

Less than fifteen minutes later, Chuck's walkie-talkie let him know that the chopper was five minutes away.

"ETA five on the Blackhawk," he told the group. "Let's get over to the field and let's get out of here."

"We have some company," said Alejandro, looking behind them. A group of infected was walking down Hooper Street towards them. They were less than a hundred yards away and stumbling towards the bus.

"Air One to CDC One."

"CDC One," Chuck answered.

"We're coming in now, over the stadium and it looks like we have some survivors running your way followed by forty Zs. I count three males and a female coming around that dorm building across from the LZ. You should be able to see them now."

"Roger, Air One. Can you have your gunner take care

of the group pursuing? We have another fifteen or twenty behind us."

"Air One clear. Engaging now. Also, be advised we're getting low on fuel. I was hoping to get back, land, pick you guys up and get out of here. We need to wrap this up quick. And the gunner says he's almost out of ammo."

The four students were running hard towards the bus and the federal police officers. The large group of zombies was only twenty-five yards behind them. The distinctive buzz of the helicopter's mini-gun cut down at least fifteen of them and then went silent. Running zombies tripped over their fallen comrades and gave the survivors a few extra seconds.

Eddie, Alejandro, and Chris focused on the group coming up behind the bus, now only forty yards away.

"Let's take them out," said Eddie.

Each man's first shot took out a window and then they started shooting the infected. Four of them managed to get to the bus before being cut down. The last one they shot was a bloody-faced man wearing the dark blue campus police uniform. Grace and Jennifer both knew him and watched with tears pouring down their faces as two bullets exploded his head and sent him sprawling to the asphalt.

The running survivors were less than a hundred yards from the bus. "Okay, guys, let's help them out," ordered Chuck.

Officers began firing at the remaining infected that were pursuing them. Another campus police officer was in this group, a sergeant. Jimmy, Chuck, Andy, and Scotty fired shot after shot into this group from the left side windows of the bus, eventually killing them all.

"Air One to CDC One, good job. The LZ looks clear. How many passengers do we have left?"

McCain turned to Marshall and Jones. "Eddie and Jimmy, go escort those people in. Make sure they aren't bit."

"CDC One to Air One. It looks like we're at sixteen with these four coming in."

"Roger, we can land and take twelve and get them to the CP at the airport, but then we're going to have to refuel there. It's going to be a while before we can get back to you. Maybe half an hour."

"CDC One clear. We'll let you take the six civilians and the two campus officers. This bus is pretty comfortable. We may just drive out of here. Can you meet us at that same mall after you refuel?"

"Roger, CDC One."

McCain turned to Grace and Jennifer. "Your ride's almost here. You'll go with Joel and Trent here," motioning at the two students, "and the four that are coming in now."

"What about you guys?" Grace asked, the concern in her voice evident.

"There's not enough room for all of us and the pilot said he's low on fuel and is going to have to fill it up. We can't sit here and risk getting surrounded so I think we're going to take our chances driving out."

Eddie and Jimmy led the four panting, terrified students

onto the bus.

"They're OK, Chuck. They'd been hiding in that dorm since everything broke loose. They saw us and the helicopter and took a chance on trying to get here. Their bad luck that a group of Zs was walking by."

"Air One to CDC One, we're putting down now. Can you get those people to the LZ?"

"Roger, they're on the way."

Grace was writing something down. She and Jennifer quickly thanked the CDC officers. Grace hugged Eddie and Chuck, kissing both of them on the cheek. She looked into Chuck's eyes and whispered, "I'm sorry," and hugged him again. Then they were off, heading for the LZ.

As the Blackhawk touched down, Eddie, Jimmy, Chris, and Alejandro ran with the survivors to make sure they got there safely. Grace paused, as she was about to board the helicopter, hugging Jimmy tightly and slipping something into his hand. Within seconds, they were on their way to safety.

Andy had the bus running and ready to go as the men rushed back from the LZ. As soon as they were onboard, the big vehicle started moving. A large group of infected stepped into the roadway ahead of them.

Eddie nudged Jimmy with his elbow at they watched for threats. "What did Grace give you?"

Jimmy smiled brightly. "She gave me one of my empty Glock magazines back and her phone number wrapped around it."

Marshall held up a fist towards Jones who gave him a

fist bump. "That was a lot of work to get a phone number," said Eddie, "but I have a feeling she's worth it."

"Smooth, Jimmy. Very smooth," commented Scotty.

"Take a right at the next street," Chuck said to Andy. "How's everybody looking on ammo?"

Five of the officers were down to two full magazines and the one in their rifle. Three of the men only had one extra mag. They had a long way to go and were critically low on ammunition.

Fleming used the bus as a weapon, steering to the right where the group of infected was the thinnest, and mowed down six of them. He turned onto Sanford Drive. Ten more zombies heard the bus and ran out into the street. There was a loud thump as Andy ran over four of them and kept going.

"Which way, Chuck?"

"Left. I'm hoping the further we can get from the stadium, the fewer Zs we'll find."

Andy slowed to turn onto Baldwin Street. At least thirty zombies were standing next to the building on the corner to their left. When the infected saw the bus, they rushed it. The CDC officers saw a door on the far side of this building fly open and several figures in military uniforms rush out, waving their arms and yelling for the bus to stop.

"Survivors on our left!" Eddie yelled.

Fleming slammed on the brakes. The zombies were behind the bus. A few of them changed direction and went for the survivors. Eddie and Scotty tried to cover the survivors and cut down eight of the infected.

The other officers fired out the back windows at the pursuing Zs. Andy put the bus in reverse and backed over several of them. Four men and three women, all wearing green army dress uniforms ran in front of the bus and threw themselves inside the open door.

More zombies came from behind the building the survivors had come out of and charged the bus. Fleming accelerated away.

"So, what's the army doing at UGA on game day?" Scotty asked casually, as he reloaded his rifle. He was down to his last mag.

A tall, slim young man answered, panting, "That was the Army ROTC building back there. We're on the honor guard and were supposed to be a part of the presentation of the colors and National Anthem. When everything started, we happened to be near an exit. Three of our team didn't make it. We managed to get out and ran up here to wait it out. Thank God, you came by. Thank you for stopping."

They saw infected throughout the downtown area of Athens but managed to get through without any problems. As they slowed down to get around several abandoned cars, four young girls and a guy ran out of a drug store behind them and rushed towards the bus. Several zombies were ripping apart and eating three bodies on the sidewalk. They were between the bus and the survivors.

The young people ran into the street, going around the zombies in front of them, trying to get to the safety of the big vehicle. Andy saw them in his rearview mirror and slowed down. The Zs on the sidewalk forgot about their meal and rushed after the survivors. Other infected saw what was happening and joined the chase. The officers could hear the growling of the pursuers.

Fleming stopped the bus but he couldn't back up because of all the abandoned cars. CDC officers began picking off the pursuing Zs. One of the escaping girls stumbled and fell. The guy in the group stopped and rushed back to help her. They were both tackled by running zombies. The two young people's screams would haunt everyone on the bus for a long time to come.

Three girls managed to reach the bus as Andy opened the door for them. They were all crying and fell into seats hugging each other. At least they were alive to mourn, Fleming thought. He accelerated as more infected charged them.

Chuck guided them out of Athens. Soon, they were clear of the downtown area, and for the first time in hours, everyone was able to relax a little. Another ammo check showed that three of them only had the magazine in their rifle and the rest only had one extra. Hopefully, they wouldn't run into any more Zs.

Georgia Square Mall, Athens, Saturday, 1940 hours

The command post was full of activity. It was in the same location where they had been earlier in the middle of the parking lot. It was full of officers and investigators from multiple agencies. CDC vehicles were parked nearby and their emergency management personnel were onscene helping the police formulate a containment plan. Everyone looked up as the tour bus with "Appalachian State University" rolling across the electronic marquee pulled in.

The big vehicle stopped and the side door opened. Seven young people wearing army uniforms exited, followed by three young, crying girls. They clung to each other and had clearly had a bad day.

McCain, Marshall, and Fleming were the next three off the vehicle. As they walked to the command post, Chief Tom Morgan could see their exhaustion. He heard one of his officers say, "Look at their mag pouches. They're all empty."

The rest of the CDC agents climbed down from the bus. A big bearded white man and a slim black man were supporting an injured Hispanic officer. He was holding his right leg up and not putting any weight on it. All of these men were sweaty, dirty, and looked physically spent.

Chief Morgan, a captain from Oconee County, and a lieutenant from Jackson County greeted them. Morgan made the introductions and the men shook hands. Three Georgia Bureau of Investigation officers were also huddled with the Chief. FBI Special Agent Thomas Burns and several other agents were on the scene and gathered around the trunk of his car, poring over a paper map. Burns saw Chuck and walked over.

"What's with the bus?"

"We needed a ride," McCain answered. Burns was curious but sensed this wasn't the time for answers.

"Is the mall secure?" Chuck asked.

"It is," Morgan answered. "Oconee and Jackson Counties both sent us some officers and we think we got them all. They killed twenty-eight zombies that were still inside. That included several of our officers who had been infected.

"We've also killed another twelve that people have called in about. Most of those were in this general area. We have no idea how many escaped but we've had several attacks in the area so it'll probably take us a while to get all of them. Can you guys stick around and help us get the stragglers?" the police chief asked.

Chuck stared at the short, fat man for a moment before answering. "No, we're done. We've been fighting non-stop for five hours. We're almost out of ammo and I have a man hurt. Do you have any idea how bad it is at the university? I'd suggest trying to find out how you can help the campus police, if there are any of them left besides the two we rescued."

The captain from Oconee asked, "So, how bad is it?"

The three CDC officers looked at each other. How could they describe how bad things were? A stadium of thousands of people fighting for their lives? A student center suddenly turned into a zombie feeding area? Groups of infected chasing students, teachers, and parents down, killing them and tearing them to pieces?

"We managed to rescue close to sixty people, including two campus officers. That's it. There are hundreds, maybe thousands of infected around the stadium. I've requested the National Guard. We'll come back out if they need us.

Good luck, gentlemen."

As he turned to leave, Burns moved next to Chuck and said quietly, "McCain, I heard. I'm sorry."

Chuck looked at him and nodded. "Thanks. You can let your people know that al-Razi is dead. That's one of the only good things that happened today."

"Air One to CDC One," his radio crackled, "we are inbound to the mall, ETA five. Confirming the LZ is still secure?"

"10-4, Air One. The CP is in the same location. You'll see the bus we drove in on. You can put down near there."

McCain told everyone goodbye. Andy would get Luis to a hospital to have his ankle checked. They would debrief on Monday morning. He walked over to the helicopter to thank the pilots and the crew. They had been the only reason that there had been any success at all today. As he turned to leave, he saw the body bag laying in the back of the helicopter. He stopped and stared.

The team climbed into the Blackhawk and the pilot started the engines. Everybody was onboard except Scotty. He followed Chuck as the big man slowly turned towards his truck. McCain opened the back door and started to take off his equipment. The large bloodstain on the backseat stared out at him. Scotty gently pushed the door closed.

"Let's put our stuff in the back."

"Our stuff?" McCain questioned.

"I'm riding back with you. I'll even drive if you'll let me," Smith said.

Chuck started to protest. He didn't want any company. He wanted to grieve alone. Somehow, he knew that it wouldn't have mattered. Scotty wasn't going to take "no" for an answer, and the helicopter had just lifted off.

They put their rifles and equipment in the back of the truck. Chuck handed Scotty the keys and climbed into the passenger seat. Sometimes, you need a friend with you when you're going through a bad dream, he thought.

Epilogue

CIA Headquarters, Tuesday, 1000 hours

He was the only passenger on the small Department of Homeland Security corporate jet. It taxied to a stop at a private terminal at the Ronald Reagan National Airport. The main terminal seemed deserted. He had heard that the zombie virus had people scared to travel. He knew that the east coast had been hit very hard. Television monitors in the terminal showed continuous aerial footage of the devastation at the University of Georgia.

A young man in a dark suit met him and guided him out of the airport to a black, government issued SUV. Chuck noted that the agent eyed him curiously. Traffic was light. Where did everybody go? he wondered. Rebecca had said the week before that the DC area had experienced some of the heaviest bio-terror attacks. The memory of her filled his heart with sadness and he stared out into space as they drove.

The email that he had received had included

instructions that he should wear a suit and tie for this meeting. He had opted for jeans, a pale blue shirt, and a blue blazer. His Glock was on his side but he knew that he would have to give it up when they got to their destination.

When they stopped at the entrance to the headquarters of the Central Intelligence Agency, his driver asked him, "Can I have your ID, sir? They'll need to see it at the gate."

Chuck handed him his ID packet, containing his badge and identification card, identifying him as a federal police officer for the Centers for Disease Control. The driver handed that and his own ID card to the security guard. He checked them against a clipboard and a computer screen before waving them through.

His guide led him inside the building, where they would have to go through another security screening.

"I was told you're armed, sir?"

McCain nodded and pulled the left side of his blazer back, revealing the black pistol.

The young agent led him to a small room next to the metal detectors. It contained an assortment of gun lockers.

"Please secure your weapon in one of these lockers and I'll escort you to your meeting."

Five minutes later, Chuck was ushered into the office of the Assistant Director for Operations for the CIA. Admiral Jonathan Williams walked out from behind his desk to greet McCain and shake his hand. He limped as he walked and his face told Chuck he was probably in his mid to late seventies but his grip was firm and strong as they shook hands. Williams' eyes were clear and sharp but he could not hide the sadness that was there as well.

"It's a pleasure to finally meet you, Mr. McCain. Rebecca told me…" He stopped for a moment and looked down. "I'm very sorry. She was a beautiful person and we're all going to miss her."

He motioned for McCain to sit in one of the two leather chairs facing the desk. The Admiral took the other. Chuck took a moment as he was sitting to do a quick scan of the office.

There were a number of photos of promotion ceremonies, family, and ships. Off to one side, however, were photos of a young Jonathan Williams wearing tiger stripe camouflage, a boonie hat, face paint, and carrying a CAR-15 rifle. A SEAL trident, the distinctive insignia worn by members of the elite unit, was in a shadow box full of medals and other awards on the shelf with the Vietnam era pictures. Williams saw McCain looking at the photos.

"I was one of the early SEALs. BUD/S Class 42. At the beginning of my second Southeast Asia tour, I stopped an AK bullet with my leg and that was that. I was able to stay in the Navy but I'd never go running through the jungle again.

"It was a tough pill to swallow. That was all I wanted to do. But I also knew that I didn't want to go back to civilian life so I threw myself into being the best officer that I could be, wherever the Navy sent me. I was very fortunate to end up making admiral before I retired and then I was asked to come work for this fine organization.

"But, enough about an old sailor. Please walk me through what happened this past weekend. I understand that it's painful. Take your time. I read your statement, but I'd like to hear about it in your own words."

Chuck spoke for twenty minutes, leaving nothing out. He didn't try to cover up the fact that he and Rebecca had started dating or the feelings that they'd had for each other. He detailed the attack at the university and how everything had transpired, including Rebecca's death. When he finished, they sat in silence for a few moments.

"Thank you for that," Admiral Williams said. "I'm sorry to have to make you relive it. Of course, you've gone through it over and over in your mind since Saturday. Do you think that there's anything you could've done differently?"

There was no accusation in the question. It was just a question, probing McCain's thought processes.

He looked into the older man's eyes. "I could have shot al-Razi in the back as soon as I had a clear shot. He was armed and I don't think anyone would have questioned the legality of it."

"And why didn't you?"

"Two reasons. Number one, I wasn't a hundred percent sure that it was him. I'd only seen pictures and I just got a quick glimpse of his face as he ran out of the student center. And number two, if we could've taken him alive, there's no telling what we could've learned from him."

"Assuming that he would talk."

"Oh, I'm sure that you guys could have persuaded him to talk," Chuck said.

The Admiral nodded and smiled. "Your instincts were dead on. Rebecca would have wanted you to try and arrest him. I'm so sorry it ended up the way that it did, but I want you to know that no one holds you responsible in any way. I understand that you just got back from visiting her parents in North Carolina?"

"I did. They're great people. They ended up comforting me as much as I comforted them."

"I know her stepfather, Danny. Good man. I hated to see him retire," the Admiral said.

Chuck had spent the previous afternoon and evening with Rebecca's mother and stepfather. Her mom was an older version of Rebecca. Tall, blonde, athletic, and graceful. Danny Johnson was a retired Special Forces operator. He and Chuck talked late into the night on their back deck, sipping bourbon and smoking cigars.

"So now, Mr. McCain, I want to discuss the future with you," said Williams. "I'd like to make your appointment permanent as the agent in charge of the Atlanta office. The war with Iran is, for all practical purposes, over. However, we know that they've sent out many agents to do as much damage here as they can. Are you willing to continue the fight?"

Chuck had expected that. It made much more sense to promote him than to bring someone else in from the CIA.

Would the Admiral accept his recommendations and suggestions?

An hour later, the men had reached an agreement. Chuck told the Admiral that he would accept the promotion. Admiral Williams had agreed to most of what Chuck asked him for. He then reached onto his desk and picked up two manila folders, handing them to McCain.

"That bag that al-Razi was carrying had a cell phone in it. We were able to retrieve some important intel off of it. We also think we know who the terrorist was inside the stadium. Everything we have on him is in the top file."

"Do we know if he's alive?"

"It looks that way. At least his phone is still in use. I can't believe that he hasn't dumped it, but for the moment anyway, he's still using it. He, or someone associated with him, killed a concessions supervisor inside the stadium and stole his car right before the infection started there.

"The victim's credit cards were used over the next two days. I'd like for you and your men to try and find this Terrell Hill. The information hasn't been released to the FBI yet. We'll sit on it for a couple of weeks and give you a chance to work."

Chuck nodded. "Thank you, sir. We'll get right to work on it. And the second folder?"

"This is some fresh intelligence about what we think is going to be the next wave of bio-terror attacks. It's scary stuff and I hope you and your people can get ahead of it."

"We'll do our best, Admiral. I'll keep you updated."

"Very good. Well, before I let you go, would you join me for a drink?"

Williams walked over to a cabinet, opened it, and retrieved two glasses and a bottle of Glenlivet 18-year old Scotch. He poured some into the tumblers and handed one to Chuck. They clinked glasses and the Admiral said, "Here's to Rebecca. She was a wonderful lady and a true patriot. God bless her memory."

They drained their scotch, shook hands, and the young CIA agent materialized to escort Chuck back to the airport. As the small jet reached its cruising speed, McCain was immersed in reading the information that Admiral Williams had given him. This war was far from over.

Coming Soon!

Thank you so much for reading *The Darkest Part of the Night*. I really hope you enjoyed it. If you did, would you consider giving me a review on Amazon? Reader reviews are so important for authors and it will help us get the word out to more people about the **Zombie Terror War Series.**

The third volume of the series, *When the Stars Fell from the Sky*, will be out soon. Iranian agents are determined to destroy America and Chuck and the guys are working hard to stop them and eliminate as many zombies as they can. Chuck is still reeling from the loss of Rebecca but he has to stay focused in the fight.

To find out a little more about me and my other books, including my non-fiction work, please check out my website at DavidSpell.com.

Made in the USA
Middletown, DE
23 September 2024

61252142R00203